THE DEAD WALK!

THE DEAD WALK!

JAMES TREYMAN

LitPrime Solutions
21250 Hawthorne Blvd
Suite 500, Torrance, CA 90503
www.litprime.com
Phone: 1-800-981-9893

Published by LitPrime Solutions   06/03/2022

ISBN: 979-8-88703-006-7(sc)
ISBN: 979-8-88703-007-4(e)

Library of Congress Control Number: 2022909072

CONTENTS

PREFACE

"When there's no more room in Hell, the
DEAD will walk the Earth."

- Peter (Dawn of the Dead '78)

Dedicated to:

Robert "Tré" Hamlin III

Dad loves you unconditionally

ACKNOWLEDGMENTS

I want to thank and acknowledge the following people who have supported and encouraged me to follow my calling as a writer. Without you guys, this book would not have been possible. You all have celebrated the great times with me and stood strong by me in the bad times of my life and for that, I love you all and am eternally grateful.

Lisa & Vic Lombard

Sharon Hamlin

Eric A. Hamlin

Brett Kleinberg

Edwin Francisco Nunez

Evangeline & Mike "Soup" Campbell

Dustin L Hamlin

David "BAMA" Hamlin Jr

MRSV-32

In a large executive meeting room on the third floor of the CDC, the top three advisors of the Viral Weapons Division sat around a large brown dark stained meeting table that contained two dozen high backed chairs. The three men sat nervously around a phone waiting for a call from senior congress members and NSA advisors. A check of the digital clock on the wall behind them read 5:29 in red numbers. The phone rang at 5:30 pm on the dot and senior chemist Joshua Stanfield anxiously hit the speaker button. Doctor Stanfield cleared his throat and nervously broke the ice "good day gentleman, how are you doing today? We…" and he was cut off when the annoyed voice on the other end sternly interrupted "what's going on with the MRSV-32 project!?" The two lead employees looked nervously at each other and swallowed hard as Stanfield answered: "We are close to optimal results sir, we just need a few more weeks; perhaps a couple of months to get it right". The voice replied "you knew we wanted this project done months ago doctor! This is the sixth call on this subject and now you are out of time! You don't have months or weeks, we will give you three days. If you don't have our viral weapon ready you will be on the unemployment line! Good luck with getting another job with no work experience, and your copious government funding will be cut! As a matter of fact, we can make you disappear, get the fucking picture!"

The third party of the CDC trio interjects "with all due respect sir, the Mutated Rabies Strain Virus is a highly volatile viral weapon and we do not have the correct antidote yet either! We aren't there yet but we are close, we just need a little more time." "Who is this, and why are you even talking?" the voice asked over the speaker. The third-party answered "my name is Robert Babcock, chief chemist and in charge of the Division of Viral Control. I oversee and approve all antidotes for the viral weapons *you* have us create. I am telling you that we currently do not have the means to control or terminate the MRSV-32 strain. If this virus gets out we are all in very deep shit! Curbing the Necrotizing Fasciitis we fused with the MRSV is proving more difficult than anticipated." There was a pause on the other end of the line as if considering the logic then the voice said "Al-Qaeda, ISIS or Korea won't give us more time, we need to rid those sons a bitches now! You have three days or you all are finished!" There was an audible click and dial tone. The room was eerily quiet for a few seconds after that major ass-chewing.

Babcock stood and exhaled deeply, then made his way to and stared out the one-way glass windows from the third floor overlooking Woodcock Boulevard. Doctors Miller and Stanfield looked nervously at each other when Miller says to Rob, "Hey, give us a few minutes will you." Rob replies "yeah, I'm going to grab coffee anyway. You want?" Both Miller and Stanfield shake their heads no and watch to ensure Babcock leaves the room before they begin to discuss a strategy. Babcock closes the door behind him and heads to the break room for a cup of stale coffee. The break room was bright with white tiled floor, white counter, refrigerator and matching microwave. The walls were light gray and white drop ceiling and the bright fluorescent lights made you squint when you first go in. Once there Robert grabs his mug from the cabinet and makes a hot cup of java tasting it to ensure its just right.

Back in the conference room, Miller says to Stanfield "we are going to give them what we have."

Stanfield responds to Miller "we can't! You and I both know it is too unstable and the DVC doesn't have the anti-virus. We would be liable if we can't control it once it is released.

"We don't have a choice!" said Miller, "Do you think they will let us live if we fail, what do you think it is we do here!? We sure as hell aren't curing anything, how long do you think we'll last is this goes south?"

"Shit", Stanfield says as he strokes his goatee and rubs his eyes in frustration and hesitation. "Alright, we'll give them what we have. Our team have been working twenty hours a day for the past month on this thing and are close to burning out, they will be glad it's over with. And what about the DVC? Are we going to tell Rob the reason his team is not getting the results they need is that the MRSV was fused with a recessive strain of Necrotizing Fasciitis and not the normal strain we told him?

Miller gets on the phone dials extension 556. Clearing his throat he says "send the correct specimens to the DVC for research, yeah right now. Thanks" and hangs up.

Robert knocks and waits before entering the conference room. He was holding a gray Yankees mug of hot coffee with the number 42 opposite the ubiquitous "NY" symbol and a pastry in the other. He sits back in his seat in front of his notepad which had scattered notations and a doodle of a cube on it. Both Miller and Stanfield stare at each other in silence and Rob stops mid-sip when he realizes the awkward silence and tension in the room. He puts the mug down and swallows as he awaits the news from his peers.

Miller clears his throat and says "Rob, we are going to give them what they want so we are going to approve the use of MRSV-32 for the government. Before we do so we need to tell you something. The reason your numbers are adding up is that MRSV-32 is fused with a recessive strain of Necrotizing Fasciitis that kicks in full strength two to three days after the other symptoms take hold. Fresh samples are being sent to your team's division as we speak."

Stanfield interjects "you're right there Bob, just tweak your approach and everything will work out fine".

"You sons of bitches!" Rob responds as he stands quickly slamming his fist on the table splashing coffee everywhere. "How could you sabotage me like this, all the man-hours and government spending poured into this project and I was kept in the dark the entire time! You forced fed me and my team false documentation and had us chasing ghosts!" He grabs his coffee-soaked notepad and mug and storms out of the conference room slamming the door behind him leaving Stanfield and Miller red in the face and silent.

Five levels underground in the Viral Weapons Division of the CDC was a clean laboratory filled with dozens of plastic beakers, containers, and microscopes. The laboratory was a secure air-tight plastic box with clear shatterproof walls that allowed for observation from a remote command center. Inside, there is a Hazmat Biochemist donned in a white level 5 protective suit who is ending his workday of twenty straight hours and his upcoming leave is the only thing on his exhausted mind. He struggles to keep his eyes open as he records the data from his observations through the microscope. He then proceeds to the decontamination room before descending down the ramp and entering the level 5 quarantine area of the lab that contained MRSV-32. He begins the painstaking process of cleaning and securing the lab properly. While picking up the sharp surgical instruments used to dissect the brains and stems for their research he punctured his glove and immediately checked for holes in his suit but didn't see any and decided to continue to clean the lab. He then handled the brain specimens, first the untainted ones that weren't used during his shift which were a fresh gray color with a touch of tan and placed them back into the cooler. He then came back to gather the two brains infected with MRSV-32 which were gray in color with a tan hue but the stem area was dark black in color and the second was divided into two halves showed the blackened stem run into the center cortex of the brain. He took one tray at a time into the cooler and on the third trip with the halved brain it began to slide to one side of the tray beginning to fall but he quickly placed his hand on the contaminated brain to stop it from falling, regained balance and proceeded to the cooler. Lastly, he takes the stainless steel containers labeled MRSV-32 and went to the cooler and opened the canisters filled with liquid nitrogen and slowly placed the containers in the canisters and sealed them.

Once finished he lets out a sigh of relief and takes a minute before he heads back up to the decontamination room, raises his arms and is sprayed from all directions with a potent sanitizing liquid, undresses and repeats the process again. As he gets undressed he notices a puncture in his glove the size of a pinhole and hastily takes his gloves off frantically checking for a puncture in his skin but doesn't see one. After checking several more times his nerves calmed and he decides to forgo the proper protocol of reporting and having to be quarantined. He showers and gets dressed in the locker room. Dave was on his way out to a much-needed vacation and as he walks down the hallway he takes two squirts from the wall-mounted hand sanitizing unit and immediately notices an intense sting as he wrings his hands together. He passes through the security gate and nods to Earl the guardsman on the graveyard shift. He waves and buzzes open the security door as Dave kindly waves in return and head out to the parking lot and get into his car taking a deep breath of fresh air.

Later that night Dave the biochemist went for a much-needed guy's night out to a local sports bar with his friends Sam, Patrick and Victor to catch a ball game then to a club for a quick nightcap. Even though it was an early night, it was exactly what he needed to blow off some steam. After he finishes his shot and chaser he says goodnight to his friends and a final unsuccessful pass at the local female he had met while there. He headed home to double-check his luggage and conduct a last-minute check on his travel itinerary. It was confirmed that his flight departed at 10:20 a.m. the next morning so he jumped in the shower and decided to shave right after to save time in the morning. In the shower, he noticed that his left hand that stung from the sanitizer earlier that evening was now very sore and discolored as if bitten by some huge insect. After showering he looks at his reflection in the mirror and notices that he seems a little pale and clammy. He had darkened circles around his eyes and quite frankly he looked like shit. He shrugs it off thinking it's from lack of sunlight from working underground this past month. "You need a vacation, my man," he says to his reflection as he lathers his face and begins to shave. He begins to feel dry-mouthed and begins coughing to the point that he nicks himself and he noticed that the minor cuts hurt like hell and bled excessively. "Shit!" he says as he applies copious amounts of toilet paper with shaking hands to stop the bleeding and finally some band-aids when done and goes to bed.

Dave wakes up to his alarm and recognizes the sports talk radio host talking about how the local professional football team was in contention for the division title. He immediately notices his entire body is really stiff and in pain especially his back. His head felt it was about to explode and he had a bad sore throat and the sniffles. He downs some daytime cold medicine with a cup of instant coffee and heads out the door with his luggage and plane ticket in hand. On the drive to the International Airport, he notices that he has a severe dry cough and his mouth was so dry his tongue kept sticking to the roof of his mouth. Taking periodical swigs of water out of the bottle of Dasani did nothing and his mouth seemed to absorb the water like a sponge. He kept trying to swallow but there was nothing there. He noticed that the spot on his hand now looked like a cigarette burn and still bothered him and as he looked in the rearview mirror he noticed that his nicks from shaving haven't healed and seemed to have grown a little in size and depth. He noticed severe reddening around his eyes, nose and his gums were very sore and irritated. None of that mattered he was on his way to Margaretville for the next two weeks and nothing was going to stop him especially the flu. He takes the exit to the airport and bears left to the long term parking lot. He grabs his bags and tickets and begins to briskly walk to the main terminal. He was now a bit worried but seceded what the hell, he could get checked by a doctor when he landed and besides, all he needed to cure his ailments was sunshine and good tequila.

Dave arrives outside the main terminal and checks his baggage with a skycap tipping him generously. He then continues inside, heads up on the escalator to the main terminal and heads for the security gate. While in line he became light-headed and coughed until he almost vomited. This drew the attention of other passengers and the security staff. He also began sneezing to the point his nose began to bleed which he plugged with a napkin. He passes through security without a problem then continues to terminal B and looks for flight 487 and settles in for the next hour before his flight boarded as he sunk into the chair and leaned his head against the wall to catch some rest.

"Flight 487 to Margaretville is now boarding. Section A, seats 1 through 20 please form to the right. Thank you" was broadcast by a female's voice and Dave sluggishly stood up and waited in line, boarded his flight and plopped down into his seat and laid his head against the window of the plane. The flight attendant noticed his pale color and asked if he was alright which he shook his head yes and went to sleep. While he rested he would cough and sometimes red dots of blood would land on his sleeve or hand which he would wipe off. The plane sped down the runway and Dave's plane takes off without a hitch and roars toward the clear blue sky and banks right toward the tropics and disappears from sight.

Meanwhile back at the CDC Robert Babcock was fast at work on the real thirty-second strain of the MRSV in the lab of the DVC. His assistant Evangeline was updating the numbers from the new data taken from the virus into the system to analyze the correct dosage to mix for the antidote of the new viral weapon that is on the fast track to being "approved" by the FDA. Babcock was due for his vacation in the next two days and was counting down the hours.

"Vange, get me the numbers on the new virus strain, would you?"

"It's still calculating Rob, we are at" she squints at the screen through her glasses "sixty-seven percent".

"Alright" Robert responded "I need those numbers as soon as you can. I'm going to the clean lab to retrieve the specimens and viral samples and begin testing."

He begins the process of donning the level 5 hazmat suit and surgical latex gloves then enters the decontamination chamber and enters the clean lab and begins work. He realizes that the now only had about twelve hours so time was of the essence and could not afford any mistakes. He takes a sample of the virus, puts it on the slide and places it under the microscope for observation. He sees something that alarms his greatly, as he peers through the microscope he watches the virus violently attack and deteriorates the living tissue cells surrounding it. He immediately makes notes and a video of his observations and later has his assistant cosign his findings. After several hours of testing and research, it was discovered that MRSV-32, unlike HIV, can live outside a living host for several hours, therefore, it can be transmitted via touch as well as bodily fluids including saliva or mucus. This new discovery needed to be reported to Miller and Stanfield. Babcock leaves the sterile laboratory then heads to the cleanroom and decontaminates. He then showers and immediately gets on the phone with the two.

"Because of you assholes, I'm behind the eight ball here playing catch up to produce a serum to combat this virus from the devil himself."

Miller tries to interject "Bob, please" was immediately cut off.

"No, you fuckin listen! This shit is bad news and it could be a grave mistake releasing MRSV-32 without the proper antidote, do not release this without it."

Stanfield gets on the line "aren't you making headway with the new serum? You were right there before just an increase here, a decrease there and you're golden. Right?"

"Yes I am almost there but still need a week or so to perfect it, plus time to run extensive testing before we can add it to the flu vaccines due to go out for nationwide distribution next Fall. I'm taking a vacation in a few hours so all my lab testing is done for now but I will take my data and do some work while at home."

After a brief pause Miller says "keep up the good work Bob and get it to us as soon as possible ok buddy?" and then he hung up.

Little did Robert know, Miller and Stanfield already had shipped MRSV-32 to the National Security Advisor with a placebo antidote which meets the deadline, to make matters worse, little did any of them know, the MRSV-32 already made it out to the secure facility and to the general public. This has started a chain of events so horrifying and macabre it would resemble a George Romero movie.

"VACATION"

Six days after infection 8:37 a.m.

It's a sweltering 96 degrees in Margaretville. The sun was beginning rise as it burned a bright orange color behind bright pink and orange clouds. The sky began to turn from pink and purple to crystal blue. The clear blue ocean waters gently crash against the soft sand and you could see the Indigenous fish in their natural habitat. Vacationers swim in the cool clear water or lounge on the sandy beaches as they soak up the sun as much as the mixed rum drinks served in fresh pineapples or coconuts. The large palm trees give shade and sway in the ocean breeze and you can just catch a whiff of coconut-scented sunscreen in the air, this is truly paradise.

Unfortunately, Dave won't enjoy any of that scenery, he is across the island at the local Saint Kimberly's Tranquility Hospital where he was admitted and quarantined. He was having several tests run to try and figure out what was wrong with him. Dave's skin was now a bluish-green around his eyes. He was now bleeding from his eyes, nose, and gums. He also ran a high fever. The cuts on his face are now the size of a half-dollar and you could see the muscles in his face. Dave now coughed continuously and his muscles were starting to contract uncontrollably causing his to seize. The monitors began beeping getting the attention of the nurses at the desk who immediately called a code. As doctors and nurses run into the room to hold him down he lets out a great open-mouthed cough spraying blood and foamy saliva in the faces of the medical staff. He thrashed around knocking a nurse on her to the floor and bites another nurse's pinky and ring fingers off then scratch the doctor tearing the skin on his right forearm. The orderlies came seconds later and were able to strap him in and the doctors gave him a sedative. The doctors were able to conduct blood tests to determine this unknown illness but little did they know they were in way over their heads.

Back in Cypress Pond, Robert is enjoying his much-needed vacation in the comfort of his own home with his teenage son Robert Jr. He knocks on juniors bedroom door "RJ, do you want breakfast?"

After a brief pause, a dry groggy voice answered "um hmm."

"Alright, game 15 then come down" and Rob heads to the kitchen to start breakfast and make his espresso fueled cup of coffee. While in the kitchen he puts the television on and turns it to the national news channel. He now starts the coffee maker and sticks his head into the fridge and grabs eggs, bacon and orange juice. In the background, the female anchors' voice is muffled as he is focused on the sizzling bacon. He notices the paperboy heading to the front yard from across the street and starts to head to meet him and get his copy of the local paper. As he quickly leaves the kitchen the national news anchor reports

"Next, a breaking story of mysterious outbreaks across the globe of an aggressive strain of the rabies virus in humans. It causes those infected to violently attack others." Reports are still unclear but we have more to follow on this breaking story, after these messages."

Robert returns with his freshly printed and folded newspaper and tosses into the kitchens island and checks the television only to see a commercial for Doritos. He changes the channel to Sports center then removes the burnt bacon form the pan as he eats a slice. He pours his coffee, cleans out the grease and begins to fry a few eggs and calls out to RJ "alright pal, time to eat".

Moments later RJ enters the kitchen, high fives his dad and sleepily pours some orange juice and begins to chug it down. Robert slides a plate of bacon, eggs, toast, and fresh sliced fruit in front of RJ and mushed the back of his head lovingly. RJ responds with a smiling "good morning dad". Rob stands at the counter and smiles at him before sipping his espresso and chomps down slices of bacon and toast as they both listen to the latest news with the local pro football team. After breakfast both take turns showering and getting dressed. RJ heads out to hang with his friends and Robert reluctantly checks his smartphone and sees the dreaded missed calls from work. He logs into his laptop and there he sees a half dozen e-mails from work RE: CLASSIFIED #32. He ignores the e-mails and surfs the web as he thinks to himself, "shit, I'm on vacation right" and decides to check in later. He was still pissed at his co-worker's antics and now that they needed him he would make them wait. The rest of the day was spent running the usual daily errands. Robert went to the market to pick up a few items, he went to the barbershop and took RJ to the shooting range to hone his skills. Little did they know how invaluable this time was spent, and afterward, the two had dinner then went to sleep. As Rob snored loudly with the assistance of a few glasses of cabernet, his cell phone lit up and vibrated in failed attempts to warn him of the deep shit that was impending.

Back at Saint Kimberly's Tranquility Hospital in Margaretville, poor 'old Dave is on his deathbed under constant supervision as he is strapped to his bed. His vitals have been dropping slow and steady since his admittance and a fever of 104 degrees is literally cooking his insides. With a final convulsion and gagging cough his last breath was taken and he flat lines. Dave is pronounced dead at 2:17 a.m., draped with a white sheet that immediately shows stains of blood from his mouth and nose area and is wheeled down to the morgue for processing.

Dave is given a toe tag and wheeled into the main autopsy room along with three other cadavers waiting their turn to go under the knife. His corpse was left under the white sheet with his stiff toes hanging out from beneath the sheet. The pathologist leaves to complete paperwork in the office then gives his day relief the proper briefing on the amount of work that lies ahead of him.

Back in the morgue a closer look at the bloodstained sheet covering our friend Dave you notice a slight movement underneath from his hands. Several minutes later the sheet begins to slip off his body as his upper torso begins to sit up slowly.

The next morning Rob has awakened from his alcohol-induced coma by the sound of sports commentators reciting game scores from the previous night. He rolls over and slowly sits up on the edge of his bed feet on the floor and he rubs his eyes and face to clear the cobwebs and notices the pounding headache from the night before. He notices on the radio a commercial for a new book "Thin Blue Line" by James Treyman He writes the title and author on his notepad to check it online when he had a chance. He gets out of bed and conducts the same coffee ritual. He puts the television on and changes the channel to the world news channel then yells up to RJ to see it he wanted a hot breakfast or Cap'n Crunch. RJ responds "I'm fine dad, cereal is ok."

Rob then makes himself a couple of pieces of toast and turns his attention to the television as he sits on the couch in the living room as he sips his coffee. He turns up the volume when he notices "Breaking News!" on the screen in white lettering against a red background and underneath "rabies outbreaks" scrolling in white letters over a red band on the bottom of the screen. His stomach twisted in knots and nausea hit him hard as he couldn't believe what was being reported. A global map was flashed on the screen with red dots, some in clusters across the world pinpointing the location of reported infections. He focuses intently as the breaking news unfolds and turns up the volume.

"Reports have been pouring in all night from across the globe that humans infected with a particular strain of rabies cause violent attacks on other humans. Some reports have cannibalism type attacks where said victims were partially devoured, bit or mauled as if by some wild animal. Again, not all these reports have been confirmed due to the speed they are coming in. Government agencies will not comment at this time but sources say they don't even know what has caused this outbreak and are scrambling for an answer. We. Hold it. Just coming in we are going live via webcam to Saint Kimberly's Tranquility Hospital for a report of an outbreak attack with local reporter Isaiah Thompson. Isaiah?

As the distorted and broken feed stabilizes the picture comes into focus. A tanned, well-groomed and clean-shaven reporter in a sweat-stained button-up shirt. Behind him shows the exterior of an emergency room filled with docked ambulances, illegally parked cars and people entering and leaving the ER some crying on their cell phones probably contacting loved ones with grim updates.

"Reporting to you live from Saint Kimberly's Tranquility Hospital where a rash reports of a mysterious illness had seemed to have overtaken about twenty-five percent of the island of Margaretville where those reporting symptoms have migrated here for treatment. Sources tell me the medical staff is overwhelmed and that indeed a vicious attack happened here not 4 hours ago".

In the middle of his opening dialogue, he begins to walk towards the ER doors and enters a scene that stops him in his tracks. The video shows a panning shot of a waiting room way over capacity and all available medical staff from Doctors, Nurses, Nursing Assistants, orderlies even receptionists giving aid to those they could as the telephone ran constantly adding to the din of the room. There were patients slumped over or laid back in chairs was loved ones wipe their faces and lightly slap them to keep them awake. Others were slouched, sitting or lying on the floor and all were pale looking some worse than others and coughing up sputum containing blood. The worse cases were bleeding from their noses mouths and eyes. There was groans of pain from all over the room and screams form family members as the infected would pass out.

In a remote corner, the camera panned in and came in to focus was several corpses wrapped in white sheets with blood stains where the mouth and nose were. The camera panned out and focused on Isaiah staring open-mouthed who was still in shock at the horror he was witnessing. As he composed himself the camera captured two armed hospital security guards wearing facial surgical masks carrying another corpse wrapped in a now bloodstained white sheet over to the far corner where flies were gathering.

"Dear God, let's talk to whoever is in charge here." They carefully move through the overcrowded Emergency Room and the smell of rotting flesh and metallic tinge from blood everywhere fills their nostrils and

makes them swallow in an attempt not to vomit. Then near the nurse's station, a doctor emerges from behind a set of double doors under a sign with arrows indicating the direction of the elevators, operating rooms and morgue. He was wiping his blood-stained gloved hands on his already blood laden white coat and pale green scrubs. He was surprised by the camera but was willing to talk briefly.

Isaiah: *"Doc, what the Hell is going on here?! What is causing this mass rush of outbreaks?"*

Doctor Rhodes: *"We are still working on the answer, as you can see we are extremely busy and trying to catch up the best we can. We have had an influx for patients for the past twenty hours or so we have been working around the clock. We froze all available staff and called back the entire roster to work on this and give the best quality care we possibly can."*

Dr. Rhodes's real attention can be seen to be focused on the war zone of the ER going on right behind the camera and he scans the room instead of looking at the camera or reporter.

Isaiah: *"Is it true that an attack happened right here from a patient that was admitted here and some of your staff was bitten and attacked?! Again Doctor, what is happening? What is causing this?"*

As Isaiah is asking his question he is positioned almost side by side with Doctor Rhodes facing toward the camera and is now facing each other. The camera catches blurry movement in the background but comes into focus as the double doors quietly and slowly open outward and a pale gray male wearing white boxers comes shambling toward the two quietly from behind. His face pale blue. The flesh rotted away exposing dead meat underneath and drawn in, eyes milky white with dried blood under them and his nose. His lips are now almost non-existent and tightly drawn around his blackened bloody gums exposing large bloodstained teeth. As he inched closer and closer without being noticed Doctor Rhodes answers the question looking into the camera with a sickening look of despair as his eyes welled with tears and begin to answer.

"Yes, there was an attack and we are completing our investigation. And as to what is causing this, well it is something never before seen and frankly......we don't know.

No sooner than he finished his statement the shambling horrid looking figure is noticed by Isaiah who falls out of the picture. The walker pounces on Doctor Rhodes from behind placing one hand on his shoulder the other around his forehead pulling his head to the left. With a snarling growl, he bites into the jugular area ripping a large chunk of meat. Bright red blood squirts from the gaping wound hitting the camera lens. A large gurgling yell was immediately drowned out by blood filling and spurting out of Rhodes' mouth. The zombie rips away the bite of flesh and the skin and sinews stretch and snaps into the zombie's mouth. Loud screams begin to fill the air as the patient's bore witness to this horrifying incident. His fingers on the face of the doctor begin to tear away skin and the second bite planted on his face now tears away from his cheek and his upper lip exposing his upper gums and row of teeth as his upper lip was torn away. The cameraman drops the camera and runs. Doctor Rhodes half-eaten face falls in front of the camera wide-eyed blood poured from the viscous founds and oozed toward the camera. Gunfire erupts from the two security guards off-screen and you could see the zombie stagger backward and fall on its back. The feed cuts out back to the studio where the anchors were caught staring in horror from what they just saw. The anchor snaps out of it addressing the camera, clearing his throat stating *"We apologize for what was just witnessed, more after these messages"*.

OUTBREAK

Robert grabs his cell phone and plays his missed messages from work. It was Miller and Stanfield taking turns calling begging for the progress of his work on the antidote and demanding to get to the office immediately for an emergency level three meeting. He hits speed dial and calls Millers office line it just rings until his voicemail picks up stating, 'mailbox is full' and disconnects. Now his hands shaking he fights his nerves and dials Stanfield only to get a busy tone. "Shit!" he says and slams his phone on the couch and yells to RJ to get up. He turns the channel to the local news and sees a breaking report is coming up next. At that moment, there was a loud explosion that shook his house to the foundation.

Rob raced out the front door and onto the lawn. A large plume of black smoke was billowing from the trees to the West. Guessing from the location it must have been the gas station a few blocks away. Rob now noticed some neighbors were outside as well pointing to the black smoke. His next-door neighbor and friend Josh Brown came over and asked: "what the hell, you think it was Jake's gas that went up like that?"

"By the location, I'd say yeah!" Rob responded. "Are you alright? "You look like you just saw a ghost."

"There's a bug going around and Laura and Katie have been under the weather the past couple days with the flu. She's really burning up and she had a really bad headache to boot. I better get back and take care of her, you take care of yourself, buddy."

Josh heads back inside and closes the door behind him. Every inch of Robert wanted to tell his good friend to leave his family before he became infected. Hearing the door slam was like a reality hitting him in the pit of his stomach knowing deep down that would be the last time he would see his friend alive.

Robert re-enters his house with his newspaper in hand and locks the deadbolt behind him. He goes and secures the back door as well. By now RJ is waking up and confused by the anxiety in his dad's demeanor.

"What's going on Dad?" RJ asks as he pours himself a bowl of Cap n Crunch.

"I think something went horribly wrong at work" Rob puts the phone on speaker and hits redial to call into work. This time he just gets a busy tone. He repeats the call several times trying different numbers including the "private" numbers all with the same results.

Frustrated he hangs up and opens his copy of the Atlanta Post and the front-page headline read "**THE DEAD WALK!**" Robert's heart began pounding and stomach began turning as he continued to read the story titled **Dead:**

Strange occurrences have been reported to the Atlanta Police Department about people becoming incredibly ill displaying severe flu-like symptoms and performing "cannibalistic" type attacks on others. From Providence, Rhode Island a man was pronounced dead at Rhode Island Hospital and reportedly returned back to life attacking medical staff. Another report from Margaretville's Saint Kimberly's Tranquility Hospital where another similar attack was reported where a corpse was in the morgue and came back to life attacking staff.

A nurse who had witnessed the attack from that day tells reporters "it's unlike I have ever witnessed, it was like a scene from a zombie movie!" Security video footage that was caught in the hospital reportedly shows the corpse rises from under the sheet and shamble its way down the hall before attacking a doctor biting him on the neck and face on live television before being shot by hospital security. "As foolish as this may seem I now believe the words from the movie Dawn of the Dead are true". Upon asking the nurse what she meant and she replied: "When there is no more room in hell, the dead will walk the earth."

Robert now knows something is really wrong and begins to dry heave over the kitchen sink. Rob rinses his face and gargles with water and gathers himself as his son watches in as much fear as apprehension.

"Dad, what's going on?!" he asks, "are we in danger?!"

Rob answers "I think we are son, I think we are."

He bites his lower lip in deep thought then tells RJ "call your mom and see if she is ok, have her get here as soon as she can alright". RJ responds with a nod in agreement and runs to his room to get his cell phone and makes the call. RJ gets through to his mom "ma, are you ok!? Dad says it is very important and for you to get to our house as quick as you can ok!?"

RJ's mom Leese responds "what are you talking about? I am not going to drop everything and ask how high when your father says jump! What does he want now?" On her end of the line, she stares at their family photo as she picks at her bottom lip then abruptly turns and says with a sigh, "put your father on". RJ calls out "dad, mom wants to talk to you!" as he runs to give his dad the phone in the living room. Rob takes the phone covering the speaker and whispers to RJ "gimme the bitch" and RJ nods with fright and excitement then disappears up the stairs again. Rob turns his attention to the phone "Hey, are you ok? I want" then he was immediately cut off by a pissed off Cape Verdean woman.

"What do you want?! Why do you have our son calling me giving me orders from you to come to see you?! You ain't nobody special!"

Robert answers "look, Le, it's not like that so calm your ass down, something very serious is happening and I just want you to be safe. Please get here as soon as you can and take the back roads alright."

Le responds "what is so important that" Robert cuts her off

"I don't have time to explain, just get here now and please be careful. I gotta go and get ready". Then he hung up the phone.

A minute later RJ returns to the living room with a twelve-gauge Mossberg 590A1 and a box of 00buck ammunition. Robert takes the shotgun and jams to capacity with eight shells, racks a round into the chamber and tops off the magazine with another shell and engages the killing machines safety. RJ is nervous and watches the television reports with his dad. Rob changes the channel to local news channel 9 to watch what caused the explosion at the gas station. It cut to breaking news as the local reporters begin to report live from the scene of a taped off police line around Jake's gas station. As black smoke billows from behind the reporter's local first responders are attending the fire and keeping the public at bay.

"Live here at Jake's service station a gruesome accident took place here in the quiet town of Cypress Pond just on the outskirts of Atlanta, Georgia. Reports from police spokesperson Chief Campbell tells us that an unidentified motorist had driven their vehicle into the service station rupturing the main fuel line causing a massive explosion killing at least eight people including the driver. Official reports are still sketchy at this time but we will keep live to get you the up to date reports as they come."

As firefighters hose down the gas station with the foam they turn their attention to a figure that emerges from the wreckage still completely engulfed in flames. The camera zooms in on the unidentified body stumbling from the wreckage as gasps and screams of horror are heard in the background from onlookers. Firefighters close in and douse the victim with foam and blankets and take him to the ground. As the fires are extinguished the camera still zoomed in on the person receiving medical treatment. It shows the person struggling to get up and the charred smoking body bites a firefighter on the arm.

The firefighter screams as he pulls away and is helped by other firefighters out of the picture of the camera. A firefighter kicked the zombie in the face knocking it back then runs out of sight of the camera to help his injured brother. Police are now closing in as the burnt corpse staggers to its feet. Once on its feet it immediately reaches for and lumbers toward the officers who have their guns drawn.

"Freeze! Police! Put your fucking hands in the air and get on the fucking ground! Last chance mother fucker!

This was broadcast live on local television. The charred smoking corpse responded to police commands with a gurgling moan as it advanced toward them. The sound of muffled gunshots rang out and muzzle flashes could be seen. Gunsmoke and brass casings filled the air and the camera shook from the cameraman flinching. Multiple hits appeared on the zombie's chest and torso area which stumbled it back a step or two every few shots until it tumbled over backward hitting the pavement with an audible thud. Police close in step by step with guns drawn and the corpse began to sit up slowly still hissing as blood spewed from its mouth. It began raising a hand toward the officers who opened up with a second volley of fire. More gun smoke and brass filled the air as the bullets could be seen striking the ground behind the corpse. Finally, one of the officer's jacket hollow points found its mark and ripped through the skull of the zombie. It caused a massive blowback creating a baseball-sized hole in the back of its head and its brains and skull fragments splatter the ground behind it.

The headshot put it down for good. The camera now zooms out and catches the local reporter staring in horror at what just happened and the camera was cut by the network and the generic "technical difficulties" picture was broadcast with that annoying high pitched tone. Rob then hit the mute button and looked at RJ,

"I gotta get to work right now and see what is going on. Get your stuff together now, we have to go."

"Mom is coming. We need to wait for her!"

Robert responded, "we don't have time to wait, we gotta go now."

In as strong but quivering voice RJ managed "Dad, its mom. We have to wait."

Robert thinks for a minute then agrees his son is right. After all, he still loved her. He turned to RJ, "go grab our bug out bags and the rest of the shotgun ammo then meet me upstairs."

As RJ's footsteps faded as he ran up the stairs Robert logs onto his laptop and pulls up all the data he has been working on with MRSV-32 and makes two copies of the files onto miniature thumb drives. He tries to call Le and see if she is still coming and if she is alright. The phone call just went to voicemail and he hung up and sent a text asking where she was and if she was still coming.

A check on the monitor shows data was downloaded ninety-three percent and he prepared the second thumb drive and once it reached one hundred percent he removed the first and inserted the second one and clicked download and began the process again. As he waits for a response from Le he yells to RJ and he responds that he is ready and waiting in his room. There is now a lot of activity outside as helicopters could be heard flying overhead spotlights flooding the area then disappearing, the distant sounds of emergency vehicles sirens whaled then faded into the distance and occasional scream from some poor bastard outside was heard. There was the sound of tires screeching and the occasional car crash and even a few smaller-scale explosions.

By now the sun is setting and the sky is quickly darkening as Rob continuously checks out of all the windows throughout the lower level of the house he hears a man's voice scream close by startling him. *"Is it Josh?"* He thought to himself. Immediately following the scream four flashes of light and four distinct bangs of gunfire causing Rob to duck.

RJ calls down to him "Dad!"

"I'm alright RJ, stay there!"

Robert ducks and runs upstairs to join his son. He goes into the closet and pulls out a gray gun box. He then hits the combination popping open the secure door exposing a nine-millimeter Glock 17. He removes the magazine checking it was loaded then slams it back home and chambers a round. He grabs the pair of short-range two-way radios, turns them on and tosses one to RJ. Rob looks at RJ and orders him to stay put and to protect himself if necessary against anybody that comes up the stairs that wasn't him and that he would be right back. RJ nodded in agreement, wiped tears from his face and took up a position behind his bed aiming the ghost ring sights of the crowd-pleaser at the door. As Robert left the room and closed the door behind him RJ took the weapon off safety.

Robert reaches the backdoor and gets on the radio trying to control his breathing and whispered " RJ, I'm at the back door, going through the back yards to the Browns yard to check on them. Over."

RJ responded "ok, be careful. Over".

Robert steadied his nerves, took a couple of deep breaths and dialed his neighbor's house number which was busy. He quietly opened his back door and closed it behind him and made his way from the deck onto the grass and crept along the rear of his house peering carefully around the corner to see if it was clear. He then quickly darted to the Browns backyard through the swing door in the wooden fence and immediately ran to the back of the house near the cement base near the glass sliding doors. He peered inside the kitchen and there was no movement. He tried the sliding door but it was locked so he retrieved the key from underneath the stainless steel propane grill and gained access through the door.

Now with his Glock nine at the low ready he switches on the light attached to the pistol. He noticed the tea kettle was whistling and spitting steam so he turns the oven off and takes it off the hot surface. Robert then hears a thud and now redirects his attention and the business end of the weapon towards the threshold of the kitchen and the hallway. Carefully he heads down the hallway littered with several family photos from the kitchen to the living room area. As he reached the end of the hallway he carefully looked around the corner to discover the living room was empty. Robert lets out a sigh of relief, swallows hard and continues to check the dining room adjacent to the living room and that two was clear.

BOOM! The thud, coming from upstairs made Rob jump out of his skin. He hesitantly heads up the stairs one at a time fighting with his jellylike legs treading lightly as to not make a sound. As he gets closer and closer to the top of the steps he can now hear a noise similar to someone chewing food with their mouth open. Instantly the metallic smell of blood filled his nostrils with the faint smell of excrement causing him to hold his breath breathing shallow and only as needed. He whispered "Josh, psssst. Josh you there?" but there was no response. He peers right Glock leading the way at the top of the steps and he notices that the master bedroom was ajar. He focuses intently on the door as tunnel vision kicks in and the slobbering chewing is growing louder. The sense that something was behind him kicked in and the hairs on the back of his neck stood on end and goosebumps filled his arms. With his heart now beating through his shirt he turns around to see Katie their twenty-year-old daughter lunge at him gnashing her bloody teeth at him trying to bite him as she quickly and stiffly shambled toward him."Shit!" he yells as he falls backward onto the floor and Katie lands on top chomping at him as she growls and spits bloody foam down her chin. He is able to kick her off and she bounces off the railing and down the steps. Robert quickly gets up and enters the master bedroom and sees a set of male feet on the other side of the bed on the floor. He closes in and as he rounds the other side of the bed and shines the light on the bodies he discovers. His good friend Josh was being eaten by his own wife. His throat was partially removed through bites and ripping from hands, his left eye was missing and now he was disemboweled as his wife Laura kneeled over him both hands holding intestines of her husband as she chewed away like a lion ripping into a fresh kill. In the midst of her meal, she begins to sniff the air and slowly turned her head toward Robert. Laura bared her tightly drawn lips over her freshly blood-soaked gums and teeth and let out a snarl letting her mouthful of meat slop onto the floor. She was met by a flash of light and a loud bang as the Glock jumped in his hand. Laura's head snapped back and body stiffened as the Glock nine sent a jacketed hollow point through her left eye angled upward and mushroomed out the back of her head. The blowback flung blood, bone and brain matter against the wall. She fell beside her husband as blood and macerated brains oozed out the golf ball-sized hole in her head. Rob had noticed that there was a large bullet hole in her chest area and a Colt 45 ACP near his departed friend. He takes the Colt and heads back into the hallway and faced the stairs.

Katie had made it up only three steps and he noticed that there were three holes in her torso as well. He aimed his Glock and put a round through her face exploding the lower part of her skull sending her flying backward onto the floor near the front door. Not believing what he just been through he sat at the top of the steps and began to cry, gathers himself wiping the tears away and tries to dial 911. An automated female voice tells him all servers are busy and to hang up and try again. "Fuck!" he says and redials 911 with the same result. He gathers himself as his radio squeals.

RJ's voice says "dad, I heard shots, are you ok?!"

Clearing his throat he responds "yeah bud, I'm coming home now."

He remains sitting with his head down so he doesn't notice that his best friend is now standing in the threshold of the bedroom doorway leading to the hallway just feet away with his small intestines hanging to the floor. His friend Josh sniffs the air and looks in the direction of Robert and begins to shamble towards him like an infant taking their first steps. As he got closer he raised his hands and chomps the air in an effort to tear into Robert.

The snarling and the chatter of teeth caused Robert to flinch as Josh had become entangled in his own intestines tripping him flat on his face. Rob immediately began pistol-whipping the head of Josh until the skull gave way with a crunching sound and Josh stopped moving.

Rob gets up re-enters the bedroom and raids the closet finding a box and a half of .45 ACP rounds. He grabs both boxes and heads downstairs into the garage of the Browns and takes his machete he lent them two summers ago. "This will come in handy," he thinks to himself with a smile. He looks at the small ammo stash he found and looked at the box and it read 230 grain Hydra Shock that was just over half full and the other white box was full of 230grain full metal jacket hardball. He releases the magazine and fills it with the matching Hydra Shocks and reseats it in the pistol and clicks on the safety. He gets on the radio to RJ telling him that he was coming in and not to shoot. Robert quickly and stealthily heads back home via the back yards, enters through the door and double locks it. He gives a last-second security check through the window then pulls the curtain shut.

BUG OUT

Robert heads upstairs to check on RJ and hugs him tightly. "Did you hear from mom yet?!" he asked and RJ shook his head worriedly no. Rob attempts to call Le again but still gets the busy signal and hangs up. "Alright, mom isn't answering her phone, she should have been here by now."

RJ notices his father is a little shaken up and splattered in blood. "What happened next door, is Mr. Brown dead?" Are you alright?"

Rob responded, "Yes I am alright, don't worry about anything but us ok. We need to get to the CDC so I can figure out what the hell happened and try and fix this mess. Unfortunately, we can't wait here forever for mom, ok".

RJ shook his head in understanding. They both ate and fell asleep with the plan to hit the road in the morning.

In the middle of the night, a frantic pounding at the rear door had startled the both of RJ and Robert as they sat up with hearts pounding quickly scanning the bedroom. Bang, bang, bang, bang came from the rear door. Then the familiar panic-stricken voice said "Robert! Robert, open the door, it's me. Please hurry!" Robert covered RJ with the .45 as RJ ran to the door and opened it for Le.

Le enters the kitchen and hugs RJ tightly and checks him for injuries. Robert now joins them both and they embrace as lovers once have. She is visually shaken, exhausted and slightly injured with a bump on her forehead dried with blood and her clothes were tattered. Rob had given her a glass of water and gave her something to eat which she thankfully devoured. Robert then gives a security check and sees a few abandoned cars in the street some with their hazards flashing. Now a few dead aimlessly staggering about caused his stomach to turn and heart rate skyrocketed.

When he returned he noticed Le had taken liberty with the use of the bathroom to freshen up and one of his New England Patriots T-shirts that hung loosely on her slender frame. They all sat around in the living room grateful to be reunited. "I'm glad you two are safe," she said with tears in her eyes as she stroked lovingly RJ's head and placing a hand on Robert's knee. I thought I might have lost you guys."

"We're just glad you were able to make it safely" Robert replied.

"What happened, we were worried sick about you!" RJ said.

"Yeah we tried to call you several times and you never answered" Rob interjected.

Le stared down at the floor as if taken back to a place she wanted to forget. "Well, here's what happened after the last time we spoke. I was reluctant to come over because you seemed very demanding and I thought to myself who the hell is he to be demanding of me! I took my time to get ready."

Knowing her Robert jokingly interrupted "I know you had to get all purty for me!' and lets out a light chuckle drawing a laugh from RJ as well. She cuts her eyes at him and continues her story.

"I was listening to the radio as I was driving and heard emergency reports being broadcast on the Jazz station giving orders to stay inside, avoid contact with anyone exhibiting illness resembling rabies or those not appearing to be in their full capacity. Things like that." Le continues to tell her story as they listened intently. She describes how the roads were littered with cars and looting has taken to the streets as well. She was no less than a mile from the house when she came to the major intersection of Broad Street and Thurber's Avenue when a minivan had blown through the red light t-boning the passenger side of her sedan.

"I blacked out for a minute or two, and when I came to everything slowly came into focus. I had pinned one of those infected people between my car and another when I was hit. As my vision came into focus I had realized it was still alive and ripping apart the shattered front windshield trying to get at me. It kept growling and gnashing its rotten teeth at me chomping at the air just a few feet from me. I looked to my right and saw the couple that ran into me and the passenger was coming to as well. She began to moan in pain and cry as she realized what had just happened.

Her doing so had caused enough noise to alert a hoard of those infected people. I was lucky enough to free myself and crawl to the back of the car. The dead had closed in on both cars engulfing the minivan and the passenger side of my car. They had easy access to the minivan and began to attack those poor people but I was able to climb out the rear driver side door."

Le continued on to explain she hid for an hour or so on the top slide crawlspace at Duarte Park waiting for the moaning of the dead to go away indicating the coast was clear. She then told how she had run a few hundred yards across the open field of the park into the woods toward the local strip mall. She ran to Brett's second-hand sports and began to pound on the door for help. A thin man wearing glasses and close-cropped beard opened the door, let her inside and then re-secured the door then barricaded it with gold clubs. There were five survivors in the store, Brett, his two sons, fiancée, and a police officer. There was an informal greet based on the circumstances as they said their first names and waived. Le thanked them for helping and Bret had informed her that they planned to stick it out at the sporting store and wait for the National Guard to come to the rescue. The officer stated that last he heard it was only a few days till the military would make its way to Cypress Pond for help.

"I need to get to my family now!" Le exclaims. "I know they are waiting for me and are worried."

The officer rendered first aid to her pump on her head as she explained her situation and replied: "you need to rest at least for a short while, you may have a concussion."

"We have a couch in the back" Brett added, "just lie down for an hour or so then make a decision after that."

After a little back and forth her acquiescence is reluctant as she is shown the back office by Brett's fiancée and given a blanket to lie on the couch. She did fall fast asleep for a few hours and woke up to a large bang sounding like an accident. She hastily makes her way back to the front of the store and rejoins the group. They were all peeking out the windows trying to see what caused the commotion. She was still groggy and sore but alert enough to get back on the road. "I have to go," she said to them startling everyone. "It's only a few blocks from here, I can make it". The officer volunteers to go with her for protection then make his way back to Brett.

Now it's nightfall and the large full moon lights up the town making it easy to see even in the shadows. The two leave the rear of the strip mall and head east toward Robert's house. While creeping down the back alley the officer dips into his black sports bag producing a four-inch blued Smith and Wesson .357 magnum and a few handfuls of ammunition which she slips into her pockets. As we round a corner now just a few blocks from the house she tells how there was a group of the dead surrounding a disabled vehicle that had screams coming from inside. "We gotta help them," the cop said and went over to try to rescue whoever was in the car but was immediately overran as he tried to shoot his way through the dead. Le said she had run off towards the house when zombies discovered he wasn't alone. "As I got closer to the house I heard gunshots from either your house or the neighbors" Le said. I waited for a bit before I was certain it was clear of the dead or looters before I came here. I noticed a faint light upstairs and just knew you were home, and here I am."

"What happened Robert?" Le asked everything is going to Hell out there. People are attacking each other and sometimes appeared to be feeding on one another!"

Rob responded "I think it's a top-secret viral weapon we created for Governmental Black Ops and I think it was unintentionally released. I've been trying to reach the office for the last day but there is no response from anybody."

"Don't you have an antidote?" Le asked.

"I was working on one but it wasn't ready. It's a long story but I am very close, I just don't have it yet. I need to get to my lab and see if I can finally crack the code of this virus. First, we need to see what's going on out there." As he turns the volume up on the television a bit he continues "we need to rest up because at dawn we have to hit the road and make the hour and a half ride to Atlanta and only God knows how that will go." She nods in agreement and they both pay attention to the broadcast.

After another hour or so passes they both tell RJ to get some rest but he puts up a fight. Rob says to him "we have a long day tomorrow. We need you to be sharp out there, ok". After a bit of a protest, he agreed kissing them both and went to his room to sleep.

Both Robert and Leese are now sitting on the couch in awkward silence as they watch the videos of chaos unfold on the television. The images of riots and looting, military units in the streets shooting both civilians as well as the dead, pictures of mass graves and armed citizens taking matters into their own hands. All reports were headlined by all capital white lettering which read "The Dead Walk!

Robert gets up from the couch and pours two glasses of cabernet returns to the couch and hands one to Le. He returns to the kitchen and begins to recheck the bug out bags. He goes through the itemized list and checks off the items one by one. Each bag contains three MRE's, two sixteen-ounce bottles of water, three pairs of white socks, two t-shirts, two pair boxer briefs, one first aid kit, one pack of waterproof matches, fifty rounds of buckshot, one hundred fifty rounds of nine-millimeter hollow points, ten rifled slugs, one hundred fifty rounds of 5.56 NATO ammunition and one combat knife.

Le saunters over and joins him in the kitchen and puts a hand on his shoulder which Robert notices and quietly watches him put the bags together. She goes to the counter and freshens her glass. Rob notices the strange yet familiar curves of her slender body and thinks back to simpler times between the two. She finally breaks the silence and asks if he had anything for her to wear to sleep in. Before he could respond she goes upstairs into his bedroom to see for herself.

A little while later and into his second glass of wine Robert is on the couch again as she comes and rejoins him wearing his favorite well-worn Yankees T, sitting cross-legged revealing a portion of her upper thigh. She sips her wine and looks intently at the television bearing the same violent news. Although she is focused on the television she also notices that he notices her as she fights back the urge to smile.

Robert gets a message via e-mail from the Cherokee Nation in Georgia of which blood flows through his veins. In the tribe, he was the elder medicine man and treated the natives on the reservation when he was not at the CDC. The e-mail read as follows:

> *Robert, we have been tracking the news on television and the web. Mother Earth is sick and is cleansing herself of the pestilence brought by man. Those who are unclean shall perish and the clean shall survive. There is NO infection with our people or on the rez. We are calling on all warriors of the tribe to return home and help protect our way of life. The secure line is still operational so please respond promptly any way you can.*
>
> *Respectfully,*
> *Chief Victor "High Eagle" Lombard*

Robert finally has a glimpse of hope and immediately responds to the e-mail stating that he would be responding to the CDC to continue his testing and find the cure. From there he would continue to the rez to vaccinate the entire tribe and help secure its survival. He would be in communication the following evening to update his progress. He copied the number to the secure line and placed a copy in each of the go bags as well as storing it in his cell phone. It was now past one in the morning and Robert tells Leese to take his bed and that he would sleep on the foldout in his office. She agreed and yawned "goodnight" and she went upstairs as Rob watched her the whole way. When he hears the bedroom door close he turns off the television and heads upstairs to his office and plops down on the couch and drifts off to sleep.

Tossing and turning in his bed Robert is awakened by a felt presence in the room. He quickly jumps up scanning the room with his pistol and sees a figure standing in the threshold. He rubs his eyes and the curvaceous and very familiar silhouette comes into focus. "Le? Is everything alright?" but there was no response. The shadowy figure began to walk toward him. The ambient light through the windows illuminated the sexy figure and he could see her erect nipples poking through her thin t-shirt. It seemed just as the pale moonlight was about to reveal her face a cloud hid it just at the exact moment to conceal her sensual eyes and juicy lips. It didn't matter much at that point, he wasn't paying attention to her face.

Now she stood at his side and he could see her thick legs that seemed to glisten in the light leading to the deep clefts of her thick meaty rear that was barely covered by the shirt. His animalistic instinct was in complete drive in his boxer briefs. He was sure she could tell as she began softly massaging him over his boxer briefs. Then in that sweet familiar voice, she said "It's been a long time baby, you can do anything you want to me. Anything."

He could barely control himself and she seductively sat on him adjusting to just the right spot and he could feel her damp warmth seeping through his draws. She leaned to kiss him passionately on the mouth and he embraced her tightly. One hand cupping her soft breast and the other on her lower back which slid down under her panties grabbing a hand full of her juicy ass. From her breast, he moves around to the back of her neck pulling her in closer returning the intensity of the kiss. Robert lightly begins tugging her hair as she let out a faint moan of pleasure. He tries to position her and look in her eyes but she turns away and responds "don't look at me!" This causes him to pause but keeps going with the moment as they continue to kiss.

Shortly after he tries to look into her beautiful brown eyes and this time her face was dimly lit by the pale moonlight. He catches her profile which was a face is of the dead! Her face had tightly drawn skin, overexposed rotted gums, and teeth and sunk in eyes that were clouded white and bloodshot. She lets out a shrieking scream, grabs his head with both hands and bites him on the lips tearing them from his face leaving a gaping wound spurting blood from his exposed gums and teeth.

Robert wakes up screaming in a cold sweat feeling his face to make sure it is intact. He jumps up and rushed to the mirror to double-check, splashes water on his face to wake up and ensure he is no longer dreaming and rechecks himself in the mirror. He goes to check on RJ who is still snoring away in his bed. Robert then opens his bedroom door quietly with the Colt .45 in tow and cautiously peers in. Leese is fast asleep also looking as beautiful as she ever did. He closes the door and heads downstairs to check the news. He looks out the front window and the street seems void of the dead, just a few cars still in the street some with the hazards still flashing. The sun was just rising to the East as the birds began chirping in the early cool morning air, it almost seemed peaceful.

He closed and locked the door and then proceeded to grab the "go bags". He then headed out to the garage and loaded them into the back of the Tahoe along with some extra ammunition, water, and canned food. He goes into the basement and retrieves his M4 carbine, case of sixty-two-grain green-tipped ammo and chest rig carrier and places it all in the SUV along with the Colt in the front center console. He reenters the house and starts the coffee machine and turns on the television. The anchor looks unusually disheveled, untucked shirt, no jacket or tie with coffee spilled his shirt. He exhaustedly reports:

"All previously reported safe refugee camps in the immediate area may be closed because we have not had an update in the past eight hours. The one thing we have confirmed to report is the dead are returning to life and feeding on the living. The only known way to stop the dead is to incapacitate the brain by shooting them in the head or severe head trauma. We will maintain broadcast of the safety camps that are still open and update as much as possible. Uh, I have just been informed we are going off the air.

Good luck and God Bless."

The television changed to its emergency broadcast system with that annoying high pitched tone with a rainbow background as the remaining emergency evacuation sites scrolled across the screen. Robert turned the television off and went to make two cups of coffee. He then goes to wake up his family. First, he goes to RJ and wakes him up and then to Leese and knocks on the door. She replies in a groggy voice "yeah, come in". Rob enters and brings her coffee in bed and offers breakfast when she is ready. She agrees to be down in a few minutes to eat before they hit the road to Atlanta. Minutes later Rob lays out some breakfast bars and orange juice. They all eat while making small talk then mount up in the Tahoe and brace for the road trip that lies ahead. Le hit's the remote garage door opener from the front passenger side visor and sunlight flooded the garage as the door slowly raised. The vehicle's DVD player came on and 2 Pac's "Me and my girlfriend" streamed through the speakers' mid-song:

"All I need in this life of sin is me and my girlfriend, down to ride to the bloody end, just me and my girlfriend……all I need in this life of sin is me and my girlfriend, down to ride to the bloody end, just me and my girlfriend……

I love finger fuckin you, all of a sudden I'm hearin thunder when you bust a nut, niggaz be duckin or takin numbers.

Love to watch you at a block party, beggin for drama, while unleashin on the old-timers, that's on my mama".

The music faded out as the Tahoe was put into drive and they pulled out headed into the Dawn of the Dead.

HIGHWAY TO HELL

The town of Cypress Pond was a complete war zone. The streets were littered with abandoned vehicles, some were just left as is and others told a different, more gruesome story. As Robert weaved slowly through the streets they stared at one car that had dried bloody handprints and smears on the outside no doubt left by the zombies. There was a broken window where blood and skin were still stuck to the jagged glass. There were cars that were totaled from a multiple vehicle pile-up and some even had zombies pinned against a wall or between two of them. The dead stayed there aimlessly looking about until they noticed the slowly moving car where they began to reach for it. They drive by Jake's Service Station which was still smoldering and across the street at Anne's Diner they noticed two to three dozen dead banging and clawing trying to gain entry.

"You think somebody is inside dad?" RJ asked.

Rob responded "I don't know. There isn't anything we can do for them now anyway."

They continue driving from the outskirts of Cypress Pond toward the main town area and the closer they got the more congested it became. They were now about a quarter-mile out till they reached the center of town when they came across a fresh car accident. One of the cars was turned completely upside down and there were about eight zombies trying to get the passengers inside. Rob gives a quick look around and sees that there were dead slowly shambling toward their location about a couple of hundred feet down the road and decided to tell Le to jump in the driver's seat.

"What are you going to do!?" she asked.

"We have to help them! We have plenty of time before the rest of them arrive. See how slow they are!" she looks as he points down the street "we can make it no problem."

"WE!?" she said.

"Yes, RJ and I are going for it, let's go, buddy. Move!"

Before she had a chance to protest both were out of the vehicle and sprinting toward the car. As they got within just feet of the dead a few zombies began to sniff the air and turn around. Robert yelled to RJ, "remember; take headshots!" RJ opened up with the unmistakable sound of a hail of buckshot, BOOM! And immediately racks in another round and sends another charge of 00 downrange CLICK, CLICK BOOM! The buckshot exploded the zombie's heads like watermelons and their now headless bodies fall to the ground. Robert also opens up with his Glock 17 taking careful shots aiming in the head area, bang, bang, bang. The dead fell one by one as their heads were blown back by the nine-millimeter jacked hollow points. They both get to the car and immediately see two terrified passengers screaming "help us please!" RJ's instincts kick in and he butt strokes the window and it crashes in. The dead are now staggering as fast as they can moaning as they slowly approached. The first passenger was a female named Brenda who was pulled out without a problem and was taken back to the car by RJ. The second female was named Jaylen and as they looked at each other they locked eyes pausing momentarily in recognition.

"Robert?" she says reaching for him. He grabs a hold of her and pulls with all his might but she doesn't budge. Unfortunately, she was stuck on something in the car that had her foot. Rob lay there trying to free her and the moans of the dead could now be heard getting closer.

By now Leese was in the driver's seat honking the horn yelling for him to come on as she kept looking back and forth between Robert and the hoard of zombies getting closer. Jaylen was struggling frantically to get free and pleaded for Robert not to leave her. Robert noticed that her shoe was stuck between the back seat and the door and he began tugging as hard as he could.

"Dad, look out!" was heard getting his attention causing him to notice a few zombies coming from between the cars on the other side of the street and were now on top of him. Rob aimed his pistol and fired. The first zombie's head snapped back, body stiffened as the bullet ripped through its head and it falls face-first striking the pavement with an audible thud. The brains and blood splattered on the street behind it slopping against the ground. The second one met the same fate falling on top of the first. The third was struck in the shoulder causing it to flinch to the right and the second shot struck the left cheekbone blowing out the right side of the head as it fell on its right side. RJ had now exited the SUV and you could hear the roar of the crowd-pleaser BOOM! Click-click, BOOM! No doubt dropping headless zombies in the street. Finally, Jaylen was freed minus her sneaker just as the hoard was close enough to hear their hellish moan and smell they're rotting flesh. They get into the vehicle just as the first zombie placed its hand on the rear window as Leese sped off.

As they drove away from the hoard of the dead they looked back as the overturned car seemed to be swallowed up by the walking corpses as they faded from sight.

"Thank God for you!" Jaylen said.

"It's not a problem. This is Robert Junior, goes by RJ and his mother Leese."

Jaylen replied with a hug and kiss for both men and Leese was none too happy. Brenda was still in shock trembling and trying to catch her breath. RJ had given them a bottle of water and a towel to wipe off. "Thank you" was mumbled from Brenda in between breaths and RJ just winked in response as he jammed shells into the Mossberg. They continued through town avoiding large groups of the dead by taking the side streets. As they made their way through town the dead were everywhere staggering aimlessly about. As the Tahoe carefully passed by, the dead slowly turned their stiff body's way too slow to even see it letting out a moan as if in frustration. Leese recommends they stop at the Cypress Pond Sheriff's office for help and everyone agrees that it's a good idea.

The silence was broken when Leese asked how the two women knew each other. Jaylen was a yoga instructor and had the toned body to prove it. She had short black hair that barely passed her ears and light hazel eyes. She was wearing a thin sweatshirt that fit tightly around her top-heavy frame and black yoga pants that clung tightly to a thick ass that wouldn't quit. She stated that Brenda who was a redhead was one of her new students and that they lived in the same apartment building so they would carpool. You could tell Brenda was new because though still well stacked, she wasn't as well-toned as Jaylen. When all this went on they stayed put the first couple days then decided to make a run for it to the evacuation site at the local mall but ended getting clipped by a garbage truck, not ten minutes before they rescued them.

They drive by the sheriff's office building which looked abandoned and there were a few dead around the front. They continue to the five-story parking garage next door and park on the top level which was clear of all vehicles and zombies. They get out and close the doors quietly. Robert goes to the rear hatch and retrieves his chest rig and M4 pulls the charging handle and chambers a round. He gives Leese the Glock and has everyone follow quietly behind him RJ taking up the rear with the crowd-pleaser. They head down the ten flights of stairs slowly checking the corners for danger until they reach the lower level which was loaded with abandoned cars. They crept along the back shielded by the row of parked vehicles to the rear of the lot leading to the rear garage exit that leads to the street between the lot and the rear of the sheriff's office. They slowly exit the heavy steel green rear door and peer around the structure and see several dead aimlessly walking the streets. Robert calmly aims through his ACOG sighted carbine placing the red chevron on the zombie's heads as they crossed his scope. He motioned for the group to quickly run across to the sheriff's lot and they did so quickly and quietly. He followed in suit and they squeezed through an opening in the rusted gate. They were about forty yards from the rear garage roll up and back entrance, but there were about five or six zombies between them and their destination. They could easily shoot them but that would bring down more dead from the report of the gunfire. RJ grabs a beer bottle from the ground and tosses it clear across the lot crashing it against the furthest parked cruiser. The shattering glass piqued the zombie's interest and they began to moan and shamble toward the far corner. They all ran in line to the door keeping a keen eye on the group of corpse's just feet away. To their surprise the door was open and they quickly enter the darkroom and locked the steel door shutting it behind them.

They all check around and realize that they are in the vehicle sally port where a cruiser and sport utility vehicle marked "supervisor". They carefully check the area and nobody could be found. Robert had them stay at the bottom of the stairs in case he had to make a hasty retreat. He clears the stairs and comes into a hallway that leads to the main waiting area. The hallway was beige with brown carpeted floor and the now familiar stench of dried blood filled the air. There were several doors along the hallway with plastic signs sticking out the top that read "interrogation room 1&2, Sheriff Hines, Holding & Processing, Armory, Detectives, etc. He waited for a few minutes listening intently for any movement. He then slowly proceeds to the first door marked Sheriff Hines and carefully rounds the corner and sees something that twists his stomach and he vomits on the spot. Robert dry heaves a second time and he spits the bile taste from his mouth. Trying not to look he takes the large ring of keys and closes the door. Robert takes a minute closing his eyes tightly trying to erase the graphic picture seared into his brain. The picture of Sheriff Hines or what was left of him reclined leaning left stiffly in his chair. His tan uniform shirt was darkened brown with blood and his name pin reading Hines ironically was untarnished and shined in the sunlight. There was a shotgun leaning on his body with the muzzle resting on the bottom row of teeth which was all that was left from the blast. The wall behind where his head used to be was sprayed and stuck with a four-square foot stain of blood, skull, brain matter and teeth. There were four shotgun shells lined up in a neat formation on his desk along with a bottle of bourbon half gone. Robert shook his head trying to erase the memory but to no effect.

72 hours earlier....

The phone rings in Sheriff Hines office. He immediately recognizes the number, it's home. His wife calling him for the umpteenth time today. A well-worn and weary un-kept Hines exhales deeply before he answers the phone.

"Look Neta, we've been over this several times. I need to be in the office to run things until FEMA arrives to help."

A crying fearful voice on the other end of the line says "your family needs you, Paul. We are here alone and are afraid! Come home damn you!"

"I don't have time for this shit! I'm losing people left and right here and I can't leave. Last I heard from the government they should be here in the next couple of hours then I will be able to come home." He now is running his hand through his hair as he looks at the family photo taken in the hospital with their newborn.

There are people attacking and eating other people all over the news. Your brother never showed up to help us and there is a lot of noise outside. We are frightened and alone Paul, you promised to protect us!"

Paul growing anxious could now hear his newborn begin in the background and loud background noise that he couldn't quite make out.

"What's that noise Neta?"

"Jesus Paul, some of those things are at the front door! Christ! They broke in the glass door and are in the house! NO!

There was a thud on the other end of the line when the phone was dropped. Sheriff Hines listened in horror as the sound of his crying infant ceased and the sound of his wife screaming NO! NO! AAAHHHHHH! Her screams ceased as the only sound on the line was of the dead as they moaned and feasted on his family.

"Shieneta! Shieneta!" Paul yelled into the phone which became disconnected. He stayed frozen as the line beeped before hanging up. He stared blankly at the phone as tears strolled down his cheeks. He hung his head placing his hands on his head and let out a boisterous cry as he swiped his desk clear as its contents crashed to the floor. Breathing heavily he wipes his face from the tears and licks his lips as he retrieves a bottle of liquor from his desk. He takes a long hard kiss from the bottle and grimaces while swallowing the strong drink. He repeats a few more times when in mid swig he coughs spraying the office. He wipes his chin as he hastily retrieves a shotgun from his closet and sits back in his chair. Taking another gulp he unloads the weapon placing the bullets in a neat row in front of him. He looks intently at them for the best-looking one takes it and kisses it before placing it into the breach closing the action. Sniffling he takes another drink and slams the bottle on the desk and takes one last look at his family photo. Closing his eyes he quickly puts the tip of the barrel in his mouth and pulls the trigger.

Back in the vehicle sally port the group anxiously await for Robert to signal the coast is clear. Upstairs Robert carefully checked the rest of the rooms which were empty then into the main area the public goes for complaints, pay tickets, etc. The main area was separated by bulletproof glass and a few dead could be seen kneeling over their victim devouring her. He goes back to the top of the stairway and whispers "all clear, come on up". When everybody is reunited he tells them to stay out the Sheriff's office, scavenge for supplies and that they were moving on as soon as possible. They quickly and quietly entered and thoroughly searched each room. While checking the break room cupboards they ended up scoring peanut butter, crackers, granola bars, power bars and a couple of jars of generic instant coffee. In the refrigerator, they find ice-cold bottles of water, sports drinks, and some spoiled leftover food.

They hit the armory last but the gun cage was unlocked and almost bare. They grabbed a couple of Glock 22 pistols with spare magazines, a Remington 870 pump gun and hunting rifle in 7.62 NATO. They also grabbed the remaining ammunition they could totaling three hundred sixty rounds of .40 Smith and Wesson Gold Dots, fifty-five shotgun shells of buckshot and slugs and thirty-seven rounds for the hunting rifle. As they make their way to the front reception area a couple of the dead must have eaten their share and wandered in search of more fresh meat. As the group ransacked the desks two of the dead approached the glass growling and clawing at the glass smearing blood and meat everywhere they touched. One was so aggressive and greedy as he was biting the glass he had actually knocked his front teeth out. All that was found was a black gym bag and they jammed all the ammo and food rations they could in it. They then headed back to the end of the hallway, they grabbed the two extra five gallons of water adjacent to the water cooler and headed carefully back to the sally port, loaded the new stash in the Sheriffs SUV and piled into the vehicle as they all looked to Robert for instruction as to what to do next.

He stands outside the driver's window and rubs his hand over his face and head. "Alright, when I open the gate, you head around to the front of the building and continue up to our vehicle atop the parking garage. We gotta move quick cause they'll be right on our asses. I will draw their attention and head back the same way through the back alley and up the back stairs and meet you there."

Le had a concerned look on her face but believed in him and that he would come through. Robert went to the glass window in the steel door and saw the dead were still clustered in the same area but were beginning to spread out into the lot again. He then checked the side near the gate they came through and he could just make out a few zombies there. "Fuck it!" he thinks to himself and goes to Le in the driver's seat and kisses her on the lips which surprises her and before she could react he taps the hood and tells her "let's roll" and runs to the gate controller. He then hits the gate opener and it begins to squeak as it raises slowly letting in more and more sunlight as it raises. The dead could be heard outside moaning and growling as they turned slowly and began to stagger toward the noisy door. Robert runs out and yells "see you in a few!" raising his M4 lining up the red chevron on the face of the closest zombie and squeezing the trigger. The back of the zombies head exploded into a pink mist as an ear-piercing crack came from the muzzle. With minimal recoil, the Colt smoothly ejected the brass spitting it onto the concrete as it fed another round from the magazine. CRACK-CRACK- CRACK- CRACK. The remaining dead were all dropped in quick succession in the same manner as the first before they knew what hit them. Le had backed over a couple of zombies as she backed out and then hit a couple more as she barreled forward and to the right out of sight. As Robert ducked under the gate he was surprised to see that almost one hundred zombies had started toward him down the side street as the closest was within arm's reach! He immediately grabbed his machete and with a mighty swing the zombie's skull crunched and the large blade stuck in its skull. The zombie fell stiffly to its knees and Rob placed his foot on the chest and used leverage to free the blade. Blood began to thickly trickle from the wound as the zombie fell to the ground face first. The dead began to quickly shamble toward him arms raised bearing their teeth. He runs across the street to the rear door of the lot and pulled on the door that was stuck! "Shit!" he said and shouldered the rifle and quickly squeezing off rounds CRACK- CRACK- CRACK dropping three more. He frantically pulled repeatedly with all his might and finally, the door gave way and swung open and the momentum from the heavy door knocked him on his side. Rob jumped up and ran into and trucking over a couple of walkers as he slipped into the stairway just out of the grasp of the hoard. He takes two stairs at a time and the legion of the dead sloppily spill into the stairway after him. The echo of the dead moaning and snarling was disheartening and though the fire burns in his lungs, adrenalin pushes him the remaining two flights of stairs.

Robert crashes through the exit door and sees both Le and RJ in their car and Jaylen and Brenda in the sheriff's vehicle waiting for him. Exhausted he slams the heavy door shut and quickly walks to the SUV and gets into the passenger seat. He takes a long swig of water and hugs his family. "Hit the road," he says to Leese and as they begin their way down the lot the dead following Robert crash through the door and spill out onto the landing tripping over each other.

Twenty minutes of weaving through abandoned cars and the dead they make it out of the heart of town and the destruction seemingly begins to lighten a bit. They finally see the sign they were looking for. A red white and blue shield with 95 N was seen hanging from the traffic light that was now blinking red. They make it to the onramp and ascend onto the main artery creeping slowly and quickly discover the interstate was surprisingly free of debris, cars or the dead. They were able to travel for over an hour passing abandoned vehicles along the way, some had a corpse or two in the seats or a zombie clawing at the windows trying to figure how to get out.

It was only mid-morning and the blazing Georgia sun was baking the survivors as they drove. Jaylen began to honk the horn and Le pulled over as everyone noticed steam billowing from under her hood. Everyone got out and stretched as they exited the vehicles. RJ had Jaylen pop the hood and listed it allowing the built-up steam to escape. Rob joined his son and they both said looking at each other "coolant." They had decided to rest for a while under the trees along the side of the highway and give the engine time to cool. They took the time rest the best they could and took turns on watch. An hour or so had passed before they tried to open the radiator which gave out a loud spitting hiss. They added some water which just seemed to boil the second it touched the engine block. The decision was made to trek the few blocks for antifreeze at the service station that they spotted from the highway.

It was now late in the afternoon and they only had a few hours of daylight to get back on the road or find adequate shelter. Robert told Leese and Jaylen to stay with the vehicles and were given one of the two-way radios. RJ had told them to call if anything happened and if it got too bad to take off and head to the CDC. RJ and Brenda then followed Robert to the guardrail and peered over the side looking down the main street leading to the service station. The street was littered with cars some with their hazards flashing, dozens of headless corpses all over the street with about a half dozen walkers still staggering about aimlessly. They quickly made their way down the grassy hill to the street and kneeled behind a parked car. They were about three hundred yards from the car shop and were peering over the hood to scan the area for threats other than the dead.

Everything appeared to be as good as it would get and as Robert prepared to move RJ grabbed his dads shoulder stopping him in his tracks getting his full attention.

"Dad, look." Robert looks at the headless zombies' stiff corpses that were scattered up and down the street. "Do you think he is still out there?" The thought came rushing to him like a ton of bricks.

"Damn sniper" Rob whispers.

They all crouch low behind the car as Rob cautiously heads back up peering intently through the 4X32 ACOG on his carbine scanning for where he thought the sniper would be. A zombies head exploded no more than thirty yards from their location and a distant crack was heard a second later. "There! Straight ahead on the right! I just saw the son of a bitches muzzle flash!" Robert said. "They haven't seen us yet. We're going to have to stay low and quiet against the buildings to the right. A single file formation like before and keep on my ass. Move!" The followed closely and they ran hugging the walls of the buildings to the right as planned. Robert led the way peering through the optic scanning for additional threats. They were halfway there when the dead were beginning to take notice and started to slowly shamble in their direction.

From the fourth floor window Thomas peers through his Burris 10X magnified scope at the dead staggering in the street and notices something or someone has their attention. He scans left but whatever it is, is just out of sight. He jumps on the radio "George, whattaya got?" On the other end, Georges voice responds "nothing yet".

Robert realizes they need to move quickly as it was a matter of time of being shot or eaten to death. They spot a second shooter on the first floor, so RJ turns and kicks in the door to the bakery adjacent the snipers perch and they file inside. They looked around checking the area for safety which was clear and while doing so they all flinched at the crack of the sniper rifle no doubt taking another walker out. Robert tells them there are two men, one on the fourth floor and the other is on the first floor. They needed a plan to distract him and try to overtake them. Robert quickly thinks to himself then says "I will sneak around the rear of the buildings, RJ you will cover my ass. Brenda, you need to go back outside and get his attention."

"Fuck you! He'll shoot me" she said.

"No, he won't. Brenda, you have to trust me ok. Take off your bra."

She looks at him disgusted as she crosses her arms covering her breasts.

"You need to get his attention and trust; that will do it!" RJ nods in agreement holding back a smirk. She turns around and complies removing her bra with her t-shirt still on saying "I can't believe I'm doing this." RJ looks at his dad puzzled and he just shakes his head and shrugs his shoulders indicating he still can't figure how women can do that. Turning around her shapely C cups could be seen hanging nicely as her nipples poked through. Robert got up close and personal and tore her shirt from the neck halfway down exposing the entire inside curves of her breasts which she didn't seem to mind. He then told her to wait two minutes then go outside and shoot the last few zombies and start calling for help. Robert taps RJ who was still staring at Brenda's tits, snaps out of it and follows his dad through the rear of the store.

They cross the small alley in the rear of the buildings and stand on either side of the door to the snipers building and pull on the door which was loose but locked from the inside. Rob pulled as hard as he could while RJ unhinged the latch and the door swung open just at multiple shots from Brenda's Glock 22 sounded. Robert and RJ quietly move into the office building which was a doctor's office. They made their way down the dimly lit hall toward the front and peer around a corner to the main entrance. From the rear of the doctor's office, Robert saw a large muscular dark tanned man now had his gun trained on Brenda so he leveled the red chevron on the rear quarter of his head and began taking the slack out of the trigger. From outside Brenda could be heard pleading "please help me! I barely got away from these, these monsters! Can I please come with you!?" He began to lower his weapon causing Robert to do the same.

Brenda could now be seen through the large glass doors and the man was intently focused on her chest. "I'm Brenda, and you are?"

"George, the names George" he replies without taking his eyes off her chest.

Brenda leads him toward the back room just feet from Robert who is waiting to knock him out. She gives him a hug showing her gratitude which he gladly accepts then everything goes black. He was knocked out giving him a nice egg on his head. The three of them hogtied and gagged him moments before the sniper came down to have his way with the helpless voluptuous redhead.

Moments earlier the sniper on the fourth floor was trying to see what grabbed the attention of the dead as he intently peered through his scope. He heard gunfire from below and the dead dropping from somebody's bullets. A young female appeared in his sights brandishing a pistol firing repeatedly at the few remaining dead missing mostly and hitting a few in the torso. She managed to get lucky and score a headshot and dropped the closest zombie as if it was a sack of potatoes. Thomas broke the gaze from her exposed chest and dropped the last zombie splitting its head like a canoe. The head exploded into large fragments as chunks of brain matter slopped to the pavement as the girl ran towards his partner downstairs. George's voice chirps on the radio "Thomas, come down here" and Thomas replies "be right there."

Thomas then scans the street for any more walkers then checks across the parking lot across the street. There was a hastily made barricade that was thrown together with a single bike chain and lock that was holding the chain-link gate together, barely. There were hundreds of zombies seen pushing and rocking the unstable fortification back and forth but it was holding so he got up from his position and headed downstairs.

Thomas was anxiously taking two stairs at a time down the flights of stairs yelling to George that he is on his way. Finally, Thomas jumps down the final three steps on opens the door to the first-floor administration office. He sees the busty redhead leaning on a table against the wall. "Where's George?" he asked and she points toward the bathroom now completely exposing one her breasts completely distracting him. He was so intently engrossed with her chest that he didn't notice Robert sneak up beside him knocking his out cold with the butt of his rifle.

Robert looks to both RJ and Brenda "stay here and watch these two, I'm going next door for the antifreeze and anything else I can grab. I'll only take a few minutes." They both nodded and RJ kept the Mossberg trained on the two who were now seated against the wall as

Brenda now tied her shirt revealing her midsection like Daisy Duke. Robert then carefully exited the front glass doors with his M4 at the low ready and heads the last fifteen yards to Jake's Service Station. He pulls on the door which was locked. The eerie sound of hundreds of zombies growling across the lot caught his attention causing his eyes to grow the size of saucers. How could he have missed them he thought to himself, and realized the rifle fire from the sniper had covered the sound of the hoard and no doubt attracted them to the area. Panic had started to overtake him but he refocused on the glass door smashing it with the barrel of the rifle and quickly entered the building.

The service station was the little sister to a Green station chain. Most of the good food was taken and a lot of the drinks were gone. Robert hurried through the aisles looking for antifreeze and finally comes across the final two bottles, slings the rifle over his shoulder and grabs both but freezes in his tracks. In the doorway to the repair garage stood a large black male in overalls. There was an oval patch reading Jake in red letters. He was holding a large revolver staring intently at Robert. There was silence for what seemed like an eternity then Jake spoke in a deep voice "first you shoot at me from the doctor's office keeping me pinned in here and now you got the balls to come into my shop and rob me! Well, I'm gonna show ya how we do it up in Jake's bitch!" Rob tries to explain he wasn't the asshole shooting everyone and he just needed some antifreeze to help his family but Jake wasn't buying it. Jake began to raise the hand cannon in Robert's direction.

Back in the medical office building both George and Thomas were awake but with a severe headache. "Why don't you untie us, we ain't done nothing," Thomas said. There was no response from RJ or Brenda, RJ was now looking through the large pane glass windows for his father.

"He should have been back by now," he says.

Brenda responds "He will just give him time."

RJ's eyes grew double in size as his mouth opened at the sight of the thousand dead pressing against the nearly downed hate. "Brenda! Look! We gotta get outta dodge!" Little did they know that while they were looking at the ocean of the dead pressing to get at them Tom was able to untie his hands and waited for the moment to make his move.

"C'mon, let us go. We are on the same side in case you didn't notice." Brenda walked towards him Glock in hand and was about to give some smart ass remark when Tom struck like a cobra lunging at her with a football tackle. Once on the ground, he gave her a swift sure backhand. RJ screams "stop!" and levels the bitch at Tom who now has the Glock and launches a hail of buckshot just missing Tom smashing the wall behind him. Flinching Tom runs toward the stairwell firing blindly behind him as one of the .40 caliber bullets strikes his partner George in the back killing him. Rob runs to check Brenda keeping the shotgun focused on the stairwell and she is dazed but ok.

In the gas station, Jake had the drop on Robert and was about to fire when the loud echo of a shotgun next door distracted Jake making him flinch. Robert seized the moment and ducked as Jake opened up with the .44 magnum BAM! BAM! BAM! The .44 spoke sending hot slugs' right by Robert and cracking into the wall next to him. Robert drawing his Glock returned fire with a double-tap POP! POP! His rounds hit the threshold sending splinters of wood everywhere causing Jake to duck back into the garage. Robert grabbed the antifreeze and made a run for it. He was again met with the heat of passing .44 slugs from Jake. The last shot had exploded one of the antifreeze jugs exploding neon green liquid all over knocking the remaining plastic to the ground. Robert ran as fast as he could to the medical building and crashed through the doors.

He sees Brenda and RJ now standing over the dead body and realized the sniper was missing. "What the fuck happened?!" he asked the two. RJ explained the situation and they decided that it would be best to hightail it out of there as soon as possible. There was a loud crack from the sniper's rifle upstairs causing them to duck. Then another shot. They couldn't understand what he was shooting at and went to the door to try and see. Robert told them that they would head out, in the same manner, they came in hugging the wall as much as they can to avoid the sniper's crosshairs. "We gotta get out before they get here" and he motioned across the lot to the dead gathered by the frail gate. Crack! The sniper rifle spoke again and to their dismay, they discovered what he was shooting at as the legion of the dead came spilling through the barricade resembling water breaking through a dam. "OH SHIT!" they said collectively. "Remember to stay quick, low and against the wall. Move!" All three burst out the door and hugged the buildings as planned. The overwhelming smell of rotten meat filled the humid evening air filling their nostrils. The moaning of the dead was nerve-wracking and the three soon realized that they couldn't outrun the hoard and were about fifty yards from the fence leading up to the highway. The dead now were only feet away now shambling as quickly as they could, arms outreached trying to grab their next meal. Robert gave the order "NOW!" The three opened up on the walkers in the way still moving forward. Brenda had decided to go right between a couple of cars the straight again which unwittingly put her in the sights of the sniper.

Back on the fourth floor Tom was drawn toward the volley of gunfire and to his enjoyment, the ginger ran into his crosshairs and he tracked her as she maneuvered through the dead. He got the timing, led her just a hair, held his breath and squeezed the trigger….Crack! No sooner did the flame leave the muzzle he watched her tumble forward as a bright red mist exploded from her front right shoulder sending her rolling over a few times. "Got you bitch" he whispered to himself as he left his sniper's nest disappearing into the evening twilight.

Now at the gate, the echo from the sniper's rifle reached them and a scream of agony came from Brenda's location. As Rob and RJ look back they see blood-soaked Brenda rolling on the ground. "No!" yelled RJ as he was pushed through the opening in the gate by his dad. Rob thought of going back but it was too late. The dead were on her as the first zombie grabbed her forehead ripping her whole hairline back literally scalping half of her head. She let out a scream of pain and another clawed into her eye socket squishing her eyeball as blood squirt from her occipital socket. Another few zombies ripped open her abdomen and bit her throat out and she was gone. The swarm of dead piled onto her and forgot about the men. They both ran up the grassy embankment to the waiting Leese and Jaylen who were now sitting in the Tahoe. They see both RJ and Robert jogging to the vehicles and ask simultaneously "Where's Brenda?!" Robert explained the whole story as he filled the Sheriffs SUV with the antifreeze. RJ stated that they need to find shelter for the night and they agreed. Everyone piled into the vehicles and continued down the highway heading toward the airport in hopes a hotel would give them a place to rest.

Shortly after they came upon a green traffic sign with white lettering that read Georgia International Airport exit 1 mile. A sense of accomplishment came over them and they continued around the curve in on the highway anticipating a smooth ride the last mile to their destination and as they clear the bend Leese slams on the brakes. The survivor's stared openmouthed at the sight of several thousand dead not more than one hundred yards from them clogging interstate I 95. "Oh, shit," Robert said. "What do we do dad?" asked RJ anxiously and the sound of their nerve-wracking moans overpowered the Tahoe's engine. There was a few dead on the right off-ramp and they decided to make a run for it. They drive the off-road area of the off-ramp bowling over six of the dead in their path and came the main artery of Georgia Airport Way. This main street was littered with various restaurants as well as hotels. They look both ways and the right was completely congested with abandoned cars telling the same grim story as the countless others before. They decide to go left and set their sights on the Springs' Motel that was about two miles down on the left. It was a bi-level building and as they drew near they saw it was closed off with the ten-foot-high red security gate and lock. A quick glance around and no dead were close by so they exit the vehicles and inspect the gate. They tried pulling and picking the lock to no avail. Robert was going to have RJ breach the lock with the shotgun and told him to blow it. Jaylen checked the rear of the Sheriff's truck and told them to wait, she had found a pair of fence cutters and ran to the gate handing them to Robert then backed off to watch for zombies. Robert easily clipped through the lock and removed the chain holding the two sides of the gate and pushed them open. Both vehicles were driven into the lot and Rob and RJ closed the gate and re-secured it tying the chain in a knot the best they could and ran around the corner to the main lot and joined the women.

SPRINGS MOTEL

It was now dusk and the sky was now a dark blue turning purple. The street lights were now turning on via the preset timer that seemed to give an artificial orange hue to the entire lot and face of the building. There was a large aqua neon sign that read Springs Motel in cursive and a rectangular-shaped five-foot pool near the main office across the lot. The building was made of white stucco slightly stained with bluish-green mold and all the windows uniformly were dressed with vintage seventies orange shades. All were drawn and everything seemed quiet. In the distance, there was an explosion drawing everyone's attention and black smoke began to fill the night sky. "We have to search this place before we settle in guys," Rob said and they all checked their weapons before cautiously heading to the manager's office. Robert quietly instructs everyone by hand signals to stand to the left side of the door. Robert peers in and can see a television was on in the back room. He doesn't see anybody and tries the door which to his surprise was unlocked. He allows the door to swing in and making eye contact with RJ indicates he is going in and RJ was to follow suit. They enter the room quietly and search the room with their weapons at the ready. There was nobody in the bathroom or behind the desk. They came to the back room where the television was glowing in the small crack in the door. With guns focused on the doorway, Robert knocked as the door opened slowly. Immediately it was clear that the room was host to the dead. Robert had Leese pull the door open and the manager wearing a v neck over a white t with a nameplate reading Jerry came stumbling out. Jerry raised his arms and began grinding his rotted teeth at them as he was met with the business end of the machete. "Shuck!" was heard as the dead skill crushed away from the blow of the sharp blade and Jerry fell face-first to the ground. Robert stepped over the lifeless corpse as thick blood began to ooze slowly from the canoe-like wound and ensures the closet of the break room was clear. Everyone checked for keys and anything else useful in the office before they clear a few rooms to bed down for the night. The ring of keys was taken off the desk and the vending machines were raided as well as the break room. They had scored several packs of beef jerky, ramen noodles, cans of soups and a case and a half of water. They grabbed the rations proceeded outside and tossed it in the back of the vehicles. Outside by the vehicles, they devise a plan on checking the rooms systematically and when done they would settle on rooms on the second level and barricade the stairways for added protection. They would take one room at a time using the keys, three would clear it and one would stay outside as watch. The motel was an "L" shape with a dozen rooms on each level including ice and vending and they started with room 1-1. Jaylen was to open the doors with the keys and Rob would be first with the Colt .45 automatic with Le with the Glock nine and RJ cleaning up with the crowd-pleaser. They gather close to listen for any activity inside the room but can't hear a thing. Robert nods to Jaylen to open the door and after nervously fumbling with the keys she gets the right one and turns the knob. Robert enters quietly and the rooms were open and only had a bathroom so he walked directly at it and could see immediately that the bathroom was empty also. Rooms 2-1 through 10-1 went exactly the same, without incident. The next room 11-1 was another story, thrashing about could be heard from the search of the adjacent room and from the sound of it there sounded to have the dead inside. They decided not to enter and barricaded the door with the now empty vending machine. 12-1 had the smell of dead meat just as the one prior filled with zombies except without any sound. They decided to enter and as soon as the door opened hundreds of flies buzzed their way past the survivors and it was discovered that an elderly couple had expired and were laying side by side on the bed holding hands. They must have been there for several days as their bodies began to liquefy into the blanket on top of the bed. They closed the door and Jaylen motioned the making of the cross, kissed her finger and pointed to the sky which was her way of prayer for the dead no doubt. They then turned their attention to the five abandoned cars in the lot and begin to wonder if they are the dead in the last room or maybe hiding someplace upstairs. They raid the cars and didn't scavenge anything worthwhile in the first four, but hit the jackpot with the last.

The last car was a blue sedan and must have belonged to a "prepper."In plain view of the back seat was a black duffle bag when picked up was heavy and uneven. When placed on the ground and unzipped, the contents surprised and strangely excited everyone. There were over a dozen homemade pipe bombs topped with waterproof fuses, a bandoleer of shotgun shells, additional seventy-five rounds of buckshot in three twenty-five round boxes, two spare magazines for the Colt .45 and one hundred fifty rounds of .45 automatic ammunition. When the trunk was popped there for the taking was an automatic shotgun, first aid kit, large tent, flares, half case of bottled water, boxes of instant oatmeal, two dozen MRE's and a Kimber .45 automatic. All of the new cache was carefully placed in the rear of the Sheriff's vehicle. It was now nightfall and the only saving grace was the cool night air.

They make their way up the stairs and now will work their way back from the far end using the same method as before. As they listen on the outside of the door they all were startled and jumped back as it swung open revealing an older man with gray straw-like hair with matching stubble. He was wearing vintage 70's glasses that fit cock-eyed and an old dingy white wife beater and greasy wrangler jeans and no shoes. He had smoked all his life and his fingers showed it. His thumb, pointer and middle finger have permanently stained a yellow-orange and severely cracked. His face was drawn and sick looking as well and from a distance could easily be mistaken for a walker. He stands in the threshold of 8-2 with a lit cigarette between his pointer and middle fingers as his hand rests on his hip and with toothless slobber, he demands "the fuck you want?"

Everyone has their weapons trained on the old mean bastard at this point. Quickly RJ answers, "We just want a room" as everyone lowered their weapons.

"Well, you got dem keys now don't ya" he responded. "How'd ya get em?"

Robert answers "grabbed em from the desk."

The old man gives him a steely look through a cluster of wrinkles and overgrown gray eyebrows as he lets smoke slowly escape through his nostrils and mouth after taking the last puff. He pinches the butt out between his fingers flicking it over the railing. Without a word, he enters back into his room and the four head to the threshold and peers in. The room looked just as you might expect to match the occupant to the very last detail. The bed was unmade, the radio was playing emergency news broadcasts of emergency operations that were still ongoing. There were old pizza boxes, and Chinese food containers distributed throughout the room old cigarette butts and ash all over the place. The smell of cheap booze and body odor filled the room as well. "Well, take care," Robert said. Leese adds "We're going to take a couple of rooms at the other end of the motel and make some dinner. You're welcome to join us." The old man kept his back toward the group and just waved them off without a word. The group continues to check the rooms without incident and take the last two on the upper level.

Robert and RJ empty both bags of supplies on the bed and began to divide it evenly. There were just over a dozen pipe bombs, seventy-five rounds of buckshot, over one hundred eighty .45 auto shells, ten MRE's, and to everyone's surprise a Vietnam Era fragmentation grenade fell out last from the corner of the bag. They restock each bag and Robert has RJ help him take the bags back down to the vehicles. As the guys are outside with the vehicles the women were preparing food for dinner. There was an awkward silence between the two as they shared what served as the kitchen. As the men returned from outside Leese told the guys to sit and get ready to eat. Le had grabbed the plate of food and a sports drink and had taken it to RJ. Jaylen had seized the moment and grabbed the plate of food meant for Robert and had taken that and a sports drink and taken it to him. As she handed it to him she politely thanked him again as she placed her right hand on his hand for saving her earlier that day and kissed him on his cheek allowing her juicy lips to linger for a second. She stared and smiled as she headed to the bathroom to take a shower and runs the water.

"Since when is she your girlfriend!" Le snapped at Robert. Stunned he responds to her "gimme a break, it's not like you want me anymore." RJ sits quietly mid-bite as his eyes dart back and forth as the two go at it. In the bathroom, Jaylen is now dressed in black and gray yoga pants and a low cut t and smiles as she hears the two argue. As she reenters the room she asks rhetorically "what's the sleeping arrangements? Le, I don't mind rooming with Robert if you wanted to be near to protect your son." Le doesn't respond and grabs the ice bucket, heads outside and slams the door behind her. RJ looks at his dad and shrugs his shoulders and continues eating his dessert of fruit snacks.

Down the hall, Terry is talking to himself as he paces his dirty room that was now thick with cigarette smoke. "Kill the bitch! Kill the bitch!" he mumbled repeatedly. Then all of a sudden he sits on the end of the mattress. He removes a large hunting knife and intensely stares at the blade as it glistens in the moonlight casting a silver reflection on his steely eyes. He hears a door slam jarring him from his trance and looks out the window. He sees a female storm down the stairs and walking quickly across the lot toward the vending area. He puts the cigarette out between his fingers and decides to seize the moment and follows suit knife in hand. He quietly sneaks in the shadows to the vending area and as he gets closer he can hear the ice being scooped from the freezer. As he rounds the corner he can see a female bent over wearing tight shorts and a t-shirt. He comes up from behind quickly covering her mouth to cover her cry for help. Startling her, she drops the ice and bucket only getting out a muffled scream. Terry hisses in her ear "got you bitch!" and lets out an evil chuckle then licks the side of her face. He pulls her into the manager's office in shadows of the building and closes the door.

Both Robert and RJ notice Jaylen and her choice of clothing but continue about their business as usual. Robert checks the window and doesn't see Leese anywhere and gets worried. "RJ, let's go check for mom." He grabs the Colt and Kimber and hands the Kimber to his dad. "Jaylen, wait here for us," Rob says and she nods with a smile looking him up and down. The men head outside and down the stairs and both begin calling out softly "Leese! Le!" "Ma! Where are you?" They check both cars and the entire lot then make their way toward the manager's office to check the vending area. Robert and RJ rounded the corner they could see the spilled ice that was well on the way to melting and bucket on the concrete. Both click off the safeties of their pistols and both backs against the wall. Robert looks at RJ and motions toward the door leading to the manager's office. They both enter and RJ let the door accidentally slam behind him. They both stop in their tracks and listen for movement and rustling came from the back room. They finally heard a scream "in here!" in a panic-stricken voice that was muffled immediately as they both close in on the back room. They enter the room and froze at the sight that befell them. Le was tied to a chair and Terry wearing his vest and name tag held a knife to her throat. She was visibly shaken and had tears running down her face.

"Drop the fuckin knife mother fucker!" ordered Robert.

Jerry hissed "you killed my twin brother you hog bitch!"

"It was an accident! I'm sorry, please let her go!"

"Mom!" screamed RJ as he began to sob.

Gnashing his green teeth and steely eyes filled with tears he hisses "fuck you and die!" as he plunges the knife in her chest and dark red blood began to flow from the wound. "NOOOOOOO!" both Robert and RJ yelled as they both open fire on Terry filling the room with smoke and hot brass. Robert fires three shots hitting him in the chest area staggering Terry back a few steps and RJ fired twice one missing striking the wall showering Terry with plaster. The second shot striking his lower left jaw jarring his head to the right causing the right side of his face to explode showering the wall with a red mist of blood, bone, and teeth. Terry went toppling over onto his right side between the love seat and the table holding the microwave. They immediately drop their pistols and attend to Leese who was now slumped in the chair. "Dad is she ok!" RJ manages to get out between breaths. "Shit!" Rob says as he checks her vitals. He immediately unties her and laid her on the floor and begins Cardiopulmonary resuscitation but inside he knew she was gone. RJ now holding her head and clearing her hair from her face "mom! Wake up! Wake up ma!" as he cries telling his dad to save her. After a few minutes, Robert again checks her vitals and can't find a pulse. Out of breath, he looks grieve stricken at RJ and they both hug each other tightly and cry in each other's arms.

Minutes later Jaylen comes into the manager's office wielding a shotgun and says "guys, are you ok I heard shooting!" Robert musters an answer "we're fine. Stay there, we are coming out." Jaylen heads outside to watch for any dead that may have been attracted by the gunfire. Robert takes the weapons and takes RJ by the arm and slowly gets him to his feet and hugs his sobbing son.

"I'm sorry son, I tri" and he was interrupted by RJ.

"I know dad, I just can't believe everything that is happening, especially this."

Rob responds "I know son, we need to stay strong to survive, ok. We will make it through this I promise." Let's get upstairs and try to rest before we head out tomorrow. I want you to rest and I will take care of her."

RJ still sobbing shakes his head yes and heads up to the room. Jaylen stares wide-eyed at the two of them and hugs Robert tightly and whispers in his ear "I'm so sorry" and kisses him on the cheek. She then catches up to RJ on the stairs puts her arm around him and they continue up the stairs and enter the room.

Robert now takes Leese's body and wraps it in a sheet from the linen closet and takes her outside and buries her in the bushes poolside. He delivers a few Hail Mary's and Our Father's and takes a few moments of silence which was interrupted by a large explosion off in the distance sending a large black plume of smoke into the sky. Tears now streamed from Rob's face which he wipes away. He heads up to the room and closes the door behind him. In the room, RJ is cleaning his face in the sink and drinking a soda to calm his nerves. Robert checks on him to ensure he is as well as can be considering then heads to the bathroom to shower. Jaylen sitting on the chair asks if she can do anything before she heads to bed and Robert shakes his head no. "I'm going to check outside every few hours so don't be alarmed, I won't get much sleep tonight." RJ is now in bed and falling asleep. Robert walks Jaylen outside and closes the door and leans on the railing under the pale full moon. "I can't believe this shit is happening," he says and hangs his head shaking it in disbelief. "I just hope junior will be ok" as he looks at Jaylen with water-filled eyes. She closes in hugging him on his left side kissing the side of his head and Robert couldn't notice how good her large breast felt squishing against his solid arm. The background noise of crickets was cut out by her voice "you're a great dad, a great man. RJ will be fine as long as he has you he can look up to." Her closeness causes Robert to stand facing her as they looked at each other for a second. She raises her right hand and gently caresses his face then places it on the back of his head saying "you're not alone here, I'm here for you too." Looking Robert in his eyes she says "In case you were wondering, I never stopped loving you." They leaned in for an open-mouthed kiss softly pecking each other's juicy lips then just the right amount of tongue making her moan in pleasure as she began to clench down there. As quickly as he pulled her curvaceous tight body into his Robert pulled away stopping cold. "I'm sorry, I can't do this" though the throbbing stiffness in his pants indicated otherwise. He backs away shaking his head and goes back into the room and lies on the other bed. Standing there on the ledge now throbbing herself in damp panties she bites her lower lip and heads to her room and closes the door.

Robert leans with his back against the door hands on his face and lowering them firmly against his face from his eyes to his chin and gives a slight exhale and gathers himself. That was the first affection from a woman since his wife divorced him years earlier and he couldn't believe such a hot woman was attracted to him. He takes his M4 carbine removes the magazine and begins the painstaking process of disassembling, cleaning and reassembling of the weapon. Twenty minutes later he tops off the magazine and reseats it firmly slamming it in the weapon. He lies on the bed next to RJ and kisses him on the head as he snores soundly. Robert then lies on the floor resting his head on the pillow and checks his watch, it's only 10:23 p.m., yet it feels like three in the morning. Even with the moaning of the dead in the background, Rob fell asleep like a newborn baby.

Robert sat up with the natural alarm to relieve his bladder. He gets up quietly not to wake RJ in the process and stumbles to the bathroom, closes the door before turning on the light and stands over the toilet. After flushing, he rinses his hands and heads back to the main room. He heads to the fridge and grabs a sports drink and takes a long swig. He walks to the chair and plops down hard. The marginal sunlight peering through the closed blind gave just enough light to see clearly. He focuses in on RJ who seemed to be having a nightmare as he began to breathe shallow and rapidly. He looks closely and sees RJ is awake staring at the ceiling and tears streaming from his eyes and his bottom lip is quivering but no sound is coming out. Before Robert could say anything RJ slowly turns his head toward him and begins to sit up twisting toward him raising his left arm across his body reaching for his father. He was mouthing without a sound "help me" as black blood began to pour from his mouth. Robert startled jumped back into his chair could now hear a loud audible slow-paced heartbeat BOOM-BOOM, BOOM-BOOM, BOOM-BOOM that seemed to fill the room. He then realizes that his torso was bleeding from a "Y cut" performed during autopsies. As RJ continued to roll out of bed his stomach skin flapped open from the weight of the clamps exposing his ribcage and intestines. The sloshing sound of wet meat sounded louder as his upper and lower intestines and gut bag slid from his abdominal cavity and splattered on the floor. Robert jumps back over the arm of the chair cupping his mouth in disbelief falling onto the floor, his back now against the wall. He begins to scream but nothing comes out......

Robert wakes up panting and immediately checks RJ who is snoring peacefully. He gets closer and sees that he is alright, then goes to the bathroom to splash his face with cold water. He pats his face dry with a towel and checks his watch. 11:48 p.m. "shit not even an hour and a half of rest," he says to himself. Anyway time to check the perimeter. He goes and grabs his M4 and heads outside and quietly closes the door behind him. He takes a few deep breathes and closes his eyes to calm his nerves and the moans from the dead could be heard from the other side of the motel. He checks Jaylen's door jiggling the knob to make sure it is locked then starts to the other side of the walkway to check the gate. He peers through ACOG scanning the area. The moonlight was bright enough at that hour even the shadows were no place to hide. Luckily the dead weren't interested in the gate but he did observe that eight were clawing at a vehicle less than one hundred yards from the entrance. A few more were seen a couple of hundred meters away aimlessly shambling between the cars. There were small fires bellowing calmly in the distance of the nearby town of Wilson what was less than for miles from the airport and their current location. Wilson was the last town before Atlanta and the possible cure for this hell on Earth.

While focused through the optic Robert was startled when he was gently hugged from behind as Jaylen's soft hands wrapped around his chest rubbing gently as her full breasts were forced against his back. Her scent of Angel perfume filled his nostrils and her hands seductively went from his chest down to his stomach then gently cupping his already stimulated crotch and began massaging his cock up and down. Robert's breathing and his heartbeat become heavy and accelerated as he bites his lower lip and closes his eyes. He turns around placing the rifle on the ground and he pulls her in tightly with one hand on her lower back and one on the back of her neck as they embrace kissing passionately. Both moan in pleasure as their lips forcefully press against one another. His hands were embracing her tightly showing his strength and at the same time showing his gentle touch. He noticed that she wasn't wearing her tight yoga pants just the tight skimpy low cut shirt that revealed her perfect breasts shape and her erect nipples as they poked through her shirt. She takes her right middle finger, slides it down her panties and inside her wet spot then removes it shoving it into his mouth. "Mmmm" he moans as one of his hands made it to the rich clefts of her ass grabbing a handful. The other grabs a breast and she responds naturally to his caresses.

He kisses her neck and works his finger along her panty line from behind to the front. Once he feels the soaking wet spot on her panties he inserts his middle finger inside her rotating it earning an audible moan of pleasure making her bite her lip and kiss him again. She works through his belt and zipper letting his pants fall as he slid her panties down. Acting on instinct and thrusts her back against the wall jolting her and he scoops her legs up as she wraps them around him. He feels her wetness on his throbbing cock and enters her tight slick exquisiteness and she squealed as he moaned. She then shoved her panties in his mouth as he repeatedly thrust inside her while pinned against the wall. Jaylen whispers in his ear between breaths "Oh yeah baby, you remember. Just like that! Oooh, right there."

They switched positions as she turned around licking her lips lustfully looked passionately at him. He thrusts inside her from behind as she moaned grinding until he explodes inside her. Robert gently bites the nape of her neck as they both rest against the wall now glistening in the moonlight panting, trying to catch their breath. Not a word was spoken between them as Robert pulls his pants up and fastened his belt. Jaylen kisses him goodnight on the lips and walks to her room and closes the door. Robert takes a minute then grabs the rifle and checks the other side of the walkway then goes in his room for the night.

The next morning Robert wakes up and RJ was missing. He quickly sits up looking around then gets up checking the bathroom which was empty. He opens the door and sees RJ kneeling beside the freshly dug grave near the pool hands covering his face. Robert goes and joins him and they sit in silence. The roar of the dead seemed to have dissipated since last night and Robert tells RJ to eat something before hitting the road so they go back to the room to eat. Jaylen exits her room and stretches her arms above her head yawning and glowing. Smiling in the threshold she says "good morning men" as she joins the guys for breakfast. Jaylen and Robert share a quick awkward glance as she discretely yet seductively licks her lips with a smile as she eats a piece of fruit. Robert finishes his cup of instant coffee and tells them to get ready to hit the road. He takes his carbine heads outside and climbs his way to the roof giving his clear line of sight to Atlanta. He raises the carbine's optic to scan Interstate 95 and to his surprise, the legion of the dead that clogged the highway yesterday had passed and now was virtually clear of walkers. He looked further north toward Wilson which seemed quiet compared to Atlanta where fires could still be seen blazing from a few skyscrapers and countless billows of smoke filled the clear blue sky. He could only imagine the sights of the big city.

He hears RJ and Jaylen gathering the equipment as the vehicle's doors open and shut. "We're good to go dad" RJ yells and Robert acknowledges with a head nod and begins his descent from the roof. He slings the weapon and makes his way to the room to ensure nothing would be left behind. The room's doors were left open and Rob headed down the stairs to the awaiting vehicles and met with RJ and Jaylen in front of them. He explained that they were just a few miles from Atlanta and they needed to go through a small town named Wilson to get there. He explained that they might find help there and if not they would continue right through to the CDC and there should be sanctuary there. They made sure the vehicles were filled with fuel and supplies the same. Robert went into the Tahoe and gave Jaylen one of the radios. "Keep it on channel one and stay off it unless you have a problem," he says to her and she nods in agreement. RJ is told to check the shotgun to ensure it was loaded and he goes to the front passenger side door, gets in and checks his weapon.

Robert then takes the Benelli and gives a crash course to Jaylen in its use. He hands her the loaded weapon and Rob joins RJ in the Tahoe as Jaylen hops in the driver seat of the Sheriffs Blazer. They head to the far end of the lot and turn left toward the tall red front gate still secured by the long-chain wrapped around keeping the two sides together.

Both men exit and RJ covers his dad with the Glock nine as he unravels the chain from the gate doors. The few dead that was a few yards away began to slowly turn and sniff the air as they realized their next meal was right behind them. They began to groan and bear their flesh and blood-covered teeth as they began to shamble their rotting corpses toward them as the large red gates squeaked open. They get back into the Tahoe as the first zombie lightly bumps into the front end of the vehicle and stumbles backward. Robert floors the vehicle and runs down the dead that was now in front of the gate and Jaylen follows close behind as they take a right and head back to I95 via Georgia Airport Way and took the onramp.

I95 was littered with a graveyard of vehicles now dirty from natural exposure as well as dead palms from the trees along the highway. The survivors carefully serpentine through the cars on the road and occasionally barreled over the dead that was in their way. They come to a green sign with white reflective lettering which read "Wilson next exit". The two vehicles peel off the interstate taking the Wilson off-ramp just miles from their final destination the Center for Disease Control in Atlanta.

WILSON

Wilson-population 1,478 is what the original sign read but the number had a black spray-painted line through it and underneath an uneven 896 was painted in its place. There was a line of yellow school buses parked blocking the main entrance into Wilson that had several dead aimlessly standing looking about. They needed to find a new route into town so they turned around and headed back the same way they came. They made their first right and continued west through a flat desolate throughway with red clay as far as the eye could see on the left where a few zombies were slowly stiffly wandering through the open plain. To the right, you could see a thick brush that met the red clay and some black smoke filling the air in scattered spots. They kept their eyes peeled for any chance of entering the town. They noticed a dirt road up on the right and decided to see if led into town. The road was uneven and continuously jostled the survivors about as they slowly went through the narrow road. The area cleared a bit and they stopped for a bathroom break. They take turns covering each other standing sentry while the others went about their business. A check of Roberts watch and it was half-past noon and the sun was unrelenting. They took out the map and plotted that the current road would indeed lead them through Wilson which was just a couple miles inbound on that road. It was a good thing because they were below a quarter of a tank in fuel. They got back in and continued down the clay road. Less than a mile from town there was a "welcome" sign that stated you are entering Wilson "Heaven on Earth" was printed below the name. This sign too was spray-painted over. The A-V-E-N was crossed out and replaced with L-L.

A few hundred feet ahead was a tunnel and yet another disturbing sight that brought tears to the survivor's eyes. As they approached the tunnel there hanging from the overpass was a family of four made up of two parents and a teen daughter and a boy no more than seven. They had hung themselves and were swinging in the wind. As they got closer they saw they were snarling trying to grab the trucks as they passed underneath. Robert told RJ not to look but it was too late, when he looked at RJ he was him he was wiping tears from his face. Robert couldn't help but allow his tears to flow as well. The radio squawked "Jesus, Mary, and Joseph. Can you believe this?" The sound of their bodies thumping the tops of the trucks could be heard as they entered the tunnel. Looking in the rearview you could see their bodies swinging wildly as their arms flailed about. "Keep off the rover unless you have an emergency," RJ said to Jaylen in which she did not respond. They pull up to another roadblock of several sedans. There were a few dead walking about the cars and were fairly spread out. Robert exit's the vehicle and takes the closest zombie using the machete with a tomahawk chop to its head. The walker stiffened and fell to her knees then over on her right side. Robert then opens the car door, puts the car's transmission to "N" then get out and slowly pushes it out of the way. The hiss of the dead gets louder from the activity and begins to stiffly shamble towards him. "BOOM!" echoed from Jaylen's Benelli and a zombie's arm went flying offspinning him to the ground. The next one's head turned into a red mist as RJ's Mossberg thundered as a blast of buckshot punches a fist-sized hole in his face exploding the remaining part of the skull.

As the dead are dropped around him Robert gets in another car putting it in neutral and rolling that one back. Dead from the other side began to head toward the noise and Rob enters the last car repeating the same routine but the vehicle only rocked and wouldn't budge.

The Benelli could be heard hard at work just feet from where Robert struggled with the minivan. Moans could be heard from behind Rob so he turned around seeing four dead closing in on him. He takes the Kimber .45 from his waistband and levels it at the walker's heads. POW! POW-POW! POW! Dropping the walkers as the large .45 auto slugs punched a golf ball-sized crater in their faces or foreheads. RJ immediately runs and joins his dad pushing the minivan out of the way crashing it into the other parked vehicles pinning and trapping a couple dead between them. One zombie's knees were severed from being pinched by the minivan and she fell over on the side of the vehicles and began crawling her legless rotting corpse toward the opening created by moving the cars. Gunfire erupted from the trio as they retreated back to their vehicles dropping walkers in their path. They make it back to their vehicles and sped through the barricade. The legless female zombie clawing her way on the ground was run over by Roberts Tahoe crunching her arms into chunks of flesh and powdered bone as they crunched under his tires. Immediately after, her head was crushed which popped like a grape under Jaylen's tires as the crushed head spit blood and brains out the top of her skull like toothpaste from its tube. The dead that were closing in were knocked over or ran down by their vehicles as they sped toward the middle of town.

Wilson was a small town that had three main roads Broad Street, Elmwood Avenue and Thurber's Avenue that ran parallel to each other and one street Wilson Way that intersected all the main streets in town. The once spotless streets of this serene little town were now littered with barricades of vehicles that tried to keep the dead at bay, bodies in the streets mostly with severe head trauma, decapitation or even burnings. Some buildings were leveled by fires left to burn or explosions and some windows that were broken had dark dried blood splattered beneath them. They continue down Wilson Way and make a right onto Elmwood Avenue and head straight to the main gas station and pull in. They exit the vehicles and check the pumps which were almost empty. Jaylen checks the door to the gas station which had a sign that read "Closed due to illness." Robert joins her and RJ keeps watch scanning the area for any type of threat. From the looks of things, it has been closed since the beginning of this thing. Robert kicks in the door and it caves easily crashing inward, as they both enter checking the generator switch flipping it on. As the generator kicks on the moaning and hissing of the dead could be heard from different locations surrounding the gas station but they couldn't be seen.

RJ yells "dad, this doesn't feel right we gotta go now!" Rob and Jaylen run back to the trucks and they could now see the dead stumbling from all directions toward them slowly forming a literal ring of death. They appeared from around corners of buildings, from between parked cars, from between alleys and even from private residences. The survivors look around and RJ points to the steeple of a church that was about a half-block around the corner to the west of the service station. "Dad, the church!" he says and the survivors hastily grab the bags of gear and sling them over their shoulders. They see a small alley between the local Mike's Hardware store and Jolene's Hoagie Hut and Robert pointed and directed the two "through the alley!" The three make a dash for it as the red chevron on the carbine rested on a zombie's head that was near the alley. Her entire lower jaw upper lip and throat area were eaten away and her tongue hung freely from the massive wound. The back to her head exploded as the high pitched crack of the Colt sent the smoking spent brass casing to the ground. Her brain matter and blood to the sidewalk behind her as she dropped like several of her friends that met the business end of the survivor's weapons. Gunfire erupted and the dead dropped with each successive shot as they ran across the street from the gas station to the alley between the sandwich and hardware stores.

The alley was a couple of hundred feet long and you could turn left or right at the end where another side of a building began. They rounded the corner to the right near the church and ran into a locked gate. The flock of the dead now began to ooze in the same alley the survivors have moving as quickly as their stiff bodies allowed to catch their next meal. "Shit!" RJ said as the smell of rotting meat and the snarling became overbearing. RJ grabs a pair of pipe bombs from the bag Jaylen was wearing, lit the fuses and tossed them around the corner. Everyone plugged their ears and seconds later KA-BOOM! A massive explosion rocked the building and a great gust of air from the blast passed over them. They check around the corner and see several dead had been blast into large chunks and stuck all over the walls and ground of the alley. There were heads and limbs strewn about and intestines stuck to the walls. There were a couple of intact heads on the ground and one was still animated as its eyes darted back and forth and tongue licked the ground. One zombie was blown almost in half and continued to crawl toward the survivors as its lower extremities were completely twisted around and hanging to the upper torso by about an inch of meat and skin. Robert peered around the corner and saw most of the dead were taken care of or knock to the ground completely stunned and weren't advancing at the moment. They turn to the locked gate and Jaylen takes aim with the automatic shotgun, BOOM! The crowd-pleaser shreds the lock and they burst through the gate and continue to head toward the church. Gunfire echoed in the streets of Wilson as the three unleashed a storm of hot lead on the advancing dead as they hurried to the church. The sign on the church read:

"Zechariah 14:12-And the Lord will send a plague on all the nations that fought against His people. Their people will become like walking corpses, their flesh will rot away, their eyes will rot in their sockets and tongues in their mouths. They will fight with their neighbors as they are terror-stricken by the Lord! The end of days is at hand, come repent now!

The three ran past it up to the dozen steps as the dead closed in behind them slowly but surely. They pull on the heavy wooden and iron door and it slowly swung open and they squeezed in as it shut forcefully behind them. They immediately began to barricade the door and lock it.

They take a rest in the large Cathedral style foyer leaning against the wall placing their hands on their knees. RJ says between breaths "They don't…. get winded!" They hear movement in the sanctuary and immediately ready themselves to fight a hoard of the dead or whatever is on the other side of the red wooded double doors. They look through the stained glass and it appears that there was a sermon taking place as the pastor was up on the altar and a dozen or so parishioners were in attendance. They slowly and quietly enter the sanctuary and the smell of death fills their nostrils and RJ vomits what little that was in his stomach on the spot. What they saw next froze them in their tracks. As the heavy door closed slowly behind them it let out a loud click as it closed against the other door. The priest was standing on the altar with his back to the churchgoers with his arms raised up as if praising the Lord. The preacher begins to sniff the air and he begins to turn around slowly.

As he stiffly pivots he bears his rotten gums and teeth. His skin was a pale tan with a bluish tint. His skin was tightly drawn around his skull like features and his eyes were sunken in, cloudy white and bloodshot. There were large holes in his skin revealing rotted flesh underneath. There were large whiteheads that were now oozing bloody puss that ran down his face, over his gums and teeth staining his white robe. As he snarls at the survivors the dozen people in the pews all simultaneously turn around stiffly as their necks cracked and bared their lipless faces at the three and snarled as they began to get up slowly. Robert mumbles to himself "Jesus, Mary and Joseph". A second later he snaps out of it and barks to RJ and Jaylen "Fuckin kill em all, let God sort em out!" As he says this he raises the red chevron to the priests head and squeezes the trigger. A deafening supersonic crack came from the rifle and the back of the priests head explodes into a pink mist as his head snaps back and his now lifeless body stumbles over backward onto the altar. RJ and Jaylen follow suit opening up on the dead making each shot count. The sanctuary was filled with gun smoke and the smell of burnt sulfur and the ground was covered with pieces of skull and brains. The dead were dropped before they could stand upright and the three now moved from the rear of the church to the front checking that all the dead were down for good. When the sanctuary was cleared they took a breather and reloaded their weapons. They noticed that there was a hallway that had a couple of little black stickers with gold lettering that read offices and restrooms. They also discovered a stairwell that leads to a dark basement. They decided to check the basement area and Jaylen was told to keep an eye upstairs.

Robert carefully led the way with the Glock nine at the ready listening for any signs of the dead and RJ covering his back with the

.45 as they made their way down the stairs. The stairs came to a short hallway which led to an open area with four steel pillars and several tables and chairs for after service functions. The walls were painted white with several religious posters and children's drawings. The floor was checkered with dark brown and tan tiles some cracked. There was a small kitchen off to the left of the basement, two doors stood to the rear of the room across the stairway Robert and RJ just came down and to the immediate right another steel door with a glowing red sign that read exit. They go to the kitchen and check for food where the cabinets yielded some rice, lima beans, corn, and the refrigerator there was some apple juice, water, and butter.

Next, they go to the far two doors and the one on the left had a light switch under a small black sign with gold trim and lettering that read bathroom. RJ quickly grabs the handle and looks at his dad making eye contact and both nodding in agreement. He opens the door quickly and Robert steps in small single toilet and sink room which was empty. They go to the next door with the same type sign which read bible study room. They hear a rustling behind the door and decide to open this one slowly. Just as RJ was about to grab the handle something on the other side of the door hand began pounding lightly and groaning causing them to jump. It sounded like a child or woman but they could not tell. RJ raised the Mossberg to the middle of the door and squeezed the trigger. A deafening blast came from the muzzle blowing the door into splinters caving it inward. After the smoke cleared they looked through what was left of the door and seen a gut-wrenching picture.

Near the gaping hole on the ground of splinters was the lower half of a child's body and its right arm was lying next to the wall feet from what is left of the poor kid's body. In the far side of the room were ten children ranging from the ages seven to ten years old. There was one adult sitting in a chair staring wide-eyed at the gaping hole in the door surrounded by the children. The blast from the shotgun had drawn their attention and as they turned around each one of them was dead with fresh blood covering their entire faces and little hands. As they staggered toward Robert and RJ it revealed that they had eaten the lower half of the poor bible study teacher. They had eaten from just below her clavicle bones exposing her sternum and ribcage, her entire intestines were missing revealing her spine and her thighs were eaten to the femur bones. RJ takes a pipe bomb from his bag, lights the fuse and tosses it into the room. They cover their ears and turn away from the doorway. KA-BOOM! They go into the room and see the child walkers and victim had painted the room red and were down for good.

They go back upstairs to Jaylen who immediately asked what happened. After a brief discussion on what just happened their next move is they head downstairs and enter the kitchen to cook some food. Robert makes some buttered rice flavored with corn and lima beans salt and pepper and as they eat their fill they make their plan to make it across the street to the Georgia State Police Barracks where they hopefully can find some help. They decide to rest for a couple of hours and head up to the office area and RJ and Jaylen both plop on a cushioned chair and sink deep into it and shut their eyes. Robert looks around and finds the closet in the office. He opens the closet and finds a pair of shoes and another robe hanging. He notices that the wall in the closet was false and he pushed it in. The door creaked outward and led to a dimly lit passageway that leads to a secret alcove of a smaller bunker-like an office. As he got closer he heard a voice from a low-frequency radio that was still broadcasting updates. There was a large desk which sat the radio and a computer. There were maps with pins marking different locations around the world and cases of rations and water stockpiled. There was a safe with the key still in the door and Robert opened it. There were six bars of gold along with two pouches of gold coins, thirty thousand dollars in cash and a pistol. "A lot of good this shit does me now!" he thinks to himself and closes the door to the safe. He goes to the radio and turns up the volume:

> *"The president has declared a state of emergency throughout the United States and has enacted Martial Law in all fifty states. Subsection four of the rules of engagement pertaining to military operations in urban terrain has been given a green light.*

U.S. forces have been authorized to shoot on sight when dealing with any civil unrest regarding the dead or civilian after nightfall. Again just enacted from the president himself, a shoot on sight policy has been authorized and a strict curfew at sundown will be enforced."

Robert smirks to himself and thinks back to how his mother used to tell him to be home before the street lights came on, but loses that grin as he realized that same rules are set upon him again but with worse consequences then punishment. He checks the computer's connection and sees that it is connected and in fact had incoming e-mails. He checked the screen and it had messages incoming in from different churches from around the world. They all were of the same genre just keeping tabs on who was still up and running and in good health. There were messages with reports who have opted out and grim updates on how the dead have overrun certain areas, even talks of some countries contemplating nuclear weapons use. Robert responds to the latest email:

To whom it may concern,

Here in the Southeast of the United States, the dead have overrun the town of Wilson and the church have fallen to the dead as well. Good luck and God bless.

Robert clicks send and the message was sent to whoever may be left. He begins a new e-mail addressed to Stanfield and Miller:

Stanfield & Miller,

I am trying to get to the office and as you can imagine the trip is proving to be quite difficult. I am currently in Wilson and plan on being there by nightfall or tomorrow the latest. What is the status of operation? Any word from the government? I tried to call several times with no answer.

*I will be there as soon as I can. Is Evangeline in the office?
Is she ok? Make sure my office is ready for me by tomorrow.*

-Robert Babcock

Click and send. He waits in anticipation like Stanfield or Miller was sitting by their laptop waiting for his to contact them. Within a minute he starts a new e-mail:

Chief,

*This is Robert Babcock. I am making my way to the Center
for Disease Control to complete my work to reverse this
abomination that is killing mankind. I plan to head to the
reservation once my serum is complete and vaccinate our
people first. Hope all is well and I will be in touch once
I reach Atlanta. I will be here for the next few hours and
can check if you reach out to me. I hope all is alright on
the reservation and families are safe. Please let me know
if you can the status of my brother Eric and cousin David
as soon as possible. I will check back in a bit.*

Take care- R. Babcock

Click and send. Robert heads back to the main office area and takes the radio with him. Both RJ and Jaylen were fast asleep and snoring loudly. He checks the time and was now 6:54 p.m and the sun was almost gone and twilight was blanketing the land. Robert decides to let them sleep for a while and stands on a table to check out the window and see what was going on over at the troopers' barracks. He saw to his surprise some movement on the third floor that he tried to figure what when his attention was drawn back to the street.

Out of the darkness came two tan military jeeps and a personnel carrier loaded with about two dozen soldiers. They all dismount and set up a hasty perimeter of barbed wire and wooden barricades. The roar of the diesel engines attracted the dead who began to slowly turn in their direction and began to stiffly swarm toward the soldiers. The squad leader ordered via megaphone to open fire. The cool night air was now lit up from muzzle blasts and filled with gun smoke as the soldiers followed orders, opening up with a hail of bullets from their M4A1 assault rifles and M249 squad automatic weapons. As hot brass casings clanged off the concrete the wall of the dead fell as their torsos exploded from being torn apart from bullets and heads popped from the high-velocity projectiles. The eruption of gunfire woke RJ and Jaylen and they both fell to the floor and scramble to pick up the guns. "What the fuck!" Jaylen says as they both look about bug-eyed. Robert explains that the military was outside killing the zombies. They join him at the window and it seemed that as one wall of the dead is dropped there was another that would take its place. The hoard seemed to inch closer and closer to the blockade forcing their way through the automatic gunfire.

A grave scream of agony was heard from outside and there was commotion from the soldiers. It appears that a piece of the barricade was knocked back and the dead have made it through. Another scream was heard and more gunfire. This time it was directed to the left of the barricade. The squad leader yells "walkers inside the left of the barricade! Kill 'em all!" The machine guns sawed the dead in half but as they went down they slowly got up until put down with a burst to the head. As their heads bursts apart their rotten corpses stayed down for good. The rest of the barricade was toppled over and then more screams could be heard and less and less gunfire was heard. Within the span of fifteen minutes, the recon team that was sent to Wilson had been overrun and like the town, the church and even the poor children now belonged to the dead.

They turn from the windows and Jaylen cupped her hand over her mouth in disbelief and RJ looked to his dad for comfort. "Look, we will make it to Atlanta we just need to be strong and stick together. We made it this far, I know we will make and I will find a cure." Robert noticed that the people in the barracks were watching the same macabre show he was and decided to make contact. He peered through the magnified optic and was able to tell there were two females and three males. He activated the flashlight on his weapon repeatedly and again looks through the optic. One of the males holds up a mini notepad and in black sharpie wrote "who?" then takes a sniper rifle and peers through the scope back at Robert's window. Robert then asks for a marker and paper and RJ and Jaylen scramble through the desks to find it. RJ grabs some paper from the copying machine and Jaylen grabs a marker from the desk and hands it to Robert. He quickly writes "three of us here, help."

RJ asks "what's going on dad?"

Robert responds "there is someone across the street in the building we need to get to."

Robert again takes aim through the optic awaiting a response. Then minutes later a response was held up which was a two-pager. The first page read "five of us here" and the next read "back door open, meet there." Robert jumps off the table and begins to plan how they would get across the street and to the back door alive. "Alright be ready to move when I tell you" and RJ and Jaylen nod in agreement and begin to pack up their gear and check their weapons. He heads to the sanctuary and tries to look out the stained glass windows for a better vantage point of the street that divided them from the brick fortress just feet away. The sightline was blurry so he broke it out with the stock of the rifle and a great crash was made as half of the tall window crashed to the sidewalk below. He stuck his head out of the window and could see to the right which was the direction of the gas station and where their vehicles were. The street was mostly clear in that direction of walkers and as he peers left there were several dozen dead laid out in piles all over the street thanks to the military. There were more still standing around but most were kneeling enjoying their latest meals. Robert signals to RJ and Jaylen to come to the window. As they arrive he explains that they would use flairs and toss them by the front of the vehicles to gain their attention as they ran behind them to the gate. Robert made a last-minute check of the office and went back to the secret alcove and checked the e-mail. There was no response from the tribe yet so he grabbed the laptop stuffing it in a backpack then rejoining RJ and Jaylen by the window. Robert jumps out first and signals them to follow. They take two flares igniting them and RJ takes the flares, takes a running start and heaves them as far as he can. The bright red glow of the flares toppled end over end in a high arc through the air casting a bright red glow over the area. The dead that were wandering about aimlessly moaned and turned their attention to the flares and began to shamble toward the bright burning lights. They waited for the perfect opportunity then dashed across the street in crouched position weapons ready. They reach the gate and try to push through the swing door but discovered it was welded shut. They were sitting ducks on the street just feet away from the dead kneeling just yards away ripping into the flesh that was left of the soldiers. The smell of their rotting flesh was unbearable and the slobbering sound of them chewing with their mouths open didn't help matters either. They either had to decide quickly which way to go, cut through the gate with the wire cutters or try and outrun them through the barricade, up to the front steps then jump down the side of the steps and make their way to the back of the building to where the group hopefully is waiting.

The dead that were eating the soldiers begin to sniff the air and groan as chunks of meat and tendons fell from their mouths. They slowly began to look around and RJ whispers "we gotta do something!" Robert grabs the fence cutters and begins to work his way through the gate. Clip...clip....clip could be heard as each piece of the fence was cut through and that noise began to stir what remained of the hoard in the street. "Hurry!" Jaylen said. The dead eating was now standing still sniffing the air and slowly turned toward the three by the fence. As the closest zombie began to open its skull-like mouth that was covered in fresh blood it was met with the business end of Robert's hunting knife as he drove it through his skull with a crunch. The corpse froze in its tracks mouth still agape as the large survival knife was turned and pulled from the skull taking a trail of black blood and thick tissue that used to serve as a brain and it fell to the ground. Other dead began to moan as they began to stiffly shamble toward the gate. Click, click sounded as RJ nervously clipped through the fence. Crack! Robert's M4 sounded dropping walker. Crack! Another bites the dust. Jaylen joins in with the Benelli twelve-gauge BOOM! Another one drops. Now the remaining of the dead began to shamble towards the survivors. "Hurry up!" Robert yelled as he now popped off rounds hitting the dead. "Ok!" RJ said. Crack-crack! Sounded as Robert double-tapped the last walker and knocks it over then turns to pull the gate apart and he pulls RJ through the hole. Jaylen was running her shotgun dry and didn't hear the guys yelling for her. As the gun spent its last casing she realized they were waiting for her and she turns to run through the gate. The dead began to close in on the gate and as Jaylen ducked through the gate a zombie had herbed a hold of her ponytail yanking her to the ground. "Aaaahhhh help!" she yelled. The zombie was stuck in the gate snapping his rotting gums and teeth as his bony fist held tightly to her hair pulling her closer. Her hands were on her head trying to free herself from the zombies grasp and her legs kicked wildly. POP! RJ had put a .45 hollow point through the walkers head splitting it in two and Robert had hacked into the arm with two chops finally severing the arm and he pulled Jaylen to her feet and they ran to the rear of the building as a dozen and a half-dead were clawing at the gate. They reach the back alley and head up the stairs to the back door. Robert's eyes are wide open and he tells Jaylen to stand still. He takes the fence clippers and clips two fingers of the dead hand that was tightly gripped in her hair and manages to pull it free and a couple of digits fall to the ground. Jaylen shaken hugs Robert and then RJ kissing him on the cheek. They pound on the back door and the door opens shining a blinding light on them from the hallway as a slender female stood in the doorway with a pistol in one hand and a knife in the other.

FORTRESS

"C' mon!" she says. "Names Sarah, follow me" and she leads the three up the stairs. As their steps echo in the long hallway she barks "Lock that shit behind you, there's five of us, you already wrote love notes to Raul at the window. My girl's upstairs her name is Tina and two other guys who are a little weird if you ask me their names are Kyle and Luke, keep an eye out for them."

"I'm Robert, this is my son RJ and Jaylen. We're from Cypress Pond trying to get to the "Center for Disease Control in Atlanta.""

As they reached the top of the steps Sarah stops looking at the three, "we just came through there from the way of Cranston. We almost didn't get out of there alive, and that was days ago when the military was in charge. God knows how much worse it has gotten."

The three look at each other and keep following her down the hallway of the third floor in silence. Before they get to the end of the hallway, Robert stops Sarah and tells them they needed to use the bathroom and all three enter their respective restrooms. Robert tells RJ to stash their bags in the trash bins and bring just enough ammunition to load his weapons which they do topping off their magazines and shoving the "go bags" into the trash canister. They go out into the hallway and Robert leans into the woman's room whispers into Jaylen, "load the shotgun and stash your bag in the trash. I don't trust these people yet and we may need to get out quick and we will need all our shit."

"Way ahead of you" she replied.

Minutes later the three continued down the rest of the hall to a room with a sign reading conference room. Sandra introduces the three to Tina, Raul, Kyle, and Luke. Tina and Raul were warm and receptive welcoming but Luke and Kyle were a different story. The men just continue to leer at Jaylen and RJ and exit the room together whispering to each other as they went down through the front entrance and down the stairs. "Don't pay any mind to those two, they're loaners" Sandra explained. Raul interjected with his broken English "No good men. Muy malo". That piqued Robert's interest and he and Raul looked at each other and nodded it was understood that they would cover each other if anything would go down. Little did anyone know that the two that made everyone leery was for a good reason.

Both Luke and Kyle were in the custody of the Georgia State Troopers and were being transferred upstate to serve out lengthy sentences. Kyle was sentenced to twenty to life for multiple rape convictions and Luke twenty-five to life for breaking and entering, murder and child sodomy. They were being held there overnight when everything went to shit. The two were now in the locker room at the urinals as they discussed Kyle's sadistic plan of attacking a woman preferably Jaylen and Luke had his eye on RJ.

"We'll do it after lights out" Kyle whispered to Luke.

"That fine ass bitch that came in with the father and son, I gotta get that!" Luke says as they now head to the sinks.

"That lil bastard got my dick hard, I'm getting that fish tonight!" After washing their hands they both grim and give each other a pound and exit the bathroom.

Back in the NARC office on the third floor the group was going through the supplies and deciding what was for dinner. They decided on a couple of MRE's and vending machine snacks and soda. They are now rejoined by Kyle and Luke and they all sat around a large conference table that had eight cushioned chairs as they begin to eat their meals. Robert is eating his food as he looks and RJ and winks and RJ mimics his father and they smile and Jaylen notices them and makes her smile. Tina is playing with Sandra's hair and ear as she eats her food and Sandra shares her food placing a potato chip in Tina's mouth. Kyle was ripping into his food and looking around at the females and eventually settled his sights on Jaylen. Luke, on the other hand, was looking between Raul and RJ and decided he liked RJ better and both Robert and Raul had noticed what both Kyle and Luke were up to. Robert breaks the ice and asks "so, what's your guy's story? How did you guys survive and make it here?"

"What the hell do you care?!" snapped Luke.

"Hey, just making conversation. I just like to know who I'm eating with is all."

Robert goes on to explain that he and RJ are from Cypress Pond and that they were making their way North to Atlanta. He explained that he was an employee at a division of the Center for Disease Control and that he was needed there to help with this problem. He also went on to explain that Jaylen was with them and helped them get this far. Sandra asked "you know about this shit we're in?! How could this happen? The dead rise and feed on the living! Did you know about this?! How could this happen?" Everybody had turned their attention to Robert who now felt like he was testifying in front of a grand jury as he begins.

"Well, I was on vacation when all this went down so I can't tell you how this got out but what I can tell you is that I believe that I can help fix this problem we have. I'm sorry I don't have much more to share at this time but right now I'm in the same sinking boat as you are…. What about you?" As he turns the conversation to someone else while he looks at everyone at the table.

Sandra begins telling her story. "Well, Tina and I came from the North just shy of the South Carolina and Georgia line. I was a bartender and Tina was an exotic dancer at a bar called the Playa's Club. A lot of the girls called in sick just days before we watched the reports on the news of people being attacked and infected with some kind of virus. We were told as things got worse to head to Atlanta for safe haven and protection. We took a road trip south to Atlanta and when we got there the military had taken over the city and was shooting innocent people in the streets. We decided to continue out of town and settled in Wilson a couple of days ago here with the state police when there were state police" as her countenance fell. "They took us in when it got bad here in town and gave us a safe haven. We were given weapons and shelter from those who wanted to do us harm both dead and alive. The last few troopers had fallen one at a time to the dead as they made attempts to save others in trouble. The last one died just hours before we spotted each other. Before he died we were able to contact the National Guard and they are coming to Wilson next to sweep the town for survivors and evacuate them. They are aware of us and we expect them in the next few days, we thought that the group that showed earlier was our rescue but turns out we were wrong. You guys should stay here with us!" Sandra said like a little kid that had a bright idea.

Robert shakes his head no "we gotta keep moving on. We are leaving in the morning. Raul what about you amigo?"

Raul clears his throat and swallows hard and says "I sorry, my English no too good." That drew a chuckle from Luke and a stern look from Robert in his direction that shut him up immediately. Raul noticeably uncomfortable begins to tell his story of survival and how he had to leave his sick kids at home with their mother a few days ago and went to work. That day there were attacks of people eating each other in the street and he had left his job as a mechanic at Jakes petroleum and attempted to get home to his family but was stopped by police and ordered to the barracks for safety. The police had taken him in and he had met Tina and Sandra here a couple of days ago and he hasn't seen his family since as he wipes tears from his face.

Everyone then turned their attention to the two guys at the end of the table and Luke had turned bright red. Kyle jumped in and began their story which was a complete lie. "I was a bus driver for the Georgia State Transit Authority and Luke here was a mechanic at our garage. One day at the end of work we were going to grab some beers at Peter's Barbecue a few blocks away when we heard screams coming from inside the bus terminal. We both went inside and saw a woman being attacked by three people that were eating her fucking face! We tried to help her but she was already gone. We tried to call the police but "911" was busy and it told us to call back later. We decided to go to the largest and safest place that was close and here we are. We were here a few days before Sandra and Tina arrived, and a week later here we are.

"So you're some kind of doctor or something?" Tina asked Robert. "What do you do that you think you can fix this situation?" Now all eyes were on him again. Robert then begins to give a little background about himself careful not to tip his hat.

"Well, I was in the military for nine years"

"Army?" as he was interrupted by Kyle.

"No, Marines before I was discharged. I went to school for chemistry and landed a job working at the Center for Disease Control in Atlanta for the past twelve years. I was in charge of the Division of Viral Control and was in charge of the antidotes for each virus known to man. My little cousin and assistant Vange were last seen in the laboratory and I hope she is still there or at least safe to help me continue my research. I tried several times to contact the office without a response."

They all continue eating their meals and leave the table at different times going about their way in different areas of the building. Robert asks Sandra about the layout of the building and she gives him a quick tour showing him the three entrances and exits. There was one main entrance which was securely locked and barricaded protected by cement barriers and bulletproof glass, the rear steel door that was dead-bolted shut and the vehicle sally port that was lowered and locked. All were set with a security alarm that was controlled by a main switch in the central armory area. The armory was about the size of an average bathroom and one cage was unlocked where the department issued Glock 19's were, spare magazines and duty ammunition. The other cage was still locked that had the heavy firepower containing sniper rifles, carbines, shotguns, and submachine guns. "The troopers opened the cage for Tina and me giving us weapons to protect ourselves if necessary."

"What about Luke, Kyle, and Raul?" Robert asked.

"As I said before, I don't trust those two, but Raul seems ok.

They haven't found this cache yet and they were here before I was. If they didn't have any weapons before me there must have been a good reason for it." They looked at each other, then Robert asks "where is the holding area?" "This way," Sandra said and nods toward the hallway as she leads him down the hall and backs down the steps. They go down another long hallway to a steel door the read detention on it. They enter through the large white steel sliding door and go in. There was a large counter that served as the officers' station that was a step up higher than the rest of the floor and had a laptop computer with mouse and printer, a file cabinet and a half dozen close circuit monitors that covered the entire cell block area. It was eerily quiet and Robert goes directly to the prisoner log in sheet and it confirmed his suspicions. The last page in the log had both names Kyle Thomas and Luke Billingsly with the caption "transfer" written in the log space titled status. "No shit" Sandra mumbled. "We just have to watch these guys closely," Robert said. Robert had taken the Kimber .45 and checked it ensure it was fully loaded and clicked on the safety and Sandra had checked her twin Glock nines as well and they both head back upstairs and rejoin the group.

Upstairs they gather in the main office area that held ten office desks all with a computer that was hooked up to a central printer against the wall. There were pictures of families or friends on the desks memoirs of happier times and desk calendars with various notes scribbled on them. The floor was white tile and the walls were painted tan and contained various law enforcement or military posters and the State of Georgia and Federal Bureau of Investigations top ten most wanted posters decorated the wall. There were a half dozen bay windows that overlooked the town of Wilson and the other set looked toward Atlanta were fires could be seen glowing in the night sky. They gathered around the front desk in the room by the door and began to plan for their escape and how they would gain one of the military vehicles by the front door that was still covered by corpses. Everyone had different ideas of executing the plan and all that was accomplished was intensifying the tension between Robert, Luke, and Kyle. The only thing that they did agree on was that there needed to be a distraction to draw the dead away from the vehicles if they were still there. After over an hour of discussion sometimes reaching the boiling point it was agreed that the best course of action was to turn in for the night and get to it in the morning. Everyone went their separate ways. Kyle and Luke went to the second floor and took their spots near the training classroom and lied in wait for their opportunity to make their move. Jaylen, Sandra, and Tina had taken the corner of the NOC office where they had laid out blankets and pillows and RJ had stayed in the other corner waiting for his dad. Raul was in the hallway just outside the NOC office lying on the floor with a blanket rolled under his head as he faced the wall and snored lightly. Robert re-enters the office and tells everyone that he is going to make security checks at the entrances and that he would be right back. RJ and the women had settled into their sleeping nests and the lights were turned out. Robert now at the door takes the Kimber and begins his rounds. He heads downstairs to the first floor checking all three doors and everything was set. Robert was really searching the building for the two that disappeared and keep tabs on them. He goes through the first-floor room by room quietly listening intently. Over a half-hour had passed and every inch of the first floor was covered and there was no sign of Kyle or Luke. Robert then heads upstairs to the second floor and enters the long hallway stopping at the first door and began to listen for any movement. The night was so quiet he could almost hear his heartbeat rushing in his ears as he peers intently through the darkness. He begins the long process of checking each room methodically looking for the two men that he thinks may do them harm. He completes the first hallway then goes into the bathroom quietly listening for anything but it was empty. As the door closes he heard some whispering from around the corner and he instinctively hugs the wall and clicks the safety of the Kimber giving off an audible click. He then crosses the hallway and peers around the corner but can see nothing in the darkness. He hears the voices getting louder and now he heard footsteps getting closer and closer. Cold sweat begins to form on his forehead and upper lip and he retreats into the shadows kneeling and raising the .45 until the sights lined up in his eyesight at chest level. Before he knew it they both came around the corner and were on top of him. He began to squeeze the trigger anticipating the loud bang and flash from the pistol until he realized at the last second that they did not see him! They were too wrapped up in their conversation planning their attack they literally walked right by him.

"We can just sneak right up on them as they sleep and before they know it they are at our mercy!" They exit the hallway and head up the stairs both wielding knives as they get ready for the attack. Robert creeps towards the same stairwell and listens for the door to close. Robert then quietly sprints up the steps and peers through the small glass window in the door and see Kyle and Luke's tiptoeing down the hallway trying not to wake Raul who seemed to sleep soundly and the two men entered the room where RJ and the girls were asleep. Robert quickly enters the hallway and is now in a full sprint to the end of the hallway as he notices Raul getting up doing the same. They both reach the door and could hear a woman's scream that was muffled as it was covered by someone's hand. As they entered the NOC office they saw that RJ had Luke at gunpoint with the Mossberg 590 as his hands were in the air and Raul had come from behind and took Luke to the ground in a headlock. Robert had rounded the corner and searched for the women and saw that Kyle was on top of Tina as she struggled underneath him while he held the knife to her throat. His pants were around his knees and he was trying to pull her panties down. Sandra and Jaylen were awakened by the commotion and immediately began yelling and were about to attack him when they saw Robert with the pistol in his hand.

He immediately wraps his left arm around his throat ripping him off Tina throwing him wildly across the floor. "Don't you fucking move ass hole!" Robert ordered. Shocked Kyle covers himself with his hands and Sandra now up went and stomped him in his balls as he let out a groan of agony, then she returns to an expectedly shaken Tina and comforts her.

"RJ!" Robert yells out.

"I'm good dad!" he responds.

While Robert was distracted Kyle made a move to grab the pistol from his hands and was in short order shot through the foot and leg by Sandra who yelled "fucker!" and was now aiming her Glock nine with its smoking barrel at his chest. Robert yells "no!" and she listens lowering the weapon in her shaking hand. Kyle now grasps his thigh now trying to stop the bleeding, grimacing and moaning in pain. Robert grabs Luke and drags him over to Kyle and tied them up together placing them against the old fashioned radiator securing them for the night. RJ comes over and whispers to his dad "he tried to stab you when he thought you were sleeping. He stuck his knife into the blankets where he thought you were laying down" as he nods at Luke. Robert gives the two a look that would kill as he holds the .45 in his hand. He walks over to Luke who is now pleading for his life and Robert yells "shut the fuck up! I'm not going to kill you." No sooner did he finish saying that he pressed the muzzle of the .45 against the front of his foot as Luke yelled "no! Plea" which was drowned out by a loud bang from the pistol and the spent casing bouncing off the wall and rolling on the floor.

A loud scream of agony came from Luke as the large-caliber hollow point ripped through his ankle blowing out the back of his Achilles tendon as blood freely poured from the gaping wound. The rest of the group had gone down to the second floor to rest as much as they could before sunrise. It was now 3:03 a.m and sunrise would be in a few hours. Exhausted, everybody looked at Robert for the next move. He notices this and says "rest up guys, we are leaving in the morning."

"How are we going to get to the vehicles?" Jaylen asks.

Robert replies "just going to walk right out the front door" as he smiles.

As they turn the lights out and get some rest the sound of the zombies outside was drowned out by the whimpering of Kyle and Luke upstairs. They all fell asleep in anticipation for the morning would bring.

The sun broke the horizon to the east and the sky began to turn a dark purple that grew lighter toward the horizon as the scattered clouds glowed a beautiful amber against the lighting of the sky. The Northern Bobwhites began singing which stirred Robert from his light sleep. He quietly gets up and goes to the bathroom and retrieves the bug out bags they stashed the night before.

He slings his M4 over his shoulder and ascended to the rooftop of the barracks and watched the sunrise feeling the quickly disappearing cool morning air against his skin. He felt a presence behind him and before he could turn around Sandra said "good morning" and he responded in kind as she joined him at his side.

They both watch the sunrise and it takes them away for a moment from the living hell they still don't believe is happening. As the sun continues to rise the sky turns crystal blue and a welcoming breeze meets their faces. The crystal blue sky is now being blacked out with dark smoke billowing from large fires off in the distance from Atlanta that was less than a few miles away. They began to focus on their surroundings and the moans of the dead a few stories down buzzed in their ears sending chills down they're spines. The smell of rotting flesh and dried blood filled their nostrils triggering their gag reflex jarring them back to the reality that this was another dawn of the dead.

As they walked back downstairs from the rooftop Sandra tells Robert that she and Tina were going to stay and wait for help. They had a secure fortress, plenty of supplies on hand and should the need arise they could go on supply runs in town. They believed that the government would sort it all out and that rescue teams would be by soon. She did tell him that they would help them get to their vehicle. She asked what the plan was and Robert replied without looking "bait."

He then goes into the NOC office and checks on Kyle and Luke who were still in severe pain, pale due to blood loss and their lower extremities were caked with blood. Their cries for help went unanswered as Robert leaned in and whispered "get ready to party boys" and he slapped them in the face and headed down to the second floor. When he reached the group they were yawning and stretching shaking off the cobwebs from their power naps. They make breakfast and eat quietly in the anticipation of what the next move will be. Robert finishes his coffee and orders them "get ready to move."

RJ, Jaylen, Raul, Sandra and Tina all gather their gear and weapons and follow Robert into the hallway where a map of the building shows the primary and secondary fire exit locations. He points to the main entrance "RJ and Raul, go to the main doors at the front steps and stay out of sight and radio when the coast is clear. Tina and Jaylen I want you both here" as he pointed to the side stairwell that led to a side door to the right side of the building. That side was divided from a large public parking garage by a twelve-foot fence with barbed wire. "I need you to go and cut through the fence in case we need to circle around to get to the vehicles or worse case jump a car somewhere in the garage. When you clip through the fence, get back inside and regroup with RJ and Raul upfront. Sandra, you come with me. We will be able to run right out the front door and if not the side door will be our secondary meeting point and we can head to the garage. Everyone to their places, go!"

Everyone understood their assignments and headed to their spots. Jaylen and Tina had reached the side door opening it and Tina had run to the gate and began cutting as Jaylen watched the alley with the shotgun at the ready. Minutes later there was a five-foot hole cut in the gate and the women were now on the way to the front to meet up with Raul and RJ.

In the meantime, Robert and Sandra head up to the third floor and check on Kyle and Luke and they mumbled the best they could that they were sorry and begged him not to hurt them anymore. Robert unties Luke and takes him by the left arm and around his neck as Luke moans in pain as he is dragged across the floor to the large window. "You wanted to hurt my son asshole!" Robert yells in his face and Luke pleads while crying "no....please" in between sobs. Robert had taken the hunting knife and rammed it into his groin and Luke squeals like a pig in pain as Robert pulled it out as dark blood now sprung like a faucet from between his legs. Robert then takes his legs and scoops him up and out of the window where a second later a loud thud of flesh smacking pavement from three stories high. Luke had shattered his legs, hip, right arm, and clavicle in the fall and was moaning in pain. Robert now with the thousand-yard stare keens in on Kyle and storms toward him who now pleading for his life as Sandra stood still in disbelief of what just happened.

Meanwhile, at the front door, RJ and Raul are joined by Jaylen and Tina. They peer out the door and see about twenty walkers still feeding on what was left of the military or aimlessly standing around the vehicles and front steps. All of a sudden they all heard a faint thud that made them jump and look at each other saying to themselves "what the fuck?" Robert gets on the radio "everyone together?" he asks.

Jaylen gets on the radio "we're all here and waiting. What was that sound?"

"Don't worry about that, just keep an eye out and tell me when the front is clear," Robert said. They all continue to watch intently as the walker's stagger out front of the building.

Back upstairs Robert grabs Kyle by the throat and dragged him to the window. "Sandra, do em!" he says and she snaps out of it. She grabs the navy knife and guts Kyle as the image of him trying to violate Tina flashed in her mind. Twisting it before she pulls it out, she drops the knife on the floor and helps Robert toss him out of the window. He fell thirty feet down right next to Luke meeting a similar fate with two broken legs and arm. As they lie there in agony praying for death to relieve their pain, little did they know He was about to answer their prayers.

The dead began to stagger from the front to the side of the building were the bloody and broken Luke and Kyle were. As they both struggled to look at what was happening they both started to scream as their eyes grew as they saw a sea of zombies slowly shambling toward them gnashing their rotten teeth and moaning as they inch closer and closer. They tried to move to get away but their broken bodies wouldn't allow it. They began to cry out to God to help them and begin saying Hail Mary's or whatever they recall from childhood. All their pleading and begging didn't help the situation as the dead were now feet away. RJ's voice came over the radio "dad they are leaving the front and going to the right side of the building. There is only a few left come down now."

Back on the third floor Robert and Sandra watch from the window as Kyle and Luke are yelling "No! No! As the swarm of the dead engulf the two blood-curdling screams follow AAAAHHH! AAAAHHHH! Then silence as the dead gather around and feast on their latest meal taking large chunks of meat with each bite from all over their bodies. "Rest in Hell mother fuckers," Sandra said as she taps Rob on his shoulder "let's get you guys a ride outta here" and the two go downstairs to join the group.

They check the area which looked clear enough to move so they begin to remove the furniture blocking the shatterproof glass doors with Georgia State Police stenciled on them. They unlock the doors and open them as Robert heads out first with his M4 at the ready. They make their way around the remaining bits of corpses left by the dead, most were bloody skeletons with some chunks of flesh still clinging to bone and a countless number of flies on each body. They could hear the dead moaning as they ate on the side of the building and kept a sharp eye on any that may come back. Robert gets into the driver's seat and to his surprise, the keys were in the ignition. He tells RJ and Jaylen to get in and he starts the diesel engine which reads it was half full. The roar of the engine got the attention of a few stragglers that were down the street near the church but weren't a concern. Sandra and Tina were covering Rob, RJ, and Jaylen at the bottom of the stairs and Raul was still at the top near the door. Robert looks back to thank them and they wave goodbye.

Robert's eyes grew to the size of saucers and as he tried to yell over the engine "lookout!" Raul was about to start making his way down the stairs when a walker that was in the corner behind the opened door had closed in on Raul and bit him on the back of the neck and shoulder area. He grimaced in pain and began to scream. The zombie pulled the chunk of flesh and blood from the back of Raul. The walker pulled the flesh from Raul as it snapped into its mouth and it began to chew slowly. It then takes a second bite out of his right bicep taking a deep chuck that reached the bone and Raul lets out a second scream. Both Sandra and Tina jump back in fear then Tina shoots the zombie in the head splattering its blood and brains all over Raul and the front steps. The dead were now beginning to get closer from the church and some were even leaving the side of the building staggering back to the front where the commotion was coming from. Raul gets up and runs back into the building spurting blood all over the floor and falls onto the chairs in the front waiting room. Robert yells to Sandra and Tina "get inside!" They head back inside and lock the doors behind them and replace the furniture. Robert then gets the vehicle in gear and speeds off running over the dead like bowling pins and gets on route 179

North toward Atlanta as the town of Wilson gets smaller and smaller in the rearview mirror.

Back in the Fortress, Sandra and Tina finish replacing the furniture as some of the dead began to claw at the doors. They run over to the main waiting area following the blood trail and they pause in their tracks as they see Raul. He is holding his hand up to signal them to stay away with tears flowing from his eyes. He was now choking on his own blood as it poured freely from his mouth as he gagged on it coughing as it is sprayed all over the floor. Literally choking to death on his own warm salty blood, he took a snub-nosed .357 magnum with his shaking hand and slowly formed the sign of the cross. He taps his right shoulder, then the left and then his stomach then to his head. He mouthed "father forgive me" as his tear-filled eyes look at the ceiling opening his mouth the death rattle could be heard as bubbled blood kept pooling and flowing out. "NO!" Sandra and Tina scream as he put the barrel into his mouth pulling the trigger, BANG! Everything had faded to black.

ATLANTA

As Robert, Jaylen and RJ approach the city of Atlanta from the South on route 137 the State Capitol's gold dome shined brightly in the morning sunlight. They pass a green sign with white reflective letters and arrows that read Atlanta 2 Miles with the arrow pointing straight ahead. This was the first time they were excited as they were close to some real help. The skyline gave the survivors and anyone who looked at it false hope as the skyscrapers seemed untouched. As they get closer black smoke billowed from the streets and smaller buildings and the destruction they witnessed brought them back to the reality of the siege the city, and possibly the entire country was under.

There was a military blockage they came across approximately half-mile from the city limits. On either side of the highway were the infamous Abrams M1A1 tank and on the road was blocked with a guard station that was abandoned with a manual security gate blocking the main road entering the city. As they slow to a stop they get out of the vehicle with their weapons ready. Immediately it was evident that the post was abandoned. y check the tanks and notice that on the backside of the turret was a corpse of a soldier that was almost only skeleton with a thin layer of leathered skin that was dry and drawn tight around the skull. Jaylen then goes to the booth and finds a portable radio that was on a charger. She shows it to Robert and RJ as she turns it on. "Anybody there? We are thee survivors at the checkpoint south of the city." They waited for a response. Again she repeats "Is anybody there? We need help!?" Again her broadcast was met with silence. Robert takes the radio and turns it to channel Bravo which was the "all call" channel and broadcast "This is Gunnery Sergeant Robert Babcock the United States Marine Corps. I'm broadcasting on assigned frequency 235.1298 Bravo. I am due south of the city, can anybody read this, over?" There was silence again. "Shit!" Robert says then repeats the broadcast which was again met with silence. They re-group at the vehicle where Robert tells them they are about four miles to the Center for Disease Control that was on the north side of the city. "I don't know how bad the city got, but judging from what we see here it can't be good. I figure we will get to the Grand Peachtree Hotel that is a little over a mile into the city, then make our way into the Underground which is about an eighth of a mile from the CDC."

They nod in agreement and get back into the vehicle and drive around the barricade heading into the congested city. There were blockades set up all over the city with military vehicles and or Atlanta police department vehicles and sawhorses. Some vehicles were still engulfed in flames with a charred corpse or two and some had a few zombies in the front drivers and passengers seats that were still clawing at the windows with bloody hands as blood and skin were smeared against the glass. Others were burnt shells of vehicles some smoking and others had crispy black skeletons still sitting in their upright positions. There were countless bodies in the street all with severe head trauma and as they got closer and closer into the city the streets became more congested and barely passable.

They were now a few blocks from the Peachtree Hotel and the dead were staggering about aimlessly. Some focused their attention at certain apartment stores and restaurant windows probably smelling survivors that were still trapped inside. They continue weaving their way through the cluttered streets until they could not go any further. Some of the dead that were close to the survivors began to turn their attention toward the diesel engine and stagger toward their location. They exited the vehicle with the Peachtree in sight and begin to head the two blocks on foot running past the dead as they slowly closed in. They headed North on Highland Street hugging the walls of the buildings hiding from the dead that littered the street. RJ had whispered, "if you need to take one out keep it quiet." They stopped in between a couple of public transit buses that had collided and took out their knives and machetes. They were now just over a block from the Peachtree and were in its massive shadow as the skyscraper blocked out the sun. They continued parallel to the hotel in a slow deliberate crouching position as to not draw attention or be seen by the dead. There seemed to be countless walkers in the main street some that still looked human but added to unnerving moan that rung in their ears. They needed a distraction to draw the dead's attention so they could make the death run to the Peachtree's front doors in hopes they were unlocked. As they got closer they could see that the front was barricaded which meant that someone might be inside. As they were just about to reach the front of the hotel a female walker has squeezed between the closely parked vehicles. RJ was side by side with his dad and Jaylen kept watch on their rear. The female walker was petite in stature, had little of her greasy blond hair left, dark bags where blood has pooled under her eyes that were milky white and no lips that exposed her rotten teeth and gums as bloody saliva freely oozed from her mouth. She only had a training bra that exposed her sternum of rotted blue-grey skin. She had the telltale bite mark on her bony arm with dried blood caked to the wound. She was wearing torn soiled panties no shoes that covered her dirty feet. She began to sniff the air and turn in their direction. As she began to snarl she was met with the business end of RJ's Navy Knife that he punctured through her skull with a mighty stroke. Her skull crunched as the reinforced blade penetrated the temple at an upward angle and the tip breaching the top of her skull. She fell like a sack of potatoes hitting the ground with a thud as RJ pulled the blade from her skull.

They all kneel together as Robert takes a pipe bomb from the bag he was carrying and lit the fuse. He then stood up and threw it as far as he could then immediately hid back behind the vehicles. The pipe bomb had landed between an abandoned city bus and two cars that were apparently in a collision. The echo of the pipe clanging off the metal of the cars and the concrete drew the walker's attention and they began to shamble and moan toward the noise. Robert, RJ, and Jaylen wait behind the vehicles for cover in anticipation of the explosion. Jaylen began to ask "was it a dud?" just as the bomb exploded under the sedan BOOM! The bomb sent shrapnel and the car shell upward in a mushroom of fire and black smoke. The explosion's massive fireball had dissolved dozens of dead and sent the zombies close enough flying in different directions. As the fire burned it set off two additional explosions, one was the other sedan and then the city bus that had killed over a hundred of the dead. The blasts had knocked the survivors on their backs and rung their ears. They could feel the intense heat from the explosions and wait for the right time to make a run for it. The zombies in the middle of Highland street and that were in front of the Peachtree were now drawn to the large fire that loomed as black smoke filled the afternoon sky. The three watched in disbelief and amazement as the dead continued to walk right into the fire as they became engulfed and their bodies lit up like a struck match.

The front of the hotel was clear enough that they made the break for the front door. They smell of burning flesh filled the air as they crossed causing Jaylen to spit up as she ran across Highland Street. They had reached the front steps to the hotel and began to ascend knocking the dead over that struggled to navigate the steps. As they reached the door they noticed that there were several corpses strewn about with their dried brain and blood matter covering the entryway from large gaping head wounds. They pulled on the side glass door which was locked from inside with wire and they could see that furniture was also put in the way as to reinforce the barricade. They began to yell inside the crack of the door "help! Is anybody in there!? We need help open the door please!" The dead began to focus their attention on the survivors that were banging on the doors. "Shit!" Jaylen said as she noticed the dead slowly getting back up and she yelled to Rob to see what was happening. Robert tells RJ to cut the chain with the bolt cutters from the bag and that he would cover until he gave the word the door was open. RJ nods ok and Robert turns around in awe at the legion of the dead that is slowly advancing toward him some of which were on fire. He raised the rifle and began firing in the head area of the advancing heard of zombies dropping them. One at a time the dead fell as their heads exploded. Jaylen was firing the automatic shotgun knocking the dead over with each shot. She took a couple of pipe bombs from the bag, lit and tossed them into the crowd of the dead. BOOM! A mushroom cloud sent dozens of walkers flying into pieces, then BOOM! A second explosion yielded the same results. As Robert and Jaylen covered RJ, he had begun to remove the bolt cutters from the bag and as he looked up startling him he saw a face of a large man in the crack of the door where the sunlight peeked into the darkness. The face disappeared from view and he could hear the barricade and chains being removed. The fire continued from Roberts now smoking M4 and Jaylen was now using the Glock nine taking carefully aimed shots. They were now backing against the building as the dead closed in on them. Robert looked to his right and Jaylen was missing and as he turned to his left he saw two large meat hooks for hands reach for him yanking him inside.

The door was immediately slammed shut and relocked. Some of the furniture that was in the lobby was used to barricade the heavy glass door. Robert immediately looks and finds RJ and Jaylen standing on the large granite design of a peach tree which covered the floor of the main foyer. The foyer was open with a cathedral ceiling and a large polished desk running the entire length of the room with a sweeping clock and the same peach tree logo centered on the wall behind the desk. To the left was a hallway leading to the stairs and elevators and to the right was the glass door entrance to the Peach Tree Tavern. Standing in front of Robert now was a large burly looking man standing 6'4 weighing well over 350 pounds. He looked like he could play lineman for any professional football team and wearing a security guards uniform that strained at the seams to contain his girth. His shoes were black no-name sneakers that were well worn and turned on their sides. His glasses looked miniature like his features on his full face.

"Names Drew, y'all ok?"

Robert thanks him patting him on the shoulder.

"We owe you our lives" Jaylen added.

The dead had begun to cast shadows in the doorway as they began to push and bang against the doors. "We should go" as Drew motioned with his revolver for them to follow him into the tavern. They follow him cautiously as he waddled into the room and switched on the lights.

"Are you here alone?" Robert asked as he looked around.

"Mhmm" Drew replied. "Something to eat?" he asked as he raised a peanut butter sandwich smashing half into his mouth.

All three refused as they took a seat to relax. While reloading their weapons Robert asked if the Underground mall was close by and if they could get to it. Shaking his head up and down signaling yes as he chewed then taking a long swig of milk as it poured down each side of his mouth. Wiping with his sleeve he answers that it was only a few blocks but might as well be a mile with all the infected all over the place.

"If ya had a car ya could drive to it, ya got a car?"

RJ, Jaylen, and Robert look at each other and RJ answers sarcastically "did you see us pull up in a car?!"

"If it is only a few blocks away we can get there on foot," Jaylen says. "We made it this far we can do it again, we just need a plan."

Drew responds "Are you kidding me! I'd be like filet mignon to those fuckers! My fat ass is staying right here." RJ lets out a chuckle and is hit with an elbow from Jaylen who is also trying to hold back a snicker. "You can take my car if you want to" Drew said tossing the keys to Robert. "It's in the garage in the basement, lower level. It's a yellow pick up." Robert takes out the portable radio from the military checkpoint and tries to broadcast again. There was no answer just static so Robert asked to be shown where the rooftop was. Drew tells them the stairwell leading to the rooftop was across the foyer as he points with the half-eaten sandwich and the three get up and go across the foyer and around the corner finding the elevator. Drew came huffing behind them holding the elevators security key that would give them access to the roof. "Here, you're going to need this" Drew managed between breaths. They all get into the elevator and Drew inserts the security key turning it clockwise and pushing the top button allowing the elevator to surpass the last security measure reaching the eighteenth floor. They exit the elevator to an empty storage area and they head to the short stairway that had a small sticker that read rooftop in red letters with an arrow pointing toward the top of the stairs. They head up single file and unlock the hatch turning it in the up position. With a screech, the steel door slowly swung open and daylight blinded everyone as they stepped out onto the rooftop.

Automatically the radio begins to pick up a mayday signal from an unknown source. Robert immediately responds "This is Gunnery Sergeant Robert Babcock, do you copy?! Over." Immediately a male's voice comes over "This is Lieutenant Pyle, U.S. Marines. Do you copy? Over" Robert replies "I copy. Where are you, over?" There was a brief silence Lieutenant Pyle responded "Due west of your location at The Underground. We see you on the roof of the Peachtree. Look for our flair, over". The group on the roof looked into the west and moments later an audible pop was heard in the air and a bright red flare attached to a parachute slowly made it's descent back to Earth. Drew points out the obvious "there it is!" "Copy your location" Robert responds on the radio. "Going to try and get to your location, I'll notify when we are on the way. Over" There was another pause about a minute. Then Pyle came over the air "Stand by for visual confirmation." There was another pause before the Lieutenant came over the portable radio again, "be advised we just received a confirmed order for a search and rescue for a one Robert Babcock. We just visually confirmed your identity and will be sending a team to escort you to the CDC. Over." Robert thought to himself had said out loud "I can't believe the fucking e-mail worked." There was a mild celebration on the rooftop of the Peachtree as everyone high fived each other and smiled. "We will be sending a team of men to extract and escort you to our current location. Over". Robert replies "fuckin roger that! There are four of us here. We will be waiting in the west end of the underground lot and will meet you once you get here. Over." Lieutenant Pyle responded, "roger that, assembling the team momentarily and will be at your location in twenty mikes." Robert tells everyone that they needed to get to the basement and prepare to move. They all headed to the door down the narrow flight of steps and headed to the elevator. They all get in and push the button for the basement.

At the Underground Mall, The United States Marines began to muster as Lieutenant Pyle calls them to formation as they stand at attention with their weapons at the ready. Pyle walks up and down the formation addressing them before heading out to start their mission. "We just received orders from the White House to bring the Marine who is currently located across the way at the Peachtree Hotel. Our orders are to facilitate his movement and ensure he safely reaches the Centers for Disease Control. This Marine may have the answer to this cluster fuck we all are in making him more valuable than all of us put together. We will complete this mission and we will survive! Semper FI!" Each Marine sounded off like they had a pair "HOORAH!" Lieutenant Pyle gave the order "fall out!" and the Marines all went their separate way as they gathered the equipment needed for the mission. They make their way up the stairs to the rear of the underground where several transport vehicles were stored. They get in the convoy and start up the diesel engines and the three-vehicle convoy proceeded to the security gate two Marines stood in the turrets and worked the charging handles on the .50 caliber machine guns. Two other Marines standing century began stabbing the dead through the gate with their bayonets as they were drawn to the fence by the roaring diesel engines. Crunching could be heard as each stab through a skull with a bayonet and the dead fell one by one. Two more Marines went to the gate to help as one covered his brothers and the other opened the gate for the awaiting convoy. As the gate swung open the three-vehicle convoy exited running over zombies in their path as the gate was closed behind them. They make a left out of the gate and then proceed down the cluttered road crushing the dead that staggers in their way as they speed toward the Peachtree.

Back at the Peachtree, the elevator had reached the basement level and the doors dinged as they opened. They stepped out cautiously into the dimly lit garage as Drew led the way to the far west corner exit. They passed several parked cars some with blinking alarms. They made their way up to the ground level where they could hear the moans of zombies that were aimlessly staggering around between the parked cars and blocked the door they needed to get through to the convoy. They all hold up backed against the wall around the corner from the door blocked by the dead as Drew and Robert peered around the corner. "Shit!" Robert says and Drew takes a look at his revolver ensuring it is loaded. He turns to the group "y'all need a distraction" and tells them good luck then begins to slowly trot around the corner as quickly as he could yelling "over here ya dumb sum bitches!" This drew the attention of the walkers as they began to growl and shamble towards the slowly moving Drew. As the last of the dead leave, the doorway unobstructed Robert leads RJ and Jaylen from around the corner and toward the blue steel door that leads to the rear parking lot of the hotel. As they reached the door gunshots echoed in the garage causing them to flinch. Robert slowly pressed against the locking bar and the door slowly opened outward letting in the bright sunlight as he led the way outside.

As the door closed behind them they realized that the rear lot was empty and the dead were being held at bay by a chain-link fence. The presence of the three survivors agitated the dead as they seemed to push and shake the fence more since their arrival. Their groans were soon drowned out by the incoming roar of the military convoy. RJ points to the other side of the gate as the convoy came into view. The vehicles sped up and crashed through the far side of the gate crushing the zombies as their bodies exploded from the impact of the vehicle. The survivors waived their hands frantically as if the Marines could miss them and they began to run toward the convoy as it came to a screeching halt. A stone-faced Marine wearing glasses and a patch on the center of his body armor that read Pyle exited the front passenger seat and said "U.S Marines, we're here to get you out! I thought there were four of you?" The dead had begun to stagger through the hole in the fence causing everyone to turn and look. Robert says "there was a guard but he drew the dead away so we could get out of the garage. I don't know where he is". Pyle responds "get into the middle vehicle and we will head back to the underground before we get you to the Centers for Disease Control."

Everyone piled into the vehicle and the convoy began its departure before the walkers were even close. As they turned around and pulled off Drew comes spilling out of the doorway completely out of breath covered in sweat as he falls to his knees. "Wait!" he gasps but it was too late all he saw was the tail lights of the last security vehicle. The sound of the diesel engines was quickly drowned out by the moans of the dead that were still pouring in through the gate. A second later he realized the grave situation he was in and staggered to his feet. His lungs burned as if they were full of acid and his feet were filled with lead, holding his chest he turned around just in time to the see zombies come spilling out of the door that led to the garage. His eyes grew to the size of saucers and he attempted to run to the far end of the lot but he tripped as his sneaker fell off. He hit the ground hard smacking his face on the asphalt knocking him dizzy. He rolled over and saw the clouds passing overhead in the blue sky and all he could hear was a slight ringing in his ears from the hit to his head. He blinked his eyes to clear the cobwebs when he felt an in intense pressure on his calf then a warm liquid filled his shoe. As he looked down he realized that the dead were at his legs and had taken a fresh chunk of flesh from him. Immediately he felt excruciating pain and began to scream as the zombies took another bite and others joined in the feast tearing into his robust stomach exposing large amounts of fatty tissue underneath his skin as the dead pulled chunks shoving it into their mouths. As they made their way through the fatty tissue his organs became exposed and blood began to spill all over the ground. The dead had finally reached him from the gate and began tearing the flesh away from his chubby face and another bit a chunk of flesh-ripping his corroded artery as bright red blood pulsated squirting from the gaping bite. Drew could no longer scream and put the revolver to his head and pulled the trigger trying to rid himself of the agony of being eaten alive. Click! The gun was empty and poor Drew had to endure being ripped apart for a few agonizing seconds that seemed like an eternity. Looking down drew was on his back now covered with walkers that disemboweled him as his dead eyes stared back at the sky.

Meanwhile, at the underground mall, the gate was opened for the returning convoy as they sped into the secure area and screech to a halt. Everyone exits the vehicles and quickly moves past the sandbag fortification to the stairway leading to the mall underground. There they passed by Marines that were standing guard with M4 assault rifles and squad automatic weapons. There were tables with computers and short-range radios where the Marines were in contact with someone on the other end. There were crates of ammunition and assorted explosives stacked to the ceiling. RJ, Robert, and Jaylen were shown to the cafeteria and given a seat. Lieutenant Pyle politely offers them to grab anything they wanted to eat or drink and that they were preparing to escort them to the CDC so he could continue his research and help save the population. As they eat their meals Lieutenant Pyle says "we are going to send a team led by myself and five other gung ho Marines that will get you to the CDC. We have been in contact with the top governmental officials and received a message with your information and was told you reached out stating that you were making your way to Atlanta but were trapped someplace in the town of Wilson. We had sent a squad sized search and rescue National Guard team in but lost contact with them last evening." "We saw them!" Jaylen said. "They were across the street from us and ran into an entire street of those things. They fought and killed hundreds of them but were overrun in the process." Lieutenant Pyle stands in deep thought to himself for a minute probably picturing the slaughter in his head. Then he comes to and says "you guys are fighters to have made it this far, and fighting together we will get you wherever you need to go. Rest up a while we will get ready to move in a couple of hours and get you to the CDC."

Robert, RJ, and Jaylen thank the Lieutenant for rescuing them from the hotel and helping them get to the Centers for Disease Control. Lieutenant Pyle responded "not a problem when you finish eating get a power nap if you can. I'll come to get you guys when we are ready to move." Robert responds "great thank you." The lieutenant nods and exits the small courtyard where they were eating to continue to prepare for the mission. The three finish their meals and make their way to the furniture store and they kick off their shoes and lounge an RJ and Jaylen find beds to plop down in and Robert settled for a comfy recliner.

They all lie in their resting place in their own thoughts. RJ lie thinking of his departed mother that made him sad but thought of his dad who was still here which helped as he drifted off to sleep. Jaylen lies there and thinks about how lucky she is to be alive. Smiling thinking back to when she and Robert were an item many years ago until they chose different career paths and how foolish of a reason it was that came between them. Then she thinks back to the night on the balcony, which makes tingle deep down. Now throbbing, she bites her lower lip, imagining Robert tasting her. Sensuously moaning she licks her middle finger, then slides her hand down her panties under the blanket and satisfies herself before drifting to sleep. Robert is nodding out as he thinks of his son and how he will handle everything. He thinks optimistically of the work he will be able to conduct once in his laboratory and that he will be able to turn this whole mess around before he drifts off to sleep. They slept like they haven't slept in weeks mostly due to the fact that they finally felt secure and that they finally found real help or they had a good feeling all things considered that everything may be ok.

Approximately an hour or so later Private First Class Dent knocked on the door to the store waking the three up from their deep sleep. "We're ready to go Sir" PFC Dent said sticking his head into the room. They all acknowledge and roll out of their sleeping areas and got dressed. As they make their way to the main control center Lieutenant Pyle greets them stating "go to the armory and get what you'll need." Gunnery Sergeant Riley stood tall at 6'4" at the armory door with his arms folded with a lit cigarette burning in his mouth. "Grab anything you need," he says out the corner of his mouth and steps aside. The three enter the small cage area and take their pick. Robert grabs additional magazines for his M4 carbine, RJ grabs a Colt himself and several magazines placing them in a carrier as he drapes it over his shoulders as well as some frag grenades. Jaylen grabs additional shotgun shells for the automatic shotgun and slings a bandoleer around her shoulder. They meet by the main computer console and watch Lieutenant Pyle communicate with someone in Washington D.C via e-mail informing them that they are about to move Babcock from the stronghold to the CDC and provide security. After he sends the message he stands up and signals to Gunny Riley. Seconds later four Marines fall into formation with a heavy combat load. Two had the M249 Squad Automatic Weapons with one thousand rounds each and the other two carried the ubiquitous M4 with eleven magazines each. All had four fragmentation grenades, two had claymore mines and two had LAWS. Private First Class Dent and Private Dosreis carried the Saws' and Private First Class Campbell and Private Blue carried the M4's. The order to fall out was given and the men headed outside to the awaiting convoy and piled into the vehicles which were uploaded for a combat mission. Inside each of the vehicles was additional ammunition for the squad automatic weapons, the M4 carbines, .50 BMG (Browning machine gun) and different explosives. Privates Blue and Dosreis jump into the front vehicle and start the diesel engine. Private First Class Campbell and Dent jumped into the rear vehicle as Robert, RJ, Jaylen, Lieutenant Pyle, and Gunny Riley jump into the middle armored personnel carrier. Robert noticed the extra ammunition, explosives, and rations in the belly of the beast as the Gunny gets in the turret and cocks the large .50 caliber machine gun. From the window, they could see the Marines that were standing guard at the base were again sticking the dead with bayonets through the fence as they approached the camp when the engines were started. As they waited for the gate to be cleared Lieutenant Pyle looked back from the driver's seat "Alright, we are going to take a left onto Grand Street, go three blocks then right onto Swan for two blocks then bear right on Woodcock Boulevard."

After a dozen or so zombies that were stuck through the skull, the security gate was opened by one Marine as the other provided cover with an M16 rifle. The three-vehicle convoy sped through the gate bowling over several more walkers that were staggering toward the commotion and their rotting bodies burst apart from the impact from the reinforced vehicles. The gate was immediately closed behind the vehicles and the Marines retreated back to the mini-tower to keep watch and stay hidden from the dead.

On the way to the Centers for Disease Control, the lead armored jeep was barreling down the street crushing any zombies in its way. Blue was driving and radioed to the trailing vehicles that a barricade of car that was parked nose to nose was blocking the route. Lieutenant Pyle ordered that they speed up and plow through it which they did. Blue had floored the gas pedal and had smashed through the front ends of a blue station wagon and gray minivan. The impact sent vehicle debris flying and a large chunk of metal had gotten run over became entangled in the front axle and tire well. This caused the lead vehicle to veer sharply to the right and collide with a yellow Ryder school bus head-on knocking Blue unconscious and jarring Dosreis in the turret. The other two vehicles seeing this came to a screeching halt. The trail vehicle had pulled up and took the point position as they tried to make communication with the disabled vehicle. The dead had begun to swarm toward the three vehicles and clawing at them in an attempt to get at the human meals inside.

Dosreis had shaken his head clearing the cobwebs and his eyes bugged out as he saw several dead surrounding the front and operators side of the disabled vehicle. He takes off the safety of the fifty caliber machine gun and opens fire. The large bore chain gun spits a large flame and the dead seemed to be sliced in half. Their bodies burst open from the large full metal jacketed bullets turning their rotting flesh into what looked like raw ground beef. The other two vehicles had opened fire with their machine guns also peppering back the dead as more bodies were picked apart sending blood, brains and bone fragments everywhere. It seemed for everyone they killed two more stiffly stepped up in their place. Dosreis had run his Ma Deuce dry as smoke bellowed from the barrel. He ducked into the vehicle and tried to get Blue to wake up with no effect. He grabs a squad automatic weapon, chambering a round and heads back up the turret opening fire peeling back the dead that was now beginning to make their slowly on the hood of the jeep. Blood, meat, and brains were splashed all over the hood of the vehicle and the side of the yellow school bus. Dosreis had run the SAW dry as he heard a click. He began to reload when he heard faint moans of pain coming from Blue who was trapped in his seat. He ducked into the vehicle and tried to free Blue with the dead clawing at the windows from the outside. Continuous gunfire from the other vehicles could be heard from the outside as well. Blue looks at Dosreis and shakes his head "no" as Dosreis slams his fist against the roof "fuck!" then goes back to the turret opening up again with the SAW peeling back the ocean of the dead.

Gunny Riley comes over the radio "we're coming to get you! Is everything ok in there?!"

Dosreis replies "Blue is hurt bad and pinned! He can't move and is hurt!"

Gunny Riley says "We're coming for you now hold on!"

Dosreis comes over "negative! Get to the fuckin CDC, I will not leave a man behind, complete the mission sir, I got these puss fucks!" The two other vehicles began to roll again on their way to the CDC.

Back at the crash, Dosreis emerges from the turret again with the SAW firing a burst in the walkers when the weapon jams. He frantically tries to clear the jam but he continuously burns his hands on the smoking barrel. He drops the SAW and removes a fragmentation grenade and pulls the pin. He nervously fumbles and winds up dropping the grenade in the vehicle. "Shit!" he says and frantically tries to recover the explosive disappearing into the vehicle. Blue in pain seemed to forget about his broken leg as he asked Dosreis "what the fuck was that?" then the vehicle went up in a large fireball. BOOM! Shrapnel and fire engulfed and shredded everything in its path creating a black mushroom cloud killing over a hundred walkers that were swallowing up the vehicle.

The explosion could be heard by the remaining convoy and as they looked back they could see the orange and black mushroom cloud rise over the row of houses that divided the streets. They were now leaving the downtown area and now in a semi-residential area where the streets were less congested with the dead. The residences were mostly boarded up or barricaded and most of the windows were broken and smeared with blood. The dead were at some residences still clawing at the front barricaded doors and windows and some were staggering in the middle of the streets and were plowed over and crushed if they were in the way of the speeding vehicles on the way to the Centers for Disease Control. The transport was just a quarter-mile from Woodcock Boulevard and the top floor of the CDC building was now in sight. They come to a stop one block from their final destination as they see a survivor atop an overturned city bus that was surrounded by walkers clawing trying to get to the survivor. When he saw the convoy he began waving a gray shirt frantically trying to get the attention of the group.

Private First Class Campbell gets on the bullhorn and orders "you on the bus keep your head down and gets ready to move!" at that moment he had slapped Dent's leg giving him the green light to open fire on the dead. Dent took careful aim with the SAW and fired a burst into the head area of the dead dropping a group of nine as their heads burst from the high-velocity projectiles. The survivor kept in a fetal position shaking uncontrollably and flinched as the armor-piercing rounds pinged and dug into the metal of the bus beneath him. The dead began to slowly turn toward the vehicles and Dent opened fire again with a long burst dropping more of the dead with headshots and cutting others in half as they fall to the ground. Dent now takes aim toward the front of the bus where more dead were coming from the opposite side of the bus and opened fire once again as a large flame spit from the machine gun. The zombie's heads burst open and they fall to the ground with large holes leaking dark coagulated blood and brain matter. "Jump!" was ordered over the bullhorn by Campbell and the man had jumped off the side of the bus hitting the ground hard as he let out a scream of agony. He slowly got to his feet and quickly hobbled to the awaiting convoy. He gets into the first vehicle with Dent and Campbell and they sped off bowling over more dead as they closed in.

They now came to and made the left onto Woodcock Boulevard and crashed through the first security gate that was covered with walkers and continued the quarter-mile drive up to the second security gate and came to a stop. Everyone exited the vehicles and joined Robert at the gate. The surrounding grounds were zombie-free but not for long as a wave of the undead came spilling through the first smashed gate. Everyone turned and looked at the dead slowly shambling toward them. "If you're going to do something, do it fuckin fast!" Riley says to Robert. Robert takes out a security pass and holds it to the bar code that turns green and clicks as the gate begins to open. The drivers get back in the vehicles and pull forward into the parking lot of the CDC and the rest walked in as the gate was shut behind them. They pull to the left side of the building where the staff parking lot was a bi-level with a ramp that had a walkway leading to the main floor of the building. There was a security gate that was pulled shut and locked that should keep out any zombies trying to get in. They all got out of the vehicles and stood in a circle as they stared at the new member of the group.

Grimacing in pain leaning against the armored personnel carrier "Names Mason, Mason Daniels. I'm a transit bus driver and that was my bus turned over. I was knocked out and when I came to I was surrounded by those things that were all over the bus. Some were inside eating other passengers so I climbed to the top side of the bus and waited for the past three days for someone to come rescue me. Thank God you guys showed!" Dent gives Mason some water and a power bar to eat which he wolfs down in a few bites taking large swigs of water in between. "Thanks" he mumbles as he chews a mouth full of food. Robert tells everyone that there are five levels to the building three administrative levels above ground and two levels deep underground. "We gotta search and secure every level and make it down to my laboratory and hope it is still intact. It is at the lowest level and will be the last place to search. We will go through the doors and take the stairwell to the right and make our way to the third floor and work our way down systematically. Everyone good?" Robert asks and they all nodded yes in agreement. They all jog to the employee entrance behind Robert as he badges his way into the building. As the door lock buzzes green and the steel door opens with an audible click they all file in a single stack as they enter through the door.

THE CDC

Robert led the way into the building with his M4 trained at the end of the hallway. RJ was right behind him followed by Jaylen then Lieutenant Pyle with his SAW, Gunny Riley with M16A4, Mason Daniels and PFC's Campbell and Dent covering the rear with M4 carbines. They make their way to the first stairwell that was halfway down the hall and took the stairway cautiously up to the top floor. As they reached the top platform a white door with red stenciling read 3rd floor which Robert slowly opened peeking inside the hallway to see if it was clear of the dead. The hallway was half-lit because of the main lighting had a short causing the lights to flicker on and off giving strobe light effect in the hallways. As they check into the different rooms it was obvious that the backup emergency lighting was on and they were able to quickly move through the third floor's third wing and move to the second which was identical. They pass through to the first wing on the third floor and the memory of the meeting weeks before with Stanfield and Miller at the end of the hall come flooding back to Robert like it was yesterday. Robert not paying attention and distracted by his own thoughts bypassed the first conference room and headed right to the same one the meeting took place. As the group passes conference room 31A they see several bloody handprints pushing against the glass right behind PFC Dent's head. Robert and RJ brace to enter the conference room and as Robert opens the door RJ enters with the shotgun ready and his dad right behind him. The room was clean and seemed like it had been untouched. Robert then looks out the same window overlooking Woodcock Boulevard just as he did weeks ago, this time at a city unrecognizable. The skyline was covered in a black smog caused by smoldering fires that continued to burn throughout the city which now belonged to the dead.

Robert breaks from his deep thought at the voice of Jaylen "where to now?" and he immediately turns to the same phone putting it on speaker as the dial tone fills the room then begins dialing Stanfield's extension. A double ring fills the room RING-RING, RING-RING, RING-RING then he hangs up. He then dials Miller's extension as the same double-ring fills the room again, RING-RING, RING-RING, RING- and the receiver was taken off the hook on the other end. "Hello?" Robert said into the speaker but the only response was some sounds of scratching as if the receiver was being dragged on the floor. "Hello, Miller?!" again no answer just the same muffled sound and what sounded like a moan then the line went dead. A busy signal beeped in the room before Robert hung up.

He looked at Jaylen, RJ and the rest of the group with a grave look of concern and immediately dialed extension 556 to his office in the Division of Viral Control and the same internal double-ring sounded from the phone's speaker. The phone rang a half dozen times before it was answered by a reluctant voice "h-hello?"

"Evangeline!" Robert exclaimed.

"Bob!" Evangeline replied. "I've been hiding in the lab since early on during the outbreak. I have been conducting tests when I could and have been hiding from the infected that are in the building. The place is crawling with them."

Robert responds, "ok, I will make my way down to you just stay put. I have some help and we will be there soon."

"Ok, hurry" Vange responds, "One last thing, be careful there are several dead in sub-level two just above me" and hung up the phone. They all go back to the hallway where Robert tells everyone the plan is to make their way to the ground floor to check Miller and Stanfield's offices before going to his on sub-level 3. They get ready to make their way to the stairwell at the end of the hall when PFC Dent turns around flinching "oh shit!" he yells getting everyone's attention and the survivors jump back as they turned training their weapons on the window. "Don't shoot! They can't get out." Robert said. "The building is in code five lockdown where all doors are automatically locked if someone trips the emergency security system. The system can only be overridden by one of the top five employees and luckily I'm one of them. My access card will unlock all the security doors secured by the emergency lockdown."

They head to the doorway at the end stairway with their weapons ready. They all make their way down the flight of stairs when the sound of scuffling feet stopped them in their tracks. Robert takes careful aim through the ACOG putting the red chevron on the top of the zombies head and begins to squeeze the trigger. A large spray of pink mist and bright red blood covered the entire wall and door to the second floor as a deafening crack echoed throughout the stairwell. The zombie fell stiffly to the floor as the colt spit the empty brass to the concrete steps chambering the next round. They wait for a second as Robert signals for a Marine to cover the bloody brain and bone stained splattered door, as the group bypassed it to the first floor where Miller and Stanfield's offices were located. Robert reaches the final step before reaching the door for the first floor and tells the group to hold. The door was opened slowly and Robert peered in and saw the hallway was like the previous floors as the emergency lighting kept the hallway dimly lit. He enters the first floor as the group follows behind him making their way halfway down the hall when a noise stopped them in their tracks. The sound of uneven footsteps coming from around the corner. The sound of sniffing accompanied by moaning and growling made everyone's hair stand on end and goosebumps race down their arms. Robert motioned to everyone to kneel against the wall as he takes aim with the M4 waiting for the first walker to stagger around the corner. The shadow of the first walker gets larger and larger as it gets closer to the corner which was fifteen feet, away. RJ creeps up and takes the safety off his Mossberg with an audible click. The zombie that first staggered around the corner was in a white doctor's blood-stained lab coat. Her hair was black with a blond patch, greasy and stringy as it loosely hung to the middle of her back from her head. The left side of her face was blue/green in color with a tint of gray and there was a distinct tattoo on the side of her neck of a musical note. As she came into the open she stopped mid-step and began sniffing the air and began growling. She turned stiffly to her left to face the survivors she reveals what was left of the side of her face. There was dried blackened blood on her chin and what remained of her lower jaw. It appears that someone had shot her in the mouth with a large caliber gun and the bullet blasted away the entire lower portion of her jaw and her tongue tended to slide out and hang through that gaping wound. She began to bear her bloody meat caked teeth and growl as she raised her arms and began to stagger toward the group. RJ steadies himself and squeezes the trigger, BOOM! A large flame spits from the quarter-sized bore of the Mossberg and the rest of the zombies head disappeared into a red mist and the headless body fell to the ground.

The deafening echo was soon drowned out with the sound of the dead staggering toward the group. Several shadows could be seen in the flashing emergency lighting causing the group to begin to back away from the corner and prepared to fight the hoard. A group of the dead began making their way from the other end of the hallway behind the group. Eight of the dead finally rounded the corner and began to shamble toward the survivors all bearing their bloody teeth. The Marines opened fire putting a quick end to the group of the dead filling the corridor with gun smoke. As the group prepares to move forward Private First Class Dent was grabbed by his body armor and pulled backward as he yells "the fuck!" Everyone gasps when they turn around and see a half dozen more dead as they began to engulf Dent ripping at him. Camp, Bell, Pyle, and Riley all open fire with their M9 Beretta pistols. Taking headshots dropping the Zombie that had tried to take a bite of Dent. Dent and the Zombie both drop to the ground as Dent pulls away from the tight grasp of the zombie's hand. Getting to his feet he yells "fuck you!" and kicks the zombies head, hearing the loud thud from his steel toe boot, as he walks away thankful to be alive!

He picked his SAW up and they all began to make their way through the CDC. They slowly make their way down the dimly lit hallway and they all felt their hearts beating in their throats from the close call they had just experienced. Stanfield's office was now just feet away as Robert has everyone stand by as he gets ready to check the office. Just before he opened the door when he realizes that there was a bloody smeared handprint on the door giving him pause. He takes the doorknob with his left hand and takes the Kimber .45 in his right and looks at the group to make sure they are ready to back him up if needed. RJ takes the Colt .45 and nods to his dad that he is ready.

Robert's heart was pounding in hi,s throat as he begins to slowly turn the knob and realizes that it is unlocked, and as soon as the lock unhinges with a faint click the door is forced open form inside and the remains of a human crashed through the door growling bearing its rotten gums and dirty teeth. The skin was torn away from most his face and the lips were nonexistent. In reflex, Robert fires a shot that strikes the wall as the zombie grabs onto Robert causing them both fall to the ground in the hallway. The corpse is now on top of him biting in an attempt to take a chunk of flesh from his face as he struggles to keep the zombie off him. Robert gets off a shot into the torso which has no effect, and just as RJ begins to take aim at his head another zombie emerges from the office bearing his teeth as he looked at the group. RJ aims at the mauled face and squeezes the trigger. The Colt punches a nickel-sized hole in the face as the head snaps back and the spray of blood flies out of the right side of the skull. The walker falls to the right side of Robert and RJ rushes to pull the dead off his dad. He takes hold of the rear collar and pulls the head of the zombie away from his dads face, at which time a third zombie had appeared in the threshold of the hallway and was met by a round of buckshot from Jaylen causing RJ to duck. The Marines move into the office as automatic gunfire erupted from within. Robert with enough room was able to take the Kimber jamming the barrel in the dead's mouth pulling the trigger sending the entire back of the zombies' skull and brains splatting the floor behind him from the large jacketed hollow point. Robert shoves the dead off him to the right onto the other dead that landed beside him. Robert gets up with the assistance from RJ, and Jaylen and they enter the office joining the Marines.

The office was now splattered with blood and riddled with bullets and a body was lying face down on the table. Robert checks the bodies and doesn't recognize anyone, of them to be Stanfield. Robert tells them to continue to make their way down to Miller's office that was down the hall about five doors. The Marines lead the way down the hallway and surround the door as they knock "U.S. Marines! Anybody in there?" There was no answer so they decided to make entry. Lieutenant Pyle yelled, "frag out!" Pulling the pin on a fragmentation grenade, Riley opens the door as Pyle tosses the grenade into the office. Moans came from inside the office and the heavy metal object could be heard bouncing about the room. BOOM! A large blast blew out the windows sending glass flying all over the hallway and papers and a gust of hot air was forced out of the open doorway. As soon as the blast sounded they entered and all began yelling in succession "clear!" Robert enters and immediately his nostrils were filled with the smell of burnt flesh and sulfur and notices a well-charred corpse whose face was half-melted as his co-worker Dr. Joseph Miller. He was bitten on the wrist and must have turned a few days later. Robert did not know how to feel, after all, it was mostly his fault that they were in the mess they were in. Robert was still looking to find Stanfield but wasn't very optimistic at this point.

Robert gets on the phone in the hallway to check on Vange downstairs and dials 556 and Evangeline answers "Bob"?

"Yeah Vange it's me, Robert replies. "How are you holding up?"

Evangeline says "hanging in there but I can't take much more here alone."

"I know, we are making our way down to you. Is the laboratory intact? Can we continue our work on the antidote?"

"I'm not sure, I have been trapped in the commissary a few doors down the past week. All I have access to is the phone, but I did see Dr. Miller head toward the lab a few days ago but haven't seen anything but the dead since. I know our security guards tried to corral as many as they could on the floor above me but I haven't seen them either. Be careful cuz, ok."

Robert says "hang in there, we'll be there in a bit" and hangs up. Robert looks to the group deciding what to say to them next. "Ok, we need to get to my laboratory that is two floors down and to my cousin. She tells me there is dead corralled on the floor between us and some are on labs level as well. We just need to keep an eye out and take our time getting there, I don't want to lose anybody else." Robert takes them to the main floors north wing of the building to the security office and they begin to check the monitors on the lower level of the Division of Viral Control and monitor the activity. The security office was gray in color, had a long desk running the entire length of the room with two dozen monitors with four main monitors to get close up identification if needed. There were three padded chairs on wheels and countless buttons and knobs to control every camera in the building. Robert punches up the cameras for sub-level two and they scan the floor and don't see any walkers in the area. They switch the cameras to the ones facing the main lab of the DVC and scans the area and they notice a few zombies gathered by the sliding doors leading to the cleanroom. They pan to the opposite side of the hallway and zoom in where the commissary doors were and saw about a half dozen corpses lying in front of the door and figured that is where Evangeline his held up.

He then switches to the camera to sub-level one and immediately they could see that floor was overrun with the dead and they could be seen standing shoulder to shoulder in the hallway. They checked the other camera and could see more dead down the hall and what looked like some pushing against the hallway door leading to the eastern stairwell. Robert points to the screen "that's our way to sub-level two. We'll take the eastern stairwell which is stairwell number nine and bypass sublevel one and make our way to sublevel two where we need to go. Lieutenant Pyle and Gunny Riley, I need you to stay here, set up communication for us and be our eyes and ears and I will take the PFC's for security." Riley and Pyle agreed and Lieutenant Pyle gave the orders to Campbell and Dent to provide security and established communication on channel three via close circuit radios.

After the equipment checks out to be in working order Pyle and Riley wish the group good luck as they exited the security office locking the door behind them. The group followed Robert in a single file as RJ was right behind his dad followed by PFC Dent, Jaylen and Campbell had the rear security. They make their way slowly down the hallway which was covered with corpses that were rotted to almost skeletons, some were half eaten had severe head trauma where the brain and blood matter had leaked and dried caking the fractured skull to the floor. Flies were buzzing all over the hall and countless maggots ate their fill of the rotten flesh that remained. The smell was almost unbearable to the point that the group tied cloths around their faces which didn't help matters as PFC Campbell vomited spitting up his remaining breakfast and bile. They made it to stairwell nine and slowly opened the door peeking in seeing the stairway was lit with an orange hue from the emergency lighting bright enough to flood the entire staircase. The sound of pounding could be heard echoing the entire staircase and muffled growls could be heard in between the bangs on the door which was very nerve-wracking. They carefully make their way down the steps one at a time carefully checking the corners as they descended. They could now see the door labeled in red lettering that reads "sub-level 1" as it vibrated from the pounding the dead was giving it from the other side. Quietly Robert motioned for Dent to cover the door with the SAW and for Campbell to tie the doorknob with tension cord to the railing on the stairwell and secured it with a half hitch knot. Dent covers the door as the group continues down the stairs slowly and they make their way around the corner and the door that read "sub-level 2" was finally in sight. They gather on the landing and look up at the camera in the corner. "Alright, we're here, how's it looking for us?" The sound of the dead moaning and aimlessly bumping into the walls and door filled the hallway as they awaited the response from the security office. "Stand by, we have a cluster right by the door. We think we should wait and see if they disperse themselves. We count about thirteen total and most are in the middle of the hallway but four or five are right by you at the door." Robert looks at the group to get their opinion on if they should make their move or wait. Dent motions they make the move saying "It's only fifteen, let's get some! Robert and RJ nod in agreement and they prepare to make their move when a voice came over the radio "alright, they are now moving away to join the rest of the walkers on the other side of the hall and they are with their backs to you. Whenever you're ready". Robert motions to the group as he draws the Kimber .45 and the others followed suit drawing their pistols clicking off their safeties. He makes sure everyone is ready and quietly counts "three, two" and placing his left hand on the doorknob "one" and quickly opens the door and the group pours into the sublevel two main hallway. As soon as the click of the door sounded the dead turned had begun to turn around and shamble toward the survivors.

Back in the security office, they watched from the monitors as bright flashes indicate the survivors opened fire dropping the walkers as their heads exploded one by one falling to the floor. Seconds later all the dead lie on the floor with dark pools of blood and tissue slowing oozing from the holes in their heads.

In the hallway, the smell of rotten meat and burnt sulfur filled the air as the group carefully checked the hallway making their way toward the commissary to where Evangeline was held up. As they approach the door they began yelling for Evangeline when she answers unlocking the door. She was not the freshest but all things considered, she was unharmed. She comes out of the commissary holding the Beretta and hugs Robert and RJ. They make their way up the slight ramp that leads to the decontamination rooms and the doors slide open with a hiss as compressed air escapes and the strong smell of chemicals fills the air. They enter the cleanroom and Robert leads them to the observation area looking down into the DVC's clean laboratory.

From what they could see the entire lab was completely destroyed by the high thermal flame containment feature as there was broken glass strewn throughout the laboratory as well as assorted papers, spilled chemicals and blood-smeared handprints all about. They look to the frozen chambers where the samples of the infected brain specimens were held was opened as cool frosty air billowed from within. Robert's countenance fell at the sight of his lab and tears began to well in his eyes. Vange and RJ come to Robert and place a hand on his shoulder as to reassure him that he was not alone. Robert then leads the group downstairs and badges his way into the laboratory for a closer look at the destruction of the lab. Up close the damage was worse than thought. The fire destroyed all the specimens fresh and infected and left burnt on the far corner table. A check of the freezer revealed that no specimens remained and all the resources at the CDC were destroyed. Robert falls to his knees and began to whimper into his hands. RJ and Jaylen comfort him the best they could but decide to let him alone for a while. After a few minutes, Rob gathers himself and RJ says "we can go the reservation dad. You have your lab there and I still have this" holding up the miniature flash drive.

Shaking his head in agreement "We have to get out of here, there is nothing I can do here" Robert tells the group. "Let's head up to the main office and get on the computers so I can see if I can salvage anything from his mess." The group follows Robert out of the burned lab and into the hallway back up to the clean rooms and through the doors. They make a left and head down the hall to Robert's office that was now just down the hall on the right. The group makes their way carefully down the hallway and are now three doors away from the office. There was an open door on the left and they turned their weapons and attention in that direction as they got closer and closer. Robert points to Mason to check the doorway to ensure it was clear and as soon as he popped his head into the threshold he was met by a large man hissing as he grabbed Mason's shoulders. The man's face was a greenish-yellow filled with puss and his lips, nose and eyes were dark from pooled blood and his hair was dirty and greasy. He had open soars on his face that were dripping a bloody puss that flowed into his eyes and mouth. His gums were rotted away bearing his large set of overexposed teeth. A toxic mixture of dark blood and saliva freely streamed from his mouth dripping onto Mason's shirt as both fell to the floor causing the group to jump back. Mason was on the floor "help!" as he rolled around on the ground trying to hold the walker at bay. "Mason!" everyone exclaimed as they pointed their weapons at the two but nobody fired in fear of hitting Mason. The zombie opened its puss infected mouth wide chomping down onto Mason's Adam's apple causing him to let out a blood gurgling yell. The zombie pulled the chunk of flesh away taking the meat, veins, and cartilage from Mason's throat. The meat and sinews stretched and snapped into his mouth and began to chew seemingly savoring the flavorful mouthful. Gunfire erupted as multiple projectiles struck the zombie as it drops to its side as the hot lead tore through its head. Mason lie on his back with a blank stare. His face and chest were covered in blood from the dead as fresh bright blood still flowed from the gaping wound. While in shock of what just happened, Jaylen steps toward the newly departed pointing the automatic shotgun at his head and squeezed the trigger. A deafening boom echoed in the hallway as the blast had completely taken off Mason's head from the nose up. The Italian made crowd-pleaser effortlessly cycled the spent shell smoothly feeding another round into the chamber. Robert then gets closer and realizes that the dead was his old partner Stanfield who must have destroyed the entire lab before he turned. After a short prayer for their friend Mason, they follow Robert the rest of the hallway to his office and they all fall into the lab as they close and lock the door behind them.

CONTRACT

Eighteen months before infection:
Washington, D.C

In the executive meeting room at the "W" hotel in Washington, D.C, the annual governmental fundraising dinner was coming to a close. The events of the evening were winding down as the President of the United States had made his appearance and departed and the remaining individuals were the upper echelon of the political word. All conversed as they nursed their choice of cabernet or scotch on the rocks. One of these individuals was the lead developer at the Center for Disease Control Doctor Miller. He was sitting with Doctor Stanfield when he was approached by a female server who had handed him an envelope and she walked away. Miller opened the crisp white envelope and in blue ink, it read *"meet in the presidential suite, a half-hour with top advisors."* Miller checks his watch and it read 10 p.m. He finishes his final snort of single malt scotch and leans over to Stansfield whispering

"Big brother wants to meet in a half hour with us."

"What for?"

Miller shaking his head "I don't know but we have to go to the presidential suite for 10:30."

Stanfield then too takes the large last gulp of his neat $50 a glass scotch and placing the empty snifter on the blue linen as both men get up and make their way through the hall. "What do we tell Babcock?" Stanfield asks and Miller responds "nothing, let's see what they want and decide from there." They both peer at Babcock as he stands to talk at the bar sipping cabernet as he exchanges pleasantries with a group across the room as they both quickly head out the main entrance of the ballroom and head down the hallway to the elevators on the main floor pushing the up button. The elevator door dings and slides open and both men enter pushing the top-level button and stand quietly as they are taken to the top floor. Moments later the elevator comes to a sudden stop and the doors ding as they open once again to a long marbled floor hallway with red walls and gold mounted lights. The hall was decorated with black and white photos of the DC Metro Area and large mirrors on either side of the wall. They step out and head straight down the hallway toward the presidential suite where they noticed two secret service agents standing guard and hold the two at the door. The agent on their left stood with his left hand extended as he put his right-hand touches his right ear as if listening to someone on the other end. He then speaks into the mini microphone attached to his wrist "they're here, are we ready? Roger that." The agent turns to his right and opens the door to the presidential suite steps out of the threshold and ushers Miller and Stanfield into the suite and closes the door behind them and reassumes his post.

Inside the suite three senior congress members, the secretary of defense, director of Homeland Security and the senior financial advisor for military funding stand around the mini bar all with glasses in their hands. They turn to Miller and Stanfield as the secretary of defense addresses the two doctors "please be seated gentleman, can we interest you in a drink?" Stanfield politely refuses and takes a seat as Miller accepts taking a neat glass of cognac then joins Stanfield on the couch. Clearing his throat of the burning sensation after taking a large gulp of the single malt beverage he manages to ask what the meeting was about. The men standing in a semicircle stared at each other before all looking at the secretary of defense. He then walks towards the two coming to the chair adjacent to the couch Miller and Stanfield were sitting on and sat comfortably as he inched forward drawing the two doctors in. The Secretary of Defense proposed that the Centers for Disease Control would be willing to create a new cutting edge viral weapon that is designed to attack the enemy's central nervous system and take them out of the fight without having to fire a single shot. He proposed a package for the timeline they wanted, the copious governmental funding and the generous bonus that would be paid upfront. They also were advised that the entire program would be Black Ops sensitive and kept off the official docket.

Miller and Stanfield discuss the terms and ask to be allowed to discuss the matter in private. "You have ten minutes" Miller and Stanfield were told as the gentlemen silently walk out of the room and close the door behind them. Both Miller and Stanfield take a few minutes and look over the ten-page budget proposal. They both agree that it would be a great opportunity not only for them but their department for future funding toward other projects.

They both anxiously look over the document and their eyes widened as the dollar amount spiked their human greed. The contract read that Miller and Stanfield would receive a total of fifty million dollars in funding for the development, testing and approval by the Food and Drug Administration within a fifteen-month period. They would each receive a full governmental retirement benefits package for their work and a bonus of five million dollars that will be paid to each of them upon agreement of the contract. Before they realized it the Secretary of Defense reentered the room after a brief knock and giving them the ultimatum. "Well doctors, have you made your choice? I have two options for you gentlemen to sign, one is the contract in which these two checks are made out to the each of you" holding up two checks made out in their names for five million dollars each, "or confidentiality agreements indicating this meeting never took place." The nature of greed was too much for them to completely comprehend what was being asked of them and the potential ramifications. They both signed, dated and initialed the contract in the appropriate places and each was handed their rich bonuses. "Thank you gentleman for your commitment and duty to your country, it is greatly appreciated. I advise you to use discretion pertaining to this matter and I will tell you this once, failure to comply with this contract will result in your termination." He took the signed contracts placing them in a silver metal briefcase and walked out the door.

That Monday back at the Center for Disease Control in Atlanta, Georgia, Miller, and Stanfield is back in their office looking through the deadly choices of stockpiled viruses they could use for their deal with the devil. Miller decided to use an aggressive strain of the rabies virus that would attack a person's central nervous system. They had already worked on a mutated strain of the virus to be immune to the current treatments. They all decided to continue their research and testing on the mutated rabies strain virus or MRSV. They ran twenty-nine variants of the strain and all were a failure, the virus would kill off its host within a matter of hours. They began their testing and evaluations on the 30th rabies virus.

Miller calls a meeting between the top three advisors at the CDC which included Stanfield and Babcock the meeting is held on the third floor in the conference room. The same place where Miller had informed Babcock that they received government funding for a special project, over the next eighteen months. If successful it would lead to uncapped funding for any project they wanted which he already agreed upon. The project was to weaponize a rabies strain that would incapacitate an enemy combatant and keep him from returning to battle by attacking the central nervous system. "Stanfield and I have decided to revisit the MRSV project and continue that avenue of study." Babcock looked intently at the two and began jotting down notes in his notebook, before asking "who authorized this study and where is the funding coming from?" Miller now red in the face snaps "its need to know Robert! Just continue with the vaccinations on the MRSV and ensure that we can control and or wipe out the virus." Going against his better judgment Robert reluctantly agrees to go forth with the program, it wasn't the first time the government funded the development of viral weapons for certain projects that never actually saw the light of day. Robert figured that the fire in Washington would die down, as usual, having wasted millions even billions of taxpayers dollars on personal agendas or projects. Babcock then responded, "Ok Miller, you're in charge, I just work here. I will go dig up what I have on the project and instruct my team to prioritize it and begin work immediately."

Babcock then gets up from his seat and departs the conference room. Stanfield and Miller smile at each other feeling that the project would be a success. With Babcock on board, it was just a matter of time the biological weapon would be complete with the antidote and they would be set for life. They both leave the conference room as they pat each other on the back and head to their respective offices.

14 Months before infection: Atlanta, Georgia Centers for Disease Control's Division of Viral Weaponry

In the white sterile testing labs of the DVW, the top chemists are working on the latest strain of the MRSV where they had successfully mutated the rabies virus and were now ready to test it on monkeys. The testing lab was now filled with a dozen animal cages that were filled with monkeys. The first two were placed in the secure observation room along with some bananas for food and various objects to keep them occupied. Test subject number one was in the observation room alpha to the left and the second in observation room bravo to the right as both were searching and looking about getting used to their new surroundings. Miller now stands by as he begins recording the next phase of testing. An assistant goes into the subzero storage walk-in freezer and goes to the liquid nitrogen containers punching in the security code as automatic locks are opened releasing nitrogen into the air. With his gloved hands, he reached into the container and stainless steel vile with a small window revealing a bright orange liquid was removed that that was labeled MRSV-32. The technician recaps the container and it seals up airtight.

Back in the observation room, the chimps are given fresh fruit to help ease them before they are infected with the virus. Miller begins to chronicle the series of events leading up to the exposure of the newly developed 32nd version of the Mutated Rabies Strain Virus that has been fused with an aggressive Necrotizing Fasciitis. The assistant carefully draws a needle and fills the syringe a quarter of the way with the neon orange virus and covers the end of the syringe's needle with a cap. He places it on a tray on the counter and leans over the counter documenting his work. The other assistant then takes the vile drawing the same amount in a different syringe this time injecting it into another vile that is inserted into a canister that was secured into a stainless steel aerosol container. That too was placed on the counter and that assistant began documenting his side of the testing.

Stanfield was monitoring the camera angles from the main control center of the Division of Viral Weaponry. The assistant with the syringe then takes the needle to the first monkey luring it to the door with a banana and quickly injects the monkey with the virus and it immediately begins screeching and hollering as he wildly hobbles about the observation room holding the site of the injection.

In the second room, the air vent's small red flags begin to flutter as the central air system is activated. Moments later an orange cloud plumes from the vent and fills the room. The monkey in the room begins to screech wildly as he rolls around on the ground with his hands covering his mouth and eyes. As quickly as the virus was introduced the vacuum was activated and the orange cloud was sucked back into the vents looking as if someone had hit the rewind button. From the observation room, Stanfield zooms in on both rooms as the monkeys have calmed down and wiped their faces as they sit in their respective corners. There was a time clock that was started once the virus exposure was completed and the night shift comes in to take over. "Exposure began 2300hrs" Miller stated into the audio recorder. The video records throughout the night as the monkeys slept balled up in a corner tossing and turning just a couple of times.

Two levels down in sub-level 2 Robert Babcock, his assistant Evangeline and his closest staff have been fast at work trying to perfect the antidote for the MRSV-31 virus. This strain of the virus is just a few molecules difference from the previous strains and they were close to perfecting the antidote. His group were a determined bunch and agreed that nobody would rest until they did. They were awaiting the newest batch of the virus that was projected to be distributed to DVC for their portion of the testing and evaluation for the development of the MRSV's antidote. When the vile of bright orange liquid had arrived in a stainless steel container it was placed on the counter next to Evangeline which she signs for and continues her paperwork. Another lab assistant dressed in the level 5 protective suit takes the canister and moves to the cleanroom where he sets it on the counter and removes it from the canister. The liquid nitrogen escaped with a hiss as the container was unlocked. The vile that was removed had a sticker with black writing which read "MRSV-31" an intentional misnomer. The assistant begins taking samples of the virus and prepares paper-thin slices of a human brain on incubation trays as well as glass slides to study how the virus would affect the central nervous system. Little did Robert, Evangeline and the rest of the staff of the Division of Viral Control know that they were given the most current viral strain, they thought they were working on the MRSV-31 virus but were indeed given the MRSV-32 that was fused with the Necrotizing Fasciitis.

The next morning at the Division of Viral Weaponry two team members donned the level five hazardous material suit and went into the observation rooms to get a closer look of the infected monkeys and to record the data. Upon entering the observation rooms the infected monkeys were very lethargic and had very little life to them. The team members had orally mentioned their observations for the record and a stenographer took a written record of said observations as well as the staff making notes on their notepads. Both examiners reported the same symptoms "the subject appears to be suffering from a severe fever and is perspiring profusely. The subject is lethargic and isn't eating or drinking the food I had brought. Small openings in the skin have formed and continued to hemorrhage. It appears that the mucous membranes are beginning to hemorrhage as well as blood is beginning to drip from the orbital, nasal and oral orifices." The monitors have shown that the test subjects have accelerated heart rates, breathing and body temperatures were a red hot 114 degrees. The assistants exit the rooms and record their finding on paper then turn all information to Miller and Stanfield.

Observations run into the late afternoon and early evening when the infected specimens began to show life and began to move around the room a bit albeit sluggishly. The monitors now showed that the heart rates of both specimens have completely stopped and the body temp now read 86 degrees and continued to drop till it hit room temperature 74 degrees. Both make their way to the fruit that was taken by them that morning and they both knock it to the floor and thrash it about the room. A close-up view of the infected monkeys via camera showed that they were salivating blood that ran down and stuck to the hair on their bodies, open sores were growing and their eyes were a cataract. Miller seeing this decides to move to the next phase and see how the infected react to non-infected monkeys. The monitors showed that their brain functions have ceased except a small portion of the central cortex which still showed small flashes of life.

Two more assistants had donned the white level five hazardous material suit and gotten two fresh specimens from their respective cages and escorted toward the observation rooms that contained the infected with pieces of fresh fruit. As they unwittingly entered the rooms the doors were locked securely behind them causing the infected to slowly notice the company just feet away as they could be seen sniffing the air. The uninfected looked at the infected and instinctively knew they were in mortal danger as they began to wail, screech and flail at the door. As the infected closed in on the fresh meal Miller and Stanfield observe from the main control console via closed-circuit monitors. They could hear the monkeys scream as they were savagely ripped apart and disemboweled and all they could do was blink their eyes in disbelief of what they just witnessed. It was far beyond their comprehension and were definitely unnerved at the effect the virus has on living organisms and both agree that more testing will be done the next few weeks and autopsies will be performed on the pilot test monkeys and their two victims.

Over the next several weeks the same tests were run and recorded with the same results and finally, Miller decided against Stanfield's objection that they needed human testing before they can ship it to the government to use. The other factor was the progress and success of the DVC on the virus. During this time Miller was well aware that Babcock was working on the wrong strain of the virus hence the reason they did not have the antidote yet though they were close. During one of the weekly meetings, the concept of human testing was presented by Miller and was met with reservation by both Stanfield and Babcock.

"Where the hell are we going to get volunteers for this testing?" Stanfield asked.

"We all watched what happen to the monkeys we've tested, I can't imagine what it will do to a human being."

Robert interjects, "we don't have an antidote yet, my group is close but there is something we are overlooking. We cannot continue onto the human testing phase without the antidote, from what our test results show it will be a complete disaster, let alone finding test subjects."

Miller now red in the face and visually perturbed retorts "I'm going to tell big brother that we are moving to the next phase of testing and that's final, it's my call, not yours", as he slams his fist on the table. Don't worry about volunteers, I will handle that." He immediately got on the phone and dials the number to the office of Homeland Security and all he says to the person on the other end "great news sir, we are moving ahead" and hung up the phone. Both Babcock and Stanfield shake their head in disgust with Miller and leave the room to get back to work to hopefully be able to cash the check that Miller's mouth had written.

Weeks later at the Peachtree hotel, Miller walks into Steve's tavern and makes his way to the far end table in the nook where he approached the back of a clean-cut man in a generic business suit. He was sipping a scotch neat and without turning around he says "Doctor Miller I presume? Please take a seat" as he gestured with his left hand. Miller sits across from the man and realizes that it is the Director of Homeland Security and Miller orders a gin and tonic as the perky waitress quickly appears taking his order with a smile then leaves just as fast.

"I need human test subjects," Miller says.

"How is the testing going? You guys have made that kind of progress already? What about the antivirus, is that side good to go as well?"

Miller was about to answer when he was interrupted by the young waitress who served him gin and tonic with a lime wedge. He hands her a ten-dollar bill indicating to keep the change.

"We are all caught up with the serum and are a go for human testing. I just need the test subjects, how are we on your end?"

Taking a long swig of his scotch and placing it on the table the gentlemen responds "You will have all you need by the end of the week. They are being selected now and will be sent on a bus to your facility." Taking another long swig he slams the empty glass down, gets up and leaves without saying goodbye. Miller sat at the table sipping his gin and tonic as he gets on his laptop and checks his e-mail before sending one of his own to Stanfield which read the following:

> *Stanfield, I just left the meeting with the wise men and I will be back in the office on Monday. I was assured that we would be getting the last piece of the puzzle to complete the testing evaluation before submitting their results.*
>
> *Be in touch,*
> *Miller*

Miller then continues to enjoy the rest of his gin and tonic. He removes his gold wedding band, folds up his laptop and leaves the tavern heads to the main lobby of the Peachtree where he meets a high-end call girl, they peck on the lips before heading to the elevators. They embrace as the elevator doors close concealing them as it begins to ascend.

That Friday 0400hrs

At an undisclosed location on the east coast, six federal detainees wearing blaze orange jumpsuits shamble their way across a tarmac shackled to each other like a pack of elephants at the circus. They were surrounded by heavily armed covert operatives scanning the area for any threat behind their reflective Oakley shooting glasses. The prisoners were escorted from an underground lift to an awaiting military transport helicopter and were loaded in single file. The helicopter lifted off the tarmac and began the flight to Atlanta to drop the cargo off at Fort Mc Pherson where a Military transport base was awaiting the cargo. The prisoners were all taken to a row of seats that were side by side and buckled in and secured through their shackles to the floor of the helicopter. While in flight one of the prisoners had continued to run his mouth to the mask-wearing operatives who said nothing. Before the prisoners could realize what happened they were all gagged with black spit hoods as other Black Operators placed them over their heads from behind. The remainder of the flight went without incident and all you could hear was the rotating of the whirly bird's blades. Seventy minutes later the transport helicopter begins it decent in Atlanta and comes to a slow bounce as it lands and another group of operatives is standing guard with their assault weapons ready. The olive drab transport bus starts its diesel engine and opens its door as the senior operator exits and signals to the chopper pilot that they are ready to take the prisoners. The helicopter opens the side door and the prisoners were unbuckled from their seats and manhandled as they were brought to their feet and shuffled out the door of the helicopter onto the tarmac. They were handed over to another group of operatives that were also dressed in military camos and also wore black masks with light gray skulls on the face. They all stood careful watch as each prisoner was eye scanned before entering the bus. As the last prisoner was seated the operatives joined them on the bus and they began the short trip to the CDC. As the bus leaves the airport grounds the helicopter could be seen lifting off into the horizon as the sun began to rise in the East. The bus was now met by the Atlanta Police Departments SWAT team who gave an official transport to the federal building which went without a hitch.

Back at the Center for Disease Control Miller and Stanfield anxiously await the transport as they keep an eye on the main gates camera. The telephone rings as Stanfield looks at the number recognizing the C.I.A. cell number. He looks at the time on the main monitor which read 0448hrs and picks up the phone answering "Doctor Stanfield here."

The distorted voice on the other end responds "we are two minutes out" and the line goes dead. Miller immediately calls the front security gate and had them open the gate in anticipation of the buses arrival. On the monitor, the front gate area could be seen opening as the steel barrier poles retract into the ground. The gate begins to pull open and four guards go outside to meet the transport. Less than a minute later the olive green bus arrives as the diesel engine roars into the underground vehicle sally port and the security safeguards return back into position. In the sally port, the bus comes to a halt causing the air dryers to spit as it hissed before being turned off. The hot engine still ticked as the side door screeched open as four of the spec ops men exited the bus forming a perimeter while the remaining to operatives began to unlock the prisoners from their seats having them line up single file on the bus before they began to exit the bus. There were a dozen security and medical personnel that met the high-risk transport in the sally port where the senior security officer had signed the transfer paperwork taking official custody of the prisoners. The heavily armed masked men boarded the bus without a word and waited until the prisoners were behind secure doors before they were allowed to depart the sally port.

Inside the hallway of the CDC, the prisoners were taken to the decontamination area where they were given a steel wool shower with bleach and other chemicals to delouse. After their decontamination was over they were given a haircut where they were shaven bald with clippers and any facial hair was now down to stubble. Each was then taken to separate holding cells with a nice plush twin-sized bed with a metal table, seat, a toilet, and a sink. On their beds were navy blue shirts and pants all with numbers that ran from 1 through 6 as well as flip flops. On the desk was a short four-inch soft plastic writing pen with a formal contract with their names on them. The contract read that if they agreed and signed the said contract they were willing to participate in a government test and if they can complete the testing they would be given a full pardon and be released. If they failed to comply or complete the testing, they would be immediately remanded to the federal government to serve their life long sentences. All of the prisoners jumped at the opportunity to regain their freedom and hastily scribbled their names on the dotted lines and slid them underneath the doors where they were collected by a lab assistant. Within the hour they were given a kings breakfast of eggs, bacon, sausage, grits, potatoes, orange juice and coffee which they ate in their cells. Afterward, they were instructed to get dressed in their blue uniforms and be ready to be taken to the testing rooms to begin the week-long testing process. The doors to the cells were buzzed open and the locks gave an audible click and the men stepped out into the hallway awaiting the next command. Two lab technicians come around the corner and instruct the men to follow them. They are led to the same testing and observation room that was used on the monkeys the week before and placed two in each cell and secured. Over the intercom system, they were told to make themselves comfortable, and that they would begin the preliminary testing in a half hour.

Miller and Stanfield began watching the subjects from the main observation room and they decided to inject the subjects in room one and aerosol expose the two in the second room and the last two in the third observation room would be the last stage of exposure, bodily fluid transference.

Thirty minutes later two lab techs responded to the first observation room both carrying a syringe full of the bright orange MRSV-32 and opened the slot in the door. Miller's voice came over the intercom system instructing the test patients to extend their arms through the slots to receive their injection of a new flu vaccine. Each of the first two complied and were given their injections without incident. The second group of men were told that they would be given a dose of a new flu vaccine as well and to stand by to receive it. The two men stood up from the lazy boys that were in front of the large flat screen where a local baseball game was being televised. Minutes later the same bright orange mist was being pumped into the room from the two air vents freaking out the two men who began to scream at the cameras and pound on the door. And just like weeks before with the monkeys, the air was reversed and the orange cloud was sucked back out of the room into the vents. The men began to calm down but were still agitated yelling into the camera. Miller's voice came over the speaker system again "calm down, that was the new flu vaccine. You must remain calm or if I feel you cannot continue you will be shipped back to where you came. You have four days to go, don't blow it by being foolish!" The men shook their head throwing their hands up in reluctant agreement and eventually went back to the baseball game.

The last two men were taken into the hallway and instructed that they would now be reunited with the others for the next few days and that they would be testing a new flu vaccine that was given to the other guys. They agreed and headed to the observation rooms, where they were divided and one went into each room. The lab techs were dressed in the level five hazmat suit's that had told the subjects that they would be fitted with monitors that would check their heart rate, blood pressure, and brain functions. Each man had stickers attached to their abdomens and temples then placed back into the observation rooms and the doors secured behind them.

Back in the observation room, Miller checks the monitors and each man 1 through 6's vitals shown strong and their body temps all read 98.6 on the thermal cameras. Now it was time to sit, wait and observe. The poor bastards didn't realize that they had signed their own death warrants and the last two entered into the rooms would have the grizzliest deaths of them all. The clock began to count as the cameras began recording the results of the Mutated Rabies Strain Virus exposure on humans.

In the Division of Viral Control Robert, Evangeline and his small staff were hard at work on the antidote for the MRSV-32. They were able to come up with the compound that can hold off the spread of the virus but not terminate it completely. Over the past few days, they would always come up short and have to start from ground zero again and again and they couldn't figure out why. The check on the numbers showed that they were off just a fraction but couldn't place it.

12 hours after exposure

Later that evening the four men exposed to the MRSV-32 virus began to show symptoms of coughing, the onset of fever and severe back pain and migraines. Their vitals began to show signs of stress as their heart rate increased as well as their body temperature and brain impulses as the non-exposed subjects still remained normal. Every slight change in the subjects was recorded and the exact time the change occurred. The next several hours were nothing to write home about observation wise, the test subjects mainly played cards, watched television or slept.

Four days after exposure

At this point then six men knew they signed up for more than they bargained for as some lie helpless on their deathbeds. A close up of the first four infected on the monitors showed how the men quickly deteriorated. Their skin was pale blue and clammy. Severe reddening around the eyes, nose, and mouth and large dark circles formed under the eyes. They now coughed up blood and moaned in pain as any movement now caused them severe pain. Their eyes began to cloud over with cataracts and blood began to stream from the corners of their eyes, nose and from their swollen inflamed gums. The four were now bedridden and their vitals were off the charts. Subject 6 was a little better off but not as bad as he was in the early stages of the infection as he began to get nosebleeds. Subject 5 seemed to have the most resistance and was just now getting headaches and starting to cough yet none to worse for wear.

Back in the main observation room, a lab assistant nudges Miller as he points to the screen were subject 3's vitals had reached maximum sustainable rates where his heart rate was off the charts and brain function seemed to cease. On camera subject 3 was now seizing and spitting bloody foam from his mouth as he let out a final exhale and gurgle and the foam flowed from his mouth. He lies staring seemingly straight into the camera at Miller and Stanfield as the screen shows his vitals are flatlined. Within the next several minutes the other three initially exposed expired in the same sequence giving the MRSV-32 a 100% mortality rate. At that time the containment team was dispatched to the observation rooms and awaited the order to terminate the testing. Now the entire staff kept a close eye on the monitor that provided the brain wave activity for rabies to reanimate the stem as predicted. Hours pass and subjects 5 and 6 were now showing the signs of infection and were too ill to move. Subjects 1, 3, and 4 began to show some activity within the base of the brain stem as the screens began to show the synapses trying to relay signals to the body. On the main screen, it could be seen as the corpses began to slowly twitch their hands and feet and eventually, they began to sit up slowly in their beds. The dead stagger to their feet and shamble their way across the large room and begin tearing into subject 6 who begins screaming and they took bites out of his chest and legs. Subject 5 rolled out of his bed and scrambled to the door and began pounding screaming for help. One of the walker's attention was drawn to the noise as he slowly leaves the others to finish their snack and goes to get his own. Subject 5 was coughing up blood as he banged on the door pleading with the hazmat suit covered operatives through the glass window in the steel door. They stood motionless watching as the dead closed in on him from behind inching closer and closer. The walker had grabbed the test subject by his face tearing into the soft eyeball as it took a full mouthful of flesh from the neck as blood spurted all over the glass window. The last victim fell out of sight as his screaming and pounding came to a stop. Minutes later the team was ordered to go in and terminate the infected, prepare and transport the corpses to the west wing for autopsy and further evaluation.

VALOR

While in the office Robert goes to his computer and immediately logs onto his e-mail and checked if there was contact from the tribe but there wasn't any. He begins clicks on the compose icon and pulls up the recent history and pulls up the address of Chief High Eagle Lombard and begins to contact him.

Dear Chief,

I have reached the Centers for Disease Control and it is overrun. All my work and supplies here have been destroyed, it is a total loss and belongs to the dead. I will try and make my way to the reservation in South Carolina and continue my work there. Any help getting there would be greatly appreciated. We are just across the state line near the Savannah River. I have the direct line to the tribal police headquarters and will try and call there momentarily.

How are things on the res? Hope all is still intact. I look forward to returning home soon.

Respectfully,
Robert Babcock

Click and send. Robert then picks up the telephone and dials the tribal police headquarters and awaits as the phone rings. The voice on the other line answers

"Charlie Eagle Tail, Cherokee Tribal police".

"Hey uncle, its Robert, how is everything on the res? Is Eric ok?"

"Hey nephew, are you alright?! Everything is ok here, got the place pretty well surrounded and our medicine man is hard at work. Eric is just fine and is now my second in command. Chief High Eagle tells me you are coming home to finish your work. Eric and I are planning to send a team to meet you and escort you back home".

"Ok, I'm still here in Atlanta but will make my way to the state line in a few hours. I have my tribal counsel's cell phone I keep in contact with you every few hours if I can keep you updated. You can track my location with the identity card. I plan to move in the morning after some rest and a decent meal".

"We just started tracking you via the phone and the signal is still strong and clear. Our people think the key to curing the infection is here on the reservation. We have come into contact with the dead and still, there is zero infection on the res. We need you here Rob as soon as you can, we will be standing by to pick you up".

"Alright, lemme go for now and get ourselves together. I will be in touch tomorrow before we head out. Love you uncle".

"Love you too nephew, get your ass here in one piece".

They both say goodbye and hang up.

Robert addresses the group as they sit in his office. "We are going to rest up here tonight and head out in the morning. Down the hallway is a staff break room with bedding and full bathrooms. The commissary is stocked with anything we need for a good meal. That is unless Vange didn't eat anything!" Everyone let out a little chuckle. "Ok, the wing is secured so if we stay in the area we should be good for the night. RJ, get on the radio and have the rest of the team make their way down here and we can hunker down for the night." Everybody exits the office and file out into the hallway where they are met by the rest of the team as they come through the door from the stairwell. "Vange, take everyone to the staff quarters and break room." Everyone followed Evangeline down the hall where the end went left and right with a white sign on the left with black lettering that read women and one to the right which read men. Everyone took their time picking their bunks and getting toiletries to shower before dinner.

Robert goes into the commissary and begins to prepare a meal for everyone to eat before retiring for the night. After everyone freshened up they all met in the commissary and enjoyed a hearty meal and some small talk about the little things each one of them missed before the shit storm was unleashed. After the talks died down, everyone went their separate ways, some going to the break room to play a game of pool, cards or hit the rack. Robert had taken the opportunity to take his shower. He takes a shower kit and Glock 17 to the bathroom, undresses and gets under hot the water stretching his neck allowing the water to wash over his solid frame as it runs down his chest and back. Taking a deep breath Robert begins to lather then rinse when he feels a presence in the bathroom. He quickly grabs his pistol looking about but doesn't see anyone in the washroom and slowly returns to his shower. As he closes his eyes to rinse the shampoo from his head he is startled as a pair of arms hugging him from behind. He jumps and turns around seeing Jaylen standing naked in front of him as water begins to spray and run down her chest. They both look into each other's eyes and begin to kiss slowly and the longer they kiss the more passionate and rougher it became. Jaylen takes her fingers of her right hand and spreads herself positioning onto Robert taking him all in at once. With a moan of pleasure, he kisses her hard picking her up as she wraps her legs around his waist and Robert pins her against the wall of the shower as water dripped down their slick shiny bodies. As Robert continued grinding in her she looked to the right she could see their reflection in the large slightly fogged mirror over the sink. Moments later Robert finished, moaning in Jaylen's ear. She climbs off exiting the shower and wraps her towel around her midsection. She winks at Robert as she bites her lower lip smiling and leaves the bathroom. He hears her voice echo "you're slippin if I was a walker I woulda got you."

Robert answers "not a chance" smiling back then quickly rinses off and exits the shower. He makes his way back to the men's dorm, checks in on RJ who is fast asleep and then takes the bunk adjacent and lies down closing his eyes.

The next morning came quickly as everyone was groggy due to tossing and turning throughout the night. Everyone slowly gets up, dressed and gathers their weapons before heading to the commissary for breakfast. There they eat a decent breakfast and make small talk before they turned to business. They begin to discuss the exodus of Atlanta to the South Carolina border, then to the Cherokee Reservation where Robert and his group of survivors would finally have a safe refuge. A map of the Northern Atlanta was laid out and everyone gathered around leaning over the table plotting the best route to cross the state line at the Savannah River. After a brief discussion, they determined that the best route would be 137 east then I95 north through Savannah and cross state lines at the Savannah River Bridge into South Carolina. They were about an hour and a half from Savannah and two and a half from the rivers crossing, if there were no problems. Since the route was planned everyone had gone back to finishing their breakfast. Before they move, Robert calls his uncle at the tribal police station.

"Bob, how are you? We kept track of the phone and the signal is still strong, it shows that you are still at the CDC."

Robert responds, "Yeah, we're good, just getting ready to head out. We plan to take route 137 east to I95 through Savannah and cross into South Carolina over the bridge." Scratching his head Robert adds "I don't know when we will get there, that's the problem. I can't give you a time to meet but I can contact you when we get closer."

Eagle Tale responds "Sounds good, we will track you the entire way and will send a team to get you once you establish a safe spot to hold up in until we arrive."

"Sounds like a plan, hope to talk to you soon."

Robert hangs up and goes to prep the group for the deadly trip that lies ahead. By this time everyone is awake and making last second checks of their weapons and they all focus their attention as they locked and loaded their weapons. As the semi-circle gathers around Robert he begins to address the group. "Look, we have to cross the border and get to South Carolina to the Cherokee Nations reservation. I am in contact with the tribal council and E.R.T which will send a recon team to meet us and escort us to the safety of the reservation. If we can get there I know I can finish my work there and come up with the antidote, I just need the sterile working conditions."

Gunny Sergeant Riley interjects "We will get you there."

Pyle, Campbell and Dent all respond "Hoorah!"

Gunny Riley adds "Rob, just point us in the right direction and we'll clear the way."

"Fuckin' A!" Pyle added as Campbell and Dent nodded their heads in agreement bumping their fists. Robert nods his head in approval as he turns his head back to the map and traces his finger along with the web of lines that indicated the roads, streets, and highways in the Northern section of Atlanta. "Ok, we're going to take Willard Avenue to the end and make a right onto Briggs Street. There we will travel north to Allens Avenue and take the onramp to 137E to 95N until the Savannah River and cross at the bridge. Hopefully, there are no hiccups in our way."

Everyone's face now had a look of determination and was ready to move. They make their way from the cafeteria to the main hallway as Campbell and Dent took point checking the area with their assault rifle and Squad automatic weapon. Robert took the lead as RJ, Jaylen, Evangeline and the rest of the group followed him down the hallway. They come to the door at the end of the hallway that led to the stairwell upstairs and listened for anything on the other side. The two young Marines open the door and lead the way into the stairwell and the unnerving sound of the dead moaning and shoving against the door could be heard echoing the entire stairway. As they approached the door it could be seen that they had broken the lock and the door was being held back by the bungee cord they tied earlier. As they got to the top step of the landing where the dead were now snarling and scratching the wall trying to grab the survivors as they passed the door. Dent and Campbell cover the door as the others passed them continuing up the stairs. As soon as the last person cleared the door the door swung open banging against the wall as the cord finally gave way. The smell of rotten flesh filled the air turning everyone's stomach as the dead spilled into the stairwell falling over each other. "Oh shit!" Everyone seemed to shout at the same time. As the dead spilled in they had separated Campbell and Dent from the group. As everyone ran up the flights of stairs gunfire erupted from the Marines below. The dead were shambling up the steps within arm's reach of Gunny Riley who was providing rear cover. Riley had fallen up the steps due to a walker gripping his feet but was able to bounce up quickly. Riley takes his M9 pistol and begins dumping rounds into the hoard of the dead scoring the occasional headshot putting them down for good. The deafening sound of the squad automatic weapon had stopped as screams could be heard echoing from below. Bursts could be heard from an assault rifle and another scream was heard followed by a single shot. The rest of the group was now back to the floor they came in on and RJ pulls the door open and heads down the hall a bit before stopping to ensure everyone made it.

While rounding the last flight both Riley and Pyle trip up the stairs as they were looking back, firing into the crowd of the dead that were just now feet behind them. Pyle had fallen onto the landing and was back on his feet and tried to pull Riley up as a walker fell onto him and began biting and scratching him. Riley took his pistol pressing it to the temple of the zombie and pulled the trigger splattering blood and brains everywhere. Riley was pulled to his feet and they both make it out of the stairwell just as Robert tosses a fragmentation grenade down the stairs. They all sprinted down the hall towards RJ and Jaylen. As the dead began pounding on the door that just closed, a loud concussive explosion sent the door flying outward into the hallway which caused the group to fall to the floor.

They get to their feet checking the doorway and there was no sign of the dead so they continued making their way back to the armored personnel carrier that awaited them. The last door that separated them from the outside was now in sight as they rounded the corner. They were halfway down the last hallway when they noticed the lights were still flickering in the last office on the right. Just then the glass broke out into the hallway from the door and walkers spilled out into the hallway blocking their only exit. Things seemed to slow to a crawl and everyone could hear their hearts beating hard and fast to the point where the rushing of their own blood was the only thing heard, BOOM-BOOM. BOOM-BOOM. BOOM-BOOM. The group all raised their weapons opening fire at the dead dropping them one by one, as their heads exploded painting the glass door and walls with dark coagulated blood and brains. The group crashes through the door leading to the elevated parking garage into a torrential downpour. They continue to the armored personnel carrier before they stop to catch their breath and scan the area.

Riley then checks himself for any bites and finds he had been bitten on his left forearm just enough to break the skin as blood began to flow from the punctures. Everyone tries to help but he pulls away and begins to wrap the fatal wound.

"We gotta deal with that arm!"

"Don't worry about it, we got a lot to do before you can afford to lose me." Riley then goes to the passenger side of the APC and gets in slamming the door. Pyle gets into the driver's seat pushing the clutch and start button causing the diesel engine to roar. Robert, RJ, and Jaylen climb into the back and take a seat. They can see the front gate where they came in which was still covered with walkers that were now rocking the security gate as close to a thousand tries to push through the gate. They decide to check the rear entrance on the other side and discover that there were walkers flooded at that entrance also. "Shit! What do you think?" Riley asked Pyle. "I'll man the .50 and you take an explosive and place it on the gate and remotely detonate it from here." Pyle goes to the back and grabs a timed C4 explosive charge, sets it and makes his way to the rear security gate placing it at the base then returns to the vehicle. Wiping his face he takes the remote detonator and turns it on arming the device at the gate. Riley gets in the turret opens the hatch and loads the large-caliber machine gun as Pyle begins a countdown "3….2….1" and pushes the button. A second later a large fireball of an explosion brightens the sky sending the security gate outward ripping the horde to pieces. As the smoke clears the dead were strewn all over the street in pieces and the ones still intact slowly began to get up and others began spilling onto the ramp like water through a dam. Riley takes aim into the crowd and opens fire. The deafening weapon spits a two-foot flame as the dead were literally ripped apart by the large caliber bullets. Pyle takes over the vehicle and puts it in drive as the vehicle lurches forward, the engine roared as they picked up speed and they crushed the dead under the massive tires and heavy metal frame. They make their way down Woodcock Boulevard and took a left onto Willard Avenue which was mostly clear of obstructions. They continued a couple of miles on Willard until they reached Briggs Street. On Briggs, they headed about a mile until they reached

As they traveled away from the dead city, the congestion became thinner and thinner and they were able to drive without incident.

There was a green reflective sign with reflective white letters and numbers that read Interstate 137 east/west ahead two miles. The interstate could be seen on the horizon where black smoke billowed sporadically no doubt from car fires which foreshadowed the same grizzly story.

"Je-sus" Pyle exclaimed, "It seems to be everywhere. Can you really fix this Rob?" Pyle asked.

"I was working on the antidote months before this shit got out but little did I know my old co-workers whom we put down were developing a different strain than what I was working on. I have the basis for the antidote I just need a sterile lab and specimens to continue where I left off. To answer your question men, yes I can."

The onramp to Interstate 137 was a quarter of a mile away and now in sight. There were cars blocking the entrance with a few walkers clawing at windows of one car and others kneeling over their latest meal. Pyle hits the gas and accelerates smashing through a couple of cars jolting all inside the APC and continue up the onramp onto 137 east. Up on 137, the survivors make their way east weaving around discarded vehicles mostly left in the breakdown lanes. The first fire could be seen about a half-mile away involving a police vehicle as the red and blues could be seen flashing in the rain. There were zombies in the area of the accident and as the survivors came to a stop the dead were immediately drawn to the engine of the APC as it rumbled in place. The rain had calmed to a drizzle and from inside of the steel beast Robert, RJ, and

Jaylen could see that the dead were clawing at the steel body trying to get to those that were inside. "Why are we stopping?" RJ asked. Pyle responds "the road is blocked from the pile-up, we gotta try to move one." Robert opens the hatch and climbs out the top of the armored transportation vehicle. RJ and Jaylen follow suit as gunfire erupted from Robert's M4. Hot brass pinged off the metal as the walkers head exploded into a red mist from the high-velocity rifle rounds. There were about two dozen gathered around the vehicle and were clawing to the point that their nails peeled back, falling off leaving bloody stumps that left blood-stained claw marks on the side of the vehicle. Jaylen and RJ join him on top of the carrier and join in the execution of the dead firing into the crowd. Moments later, the dead that swarmed the carrier was now terminated and Robert and Jaylen hop off and move to the parked vehicles. Jaylen gets into the abandoned minivan and starts the vehicle backing it to the side of the highway. Robert opens fire with the assault rifle as the scattered zombies begin to turn their attention in their direction. Jaylen moves to the next vehicle and does the same clearing a small crease in the vehicle boneyard. Three walkers emerge from the vehicle fire involving the police cruiser where they were charred black and smoking. The smell of burnt flesh caused RJ to vomit down the side of the armored carrier. Riley had taken the Ma Deuce and opened fire on the charred walkers turning them into chunks of cooked meat. Robert and Jaylen make their way back to the APC and climb aboard as Pyle begins to drive forward through the small opening as the vehicle jumped the smaller cars like a monster truck at a truck show. The rest of the drive on 137 east was without incident and the group noticed that the sky was beginning to break and the rain had stopped. The group had traveled the length of 137 without incident making their way around vehicles and crushing the occasional walker where they read a similar traffic sign that read 195 North 10 miles. Before they realized it their turn off came and they took the exit. They peel off and make their way onto 195 north and begin making their way to the state line toward Savannah. The main artery was surprisingly obstacle-free and the group had traveled the next few hours event free. They had passed numerous cars abandoned on the side of the highway and the occasional zombie that wandered aimlessly. Every ten to fifteen minutes a sign would appear to the right of the highway reading Savannah 30 miles and the number would decrease with each passing sign. The last read Savannah 5 miles and as they drew closer the trees and weeds gave way to more and more pavement and concrete as the city of Savannah's skyline came into view.

The city of Savannah was the little brother to Atlanta and was a small bustling metropolis any other day but today, as the survivor's approach it told a different story. They took the off-ramp and coasted into the desolate city keeping north making their way to the city bridge to cross into South Carolina. Inside the APC Pyle yells over the roaring diesel engine "we need fuel! Almost on E." Robert responded, "keep due north heading to the bridge and look for a fueling station on our way, maybe we'll get lucky." Pyle nodded in agreement. The day had turned into another scorcher as the heavy dark ominous clouds from the morning had burned off and the sun showed white-hot in the pale blue sky. By the time they reached Savannah the temperature had reached over a hundred degrees and sitting in that metal toaster oven increased the temp by thirty degrees. Along with their drive north on the outskirts of the city, there were only sporadic sightings of walkers some in small groups but no large hoards. They finally come upon a petroleum station, pull in by the diesel tank and hiss to a stop and the engine shakes the vehicle as it shuts off. Everyone exit's the armored vehicle and stretches as they look around for any danger. Riley was now showing symptoms of the virus as it was well on its way killing him slowly. Robert attempts to check and dress the wound but Riley again refuses any help walking away as he begins to check the pump for fuel. Pyle goes with him and Robert, Jaylen, and RJ begin to check the immediate area for any danger but it was a ghost town. There were noting but abandoned vehicles and dried palm leaves that had fallen from the trees and now blew in the hot breeze. There were no walkers in the area but the smell of death was still in the air. Two blocks south of their location they had passed a small strip mall when out of the blue a single gunshot sounded from that direction causing everyone to hit the ground. They get to their feet and make their way across the street and enter a school bus's front windshield that turned over on its side. They climb on the side and get prone taking aim scanning the small plazas stores that contained Dave's Bar and Grill, Dustin's house of pain gym, Pete's bus tours and Savannah's credit union. The bus was about forty yards away from the plaza and through a set of bushes came two good ole' country boys complete with straw cowboy hats, tight wrangler jeans, greasy sweat-stained t-shirts, dirty sneakers and a mouthful of chew. One brandished a well- worn pump shotgun and the other a scoped hunting rifle. Through the ACOG mounted M4 rifles Robert and Pyle kept a close eye on the two as they lined the red chevrons on the two heads of the men. The heavyset one takes a swig from a small bottle taken from his back pocket and passes it to the thin one with a scruffy patched chin. He takes a swig handing it back to his friend. The gunshot had stirred some activity within Dustin's gym as three zombies exit the building shambling out the glass doors. The thin one takes aim with the shotgun firing a blast sending the first walker stumbling onto its back, pumps the shotgun and fires a second time knocking two down as he scored a double-leg shot blowing their limbs clean off as they fall on their faces. As he stops to reload nervously jamming shells into his weapon the heavyset one takes a pistol from his waistband firing at the remaining walker. He then walks up to the other three zombies now clawing their way on the ground shooting them in the head.

"You see dat Les! I kilt dem sum bitches!"

Les replied, "you got em Cooter"!

Everyone back on the bus chuckles at the two but notice more movement from within the gym. The two men were admiring their work on the walkers when all of a sudden, out of the door crashed a hulk of a zombie. He stood all of six-plus feet, wearing a muscle t-shirt that was stained with dried blood and warm-up basketball pants also torn and stained with dark dried blood. His eyes were cataract and dried blood formed in his nostrils and teeth. His body wasn't rotten and must have died within the last day or so. He immediately grabbed the heavy set Cooter taking a deep chuck from his thick neck spurting bright red blood all over his face and onto the ground. Cooter lets out a high pitch scream and tries to pull free from the hulks grasp to no avail. This attack catches Lester off guard as he stumbles back onto his ass pulling the trigger firing a shot into the air. The second bite now rips out the Adam's apple as blood continued to flow freely from the gaping bite wounds. The hulk pulls the mouthful of flesh, tendons, and cartilage from the body and the skin rips and snaps into his mouth as he chews on the savory bite. Les yells "Noo! You mother fucker!" as he gets to his feet and fires a blast into the hulk which tears a large chunk of meat from his arm breaking it spinning the walker around. The second shot misses him completely hitting a parked car igniting the gas tank and the sedan becomes engulfed in bright orange flames. He then fires a third shot center mass creating a fist-sized hole in the chest cavity sending the hulk into the flaming vehicle. The huge muscle clad zombie was lit on fire as it tried to get back on its feet. As it tried to get back up the arm damaged by the gunshot was shattered and as the bone ripped through the skin it caused it to lose balance stumbling to the ground again.

As the hulk sat up his head snapped back as the back left rear side of its head exploded into a pink mist and an echoing crack of Roberts M4 could be heard from across the street. This got the attention of Lester as he realized for the first time he wasn't alone. As the attack happened both Marines had made their way closer and were now on top of Les making him jump as he was now staring down the barrels of automatic weapons. He drops his shotgun without a thought and Pyle and Riley lower theirs. "U.S Marines, we're on our way out of the state. You will be safe with us." Les lamenting says "that was my cousin Cooter. We were out huntin' and gatherin' supplies for our group." Steel faced Riley says "you gotta shoot em in the head dumb ass!" and fires a burst into the head of Cooter as he lies in a spreading pool of blood and walks away toward the bus and APC. Riley wishes Les good luck and hurries to rejoin the others.

Back at the gas station, they hit up the pump but it was almost empty. They began to pump what was left as RJ and Jaylen climb back into the blood and meat splattered vehicle. Robert and Riley provided security as Pyle took care of the refueling. A slight breeze came through the lot of the gas station and a second later their nostrils and lungs were filled with the unmistakable smell of rotten flesh causing them to cover their noses and struggle to retain their lunch. The smell was accompanied by a shotgun blast and a scream from across the way where they last saw Lester walking. They make their way around to the overturned bus to see a legion of the dead shambling their way across the street. They had just made it to the bus when the car by the gym finally exploded into a large orange mushroom-shaped fireball shattering the windows of the adjacent stores. This gained the attention of the walkers as some turned their attention to the fire and began in that direction. The men ran back to the vehicle jumped in and started it. It took a couple of tries before it turned over and when it did everyone thanked God in their own way. Riley had jumped in the turret and observed that the swarm of the dead had made it to the gas station and were just about to surround the vehicle. He opened fire with the .50 caliber BMG spitting a two-foot flame as the dead seemed to explode into dark red chunks of meat and bone as they fall to the ground. The vehicle lurches forward circling the gas station pulling the gas hose off the pump before getting back on the street out heading north again. As they accelerated down the street zombies that were in the way exploded on impact from the reinforced metal grates or were crushed under the massive tires popping the brains out the top of their heads like toothpaste squirt from its tube. Pyle had noticed that the fuel needle hadn't moved at all but the warning light wasn't on anymore as they continued northbound toward the state line.

The rest of the city seemed to be barricaded in certain areas and even in some buildings, they could see survivors waving white towels, shirts or sheets out of windows praying to be saved as they rolled by. "Poor bastards," Pyle says as he looks up at the buildings as they fly by. The sign for the Savannah Bridge read it was a mile straight ahead. "We're almost there!" Pyle shouted giving everyone a boost of confidence. As they continued down the street the tall concrete structures gave way to dried yellow tall grass and the onramp to the bridge was saturated with the dead shambling their way onto the bridge. "Shit! We can't get through all of them. What are we going to do?"

Pyle exclaimed as he hit the brake. Riley slides down from the turret "go through the river, this baby is made for water too." He leans forward flipping several switches and pushes a few buttons. The beast lurches forward as it angles to the right and splashes into the muddy Savannah River. The beast accelerates kicking a white cloud of smoke behind it. Halfway across the river the fuel light came on again and began buzzing warning the occupants. They look to the left and see the swarm of the dead slowly making their way across the state line bridge. Riley decides to gun the engine picking up speed finally making it across the river and onto the muddy incline where they had gotten bogged down. The more the wheels were spun the deeper the heavy vehicle sank. Riley had reloaded the .50 and Pyle had climbed out of the driver's seat telling Jaylen to take over. Robert had joined Pyle on the side of the vehicle as they looked at the half-sunk vehicle. "Grab the tow line and hook it to the beam of the bridge!" Robert ordered Pyle, "I'll cover you, RJ cover!" Pyle rushes to the winch and nervously takes the large hook switching the security stop to off and clumsily makes his way through the red clay mire. The walkers on their side of the bridge had begun to turn their attention to the group as Robert opened up on them with his assault rifle. RJ also had joined his dad providing gunfire from the side of the APC. Riley also joined in the large-caliber machine gun again turning the crowd of walkers into raw hamburger and bone fragments quickly eliminating the dead. Pyle had made it to the beam and secured the line signaling Jaylen to start the winch and to hit the gas. The steel line tightened as the beast began to be slowly pulled from the muck and the tires began to spit red clay everywhere as it was freed and sped toward the bridge. Jaylen had applied the brakes hard causing the vehicle to come to a skidding stop. The vehicle crashes into the side of the bridge abutment violently jolting Riley and crushing the wheel well into the front driver's side tire. Riley ducked into the beast taking control backing a little then driving the damaged vehicle onto the bridge fighting to keep it straight, then pulls it sideways blocking the bridge along with other cars. Robert, RJ, and Pyle run to catch up to the vehicle as Jaylen and Riley exit and meet them at the rear of the carrier. "Look," Riley says looking at the group "the vehicle is done, grab one of the sport utility vehicles over there and get to the reservation. I'll cover you guys." "No!" Jaylen exclaimed. "I'm not fuckin leaving ya bro" Pyle added.

Robert tells RJ, Jaylen, and Evangeline to find a good vehicle and start it up. Robert and Pyle get into the back of the beast and gather some supplies in backpacks and tossed them in the four-wheel-drive vehicle. The moans and snarls of the dead were now in earshot as they continue to shamble their way toward the group and that smell of death filled the air. "What about you?" Robert asked Riley looking at the group. Finally, he removes his sunglasses revealing the dark circles under his eyes as blood filled tears streamed down his face. "It's too late for me, now go!" As the group heads to the vehicle Riley grabs Robert's arm looking him square in the eyes "complete the mission. Get your ass to the reservation!" and pushes Robert away. Riley gets into the beast and takes a squad automatic weapon and a rocket launcher. He gets on top of the vehicle takes aim with the LAW and fires it into the crowd of walkers creating a large explosion sending bodies and limbs flying. "Get outta here!" he yells to the others without looking back. The dead were now weaving their way through the cluster of cars left on the bridge that were less than thirty feet from the group. They began to snarl and snap their teeth together in anticipation of fresh meat. Riley begins firing bursts into the rows of walkers as their heads burst open like split watermelons from the high-velocity rounds. Pyle gets his machine gun and opens fire as well into the crowd. RJ gets the vehicle to start and calls for his dad. Robert grabs Jaylen and they head for the truck. Riley empties his weapon and tries to reload but drops it to the ground and jumps down to retrieve it. "Mother fucker!" he yells as he jams another 200 round box into the holder, feeds the belt of ammunition into the chamber closing the upper receiver and pulls the charging handle and takes aim to fire but the swarm of the dead were already on him. He fires a long burst into the torsos of the zombies stumbling them back a step and he runs to the rear of the beast and jumps in. As he scrambles to get up he screams as a walker takes a chunk out of his calf. He turns yelling "fuck you!" and kicks the walker in the head sending it to the ground. Pyle was still on top of the beast still dumping fire into the dead as hot brass falls into the belly of the beast onto Riley as he climbs into the turret.

"You crazy bastard, what's wrong with you! I told you to leave!"

"Never leave a man behind right" Pyle responds, tapping him on the shoulder. At this point, the dead engulf the beast and claw at the metal frame trying to get to the men on top.

Robert now in the driver's seat looks behind them with RJ and Jaylen to the crowd of zombies over one hundred yards away that is preoccupied with the two Marines in hopes they change their minds. They then notice both men climb into the vehicle out of sight.

Inside the APC Riley was now in bad shape and bleeding out fast. Pyle begins to cough and notices blood in his hand. Both look at each other and realize it was the end of the road. Pyle reaches into his pack and pulls out a bottle of whiskey spinning the cap off taking a long slow swig before passing it to Riley who mirrors Pyle's taste. "Where's your special fireworks?" He asks Pyle. Reaching into another bag he removes a white bundle about the size of two loaves of bread taped side by side showing Riley. "This is a six-pound thermometric charge made it if we needed to level a building." Taking another swig Riley says "fuck it, set it and forget" getting to his feet climbing into the turret. Riley sets the timer and hit's the start button. He grabs an assault rifle and begins shooting whatever he can out of the windows and Riley ran the BMG yelling "come on, get some!" over and over again. In a split second, everything had turned white and went silent.

Back in the truck, Robert decided to leave as the dead became focused on the running engine. A few hundred yards down the road a bright flash followed by a sonic boom rocked the vehicle causing Robert to stop. They looked in back and could see a bright white fireball mushroom cloud as it cleared the tops of the trees. The explosion had cooked everything within fifty yards and created a ten-foot gap in the bridge separating the two states. They continued to drive on the road heading north as they pass a sign on the right that reads welcome to South Carolina!

THE CABIN

The back roads in South Carolina were almost serene as the sun began to set casting a bright orange blaze in the sky that met the tall evergreens that flanked the road. The forest floor seemed to be covered in a sea of dead orange pine needles and pinecones, and as the survivors looked at the quiet stillness they almost forgot the grave peril that they were in. As they continued to drive they would even see the occasional chipmunk, squirrel, and buck. "We need to find shelter for the night," RJ says and Robert agrees. They continue to the remote town of Midland which had the appearance of a ghost town. All the roads were unpaved and the grass in the town was overgrown. Loose papers blew in the evening breeze as the explorer Robert was driving came to a stop in the center of town. A gust of wind had blown the local town's newspaper towards and up onto the front windshield where it comes to rest held open by the breeze. The front-page news in large black bold lettering read "THE DEAD WALK!" It was like a sick joke by God himself as an unsettling feeling had overtaken the group. Robert lets out a nervous chuckle as he mumbles to himself "un fucking believable" getting out of the truck.

As the group gets out they notice at the far end of the main road four walkers could be seen aimlessly staggering about but were no immediate threat. They look around and could see what appeared to be an abandoned mill on the edge of town and they decide to check it out and that it would be the safest place to fortify for the night. Robert has everyone get back into the vehicle and they take the beaten dirt road up to the entrance of the mill throwing the dust into the air behind them as they flew by the walkers spinning one down to the ground when it was grazed by the side-view mirror. The truck comes to a stop at the gate as RJ jumps out and opens the gate inward and the truck is pulled into the lot. Vange gets out and helps RJ relock the gate. Robert and Jaylen exit the vehicle and everyone check the front staff parking lot which still had four abandoned vehicles and two semi-trailers. Robert and RJ go to the first trailer and carefully check the door to see if it was unlocked. When the door creaks slightly outward, they slowly open the door in anticipation of a zombie to spill out but nothing happened. The small building was empty and was the next one. Evangeline and Jaylen had checked the vehicles and perimeter fence and all was secure. The four then turned their attention to the interior gate that led to the old mill. The fence was secured with an industrial chain and lock so getting in wasn't an option. They pause for a moment and listen for any noise coming from inside the mill but all they could hear were crickets, which was a nice change from the moans of the dead they've been enduring. They decide to make the trailer their home for the night. Evangeline grabs some supplies from the vehicle and the four barricade themselves in a trailer for the evening. While eating dinner they find and study a local map of the area and figure that the town of Spearpoint will be the place they will fortify and wait for the tribal team to rescue them taking them back to the reservation of Hilton Head Island. Studying the map RJ notices and points to a spot on the map adjacent to their current location. "Dad, look a campground, maybe somebody's alive there!" Rubbing his goatee thinking, Robert nods in agreement, "we'll check there tomorrow on the way to Spearpoint." Robert addresses the group, advising that he would take first watch, for them to rest up and that they would take turns on watch every two hours. Robert scans the campgrounds and road just a couple of hundred yards away as he takes a look through the scope of his rifle as turns off the lamp so he doesn't give away their position. From outside the soft amber light is given off by the kerosene lamp could be seen lowering to the point darkness filled the camper as the flame was extinguished. The line of sight wasn't clear and he needed a better vantage point so Robert exits the camper and climbs onto the roof for a better vantage point of the main road and the campground.

Just a stone's throw from the mill site the Midland campgrounds had one blazing fire that soon would be accompanied by another fire so to speak. The glowing orange and yellow flames of the campfire glowed against the car and trailer casting the shadows to two lovers intertwined on the ground. The heat of the fire warmed their bodies as they kissed passionately undressing each other under the stars. Jasmine lies on her back as George begins to slowly slide down her pink panties taking them completely off tossing them over his head. George begins to kiss Jasmine on her tight soft stomach causing her to moan with her eyes closed she softly bites her lower lip. She takes her hand and pushes his head lower between her widespread shaking legs and let out a moan of pleasure as he tastes her.

While preoccupied George wasn't aware of his surroundings and did not hear movement in the bushes surrounding them. From a distance, you could see the bushes and low hanging tree limbs moving as the horrifying sight of stiffly staggering corpses emerging from the darkness.

Back at the mill Robert keeps watch scanning and listening for any movement praying that the unforgettable smell of rotting flesh doesn't fill the air indicating zombies were near. From the rooftop of the trailer, the main road could be seen and something in the darkness catches his eye. It was a faint glow of orange-yellow through the thick pines that told him someone was indeed alive giving him hope that they could meet up with other live people. Robert checks the area of the light source through his scoped carbine panning left to right when the silhouette of a shambling walker gets his attention. As he follows the walker it's revealed that he was the last in line as a swarm had entered the woods heading straight towards the campfire. "Shit!" he says to himself as he anxiously peers through his scope. Minutes later screams could be heard from the Midland Campgrounds. Robert shook his head in disgust as he closed his eyes swallowing hard.

Back by the campfire, George was busy pleasuring Jasmine and neither could hear the moans of the dead as they approached the opening from the trees. The dead began staggering as fast as their rigor riddled legs would allow and formed a semi-circle of as they approached the two lovers. Breathing heavily through her mouth Jasmine opens her eyes slightly, which now turns to the size of saucers as she lets out a scream of horror. She sees a walker stagger through the flames of the fire becoming engulfed as it falls on top of her. George startled tried to get to his feet but backed into a dozen walkers. He screams "Jasmine!" as the dead begin clawing at his body. As they tear the skin away from his face revealing his skull underneath, screams of pain take over. They bite his legs and arms as he is taken to the ground. Jasmine catches fire from the walker that fell on her and is ripped apart in the same manner as George. The dead knelt down and ate their victims panting in an eerily similarity to campers eating dinner by the campfire.

The rest of the evening went without incident as everyone took turns on watch. The sky began turning bright purple as the sun began to rise in the east. The sound of hawks circling over the campgrounds woke the group as they screeched overhead. Immediately everyone could tell it was going to be another dog day of summer. They woke up drenched in sweat as the morning temp felt like a hundred with the humidity. Everyone stretched and shook the cobwebs of sleep off as they carefully check the driveway and fence which was clear. They take the supplies and reload the truck then break for breakfast. Robert takes the phone and contracts the tribal police connecting with the dispatcher this time.

"Hello Robert, this is Teresa, Chief Eagle Tail has led the team to retrieve you and we are in direct communication with them. I have your location in the town of Midland and the signal is strong, is everything ok?"

Robert responds, "everything is ok were going to move soon. I plan to wait in the town of Spearpoint for the rescue team. The place, I don't know yet but I will begin transmission once I find it were getting ready here, so I will be in touch. Take care."

"You to hun, be safe now" as Teresa hangs up.

Robert takes the phone and puts it in the pocket of his plate carrier slinging it over his shoulder he heads to the vehicle where the group was eating breakfast. RJ looks at his dad with sadness "I know we don't need to check the campgrounds, I could hear them last night." Robert looks at RJ seeing his saddened expression and hugs him as RJ grabs around Roberts' waist. "It'll be ok son, were gonna make it! Hang in there, once we get to the reservation I can finish my work on the serum and get things back to normal." RJ just shakes his head in a yes motion turning away from Jaylen and Evangeline to wipe his eyes. They finish breakfast and gear up for their trek to the city of Spearpoint which is the largest town in South Carolina. They pile into the vehicle and leave the mill making their way through the dusty streets of Midland and find the main artery north towards Spearpoint. While making their way to town they come into some heavy forest that surrounded the curvy road. Robert looks in the rearview to Evangeline who was staring out the window as the warm air blows her hair. "Hey Vange, how did you survive all that time?" She snaps out of her daydream and begins to tell her story as she looks down she recalls the dreadful ordeal. "Well, this is how things happened for me" as she begins her story her words seem to fade away as a vivid picture was painted in everyone's mind and a movie seemed to fill their heads.

"I was on vacation like the rest of the team, when I came across a breaking story in Margaretville where an outbreak of an unknown illness had plagued a quarter of the island. I saw the inside of the emergency room with all those sick people and dead ones stacked in the far corner. Anyway, they cut away to a doctor they were interviewing and from behind him through a set of doors came Dave from the research team. He didn't look like himself but I could see it was him. All of a sudden he attacked the doctor biting his face off. I continued to watch the news as reports from all around the world kept flooding in of the dead coming back to life and attacking the living. I immediately headed back to the office where Stanfield and Miller were hard at work in the labs. I never saw what they were up to as they ordered me to get to the DVC and start working on the MRSV antidote until you arrived. I continued our work for the next few days when all of a sudden, I heard a scream from down the hall so I hurried to see what was going on. I saw Miller on the floor with blood tearing from his eyes, nose, and mouth. He wasn't breathing and I saw the group of people around him was covered in droplets of his blood. Then Emergency personnel began performing Cardiopulmonary Resuscitation but I heard someone say he had expired. Everyone was upset as you could imagine, but we needed to get back to work on this thing. The next day at lunch I was in the cafeteria when Miller had slowly walked into the busy cafeteria looking like Dave in the video on television and the first person that was within arm's reach he bared his teeth like a rabid dog and tore into him taking a huge chunk of flesh. Everyone began scrambling for their lives and in the fray, he was able to get four more. I headed back to the office but was cut off by more dead, they were the ones who were splattered in his blood so I ran into the commissary and locked the door. For the next few days, I heard screams and the occasional gunshot. One night a security guard came to hide but I wouldn't let him in when I noticed he had deep scratches. Another came shortly after and gave me this Beretta 9 millimeter and a box of ammunition. I tried to call out but the emergency protocols kill the exterior lines so I was stuck. The only thing I heard was the dead that pounded on the door, so I shot them as they came one by one. You are the only living people I have seen in the past few weeks! I guess you know the rest."

As Evangeline's story ends the vision of the road and the breeze come back to the forefront of Robert's senses as he navigates the winding road. All of a sudden, the vehicle begins to sputter and steam begins to plume from underneath the hood as the dashboard lights up like a Christmas tree with red and orange lights. Just then the engine seizes as Roberts struggles to control the vehicle he manages to pull the truck over to the side of the road. Robert puts the vehicle in park and engages the emergency brake. Robert gets out and smoke gushed out from under the hood as the engine sizzled as he opened the hood. Robert tried to fan it away with his right hand so he can get a look at the problem. The rest of the group quickly exited the vehicle and gathered at the front of the truck. "She's dead dad," RJ says looking the engine over. "I know, buddy. We don't have anything to fix it either." "We gotta walk it?" Jaylen interjects. "Looks like it," RJ says as he heads to the rear of the vehicle and begins retrieving the bags. Everyone takes a bag slinging it over their shoulders and surveying the trunk, making sure they took everything they needed. They cautiously begin the dreaded walk down the hill to the highway in the mid-day heat. They reached the bottom of the slope and find that the road is shadowed by the trees, leaves, and debris which gave little relief from the sweltering humidity.

The heat seemed to drain the life out of the group as each step they took seemed harder and harder and the gear seemed to get heavier just as fast. Just off the road in the woods, the unmistakable moans of the dead could be heard putting the four on high alert as they quickly forgot about the heat and began to pick up the pace. About fifteen yards behind them eight walkers staggered onto the road and began shambling after the survivors. About a quarter of a mile down the road the group heard the revving of an oncoming vehicle so they dart into the woods taking aim at the oncoming vehicle.

From inside his vintage 1984 Chevrolet Blazer, the driver could see a group of people running into the woods. Venus, his German Shepard became excited and started to scratch at the window as they approached and skidded to a stop just feet from Robert and the group.

Through the ACOG on Robert's carbine, he sees the curled mustached man put the truck in park and waives a white shirt out the window. The red chevrons apex was centered on the man's forehead between his yellow shooting glasses. He slowly opens the door and steps out checking all around as he shuts the door leaving his dog inside the vehicle now barking and pacing back and forth. The man stood six feet tall with a stocky build and high and tight haircut. He wore an olive drab shirt and matching cargo pants with tan boots. He obviously was military and his license plate read "BADASS."

"You can come out, I mean you no harm. I saw you coming and was going to offer a ride." Slowly, the four came out of hiding and approached the large man. "That's my dog Venus in there and you can call me Mad Dog," he says as he lowers his hands.

"I'm Robert and this is my son Robert junior, my cousin Evangeline and Jaylen."

Mad Dog's attention was grabbed by the walkers that were coming after the group. Their attention was drawn to the distant snarls of the dead as they slowly drew closer and closer. "Come on, I gotta place!" Mad Dog tells the group. They all begin to pile into the back of the truck when he grabs a pump shotgun from his front seat and a shovel from the back seat. "Mother fuckers!" he yells as he throws the shovel into the zombies striking one in the face causing a laceration. He takes aim with the shotgun and begins blasting the dead with buckshot bursting their heads like watermelons until his gun ran dry. He takes the stock of the shotgun hitting the remaining two in the head knocking them to the ground. With death in his eyes, he begins ramming the butt of the shotgun into the skull of the closest walker as it hissed and tried to grab him. He hit harder and harder until the sound he was looking for rang music in his ears. An audible crunch could be heard as the skull finally gave way and the zombie stopped moving. Robert goes to Mad Dog and gets him to his feet. The last zombie began to sit up slowly and Mad Dog pulls away from him taking the shovel and swings for the fences making contact with the skull causing a ping sound to echo. He then takes the shovel and jams the blade through the walker's mouth splitting the upper and lower jaw causing the zombie to make a gagging noise. Robert tells him that was enough and that we needed to get out of here but he doesn't listen. He then uses his foot for leverage as if digging a hole and begins working the shovel through the remaining cartilage and bone of the spinal cord as blood pours all over the road. The sound of metal scraping pavement could be heard as the last pieces of skin snap as the top part of the head was removed from the body and rolled down the street. Robert in shock looks at Mad Dog "shit man. That went too far! Are you fucking crazy?" Mad Dog wiping the spit from his mouth looks bug-eyed at Robert and responds "too far? When the dead walk, ain't no such place. Come on friend, let's go before more of these puss fucks show up."

They finally get into the truck turn around and speed away. The top half of the head that was severed lie on its side and the zombie's eyes looked back and forthcoming to rest as it stares right at you.

"Do you trust this guy?" Jaylen whispers as they continue to travel along the winding road. Robert answers "no choice now, just gotta ride it out. Be ready though guys." Everyone nods in agreement gripping their weapons tightly. They look around the back of the blazer and see some of Mad Dog's choice of well-used weapons. There was a blood and meat cakes chainsaw, a sledgehammer with dried blood and a machete that was fairly clean. There were several boxes of shotgun ammunition and a few hunting knives that were also bloody. Mad Dog yells back without looking "almost there!" as Venus keeps a close watch of the strangers in her vehicle. They take a left turn and head up a dirt road which jolted the passengers about the vehicle leaving a trail of dust and debris behind them. In the spacious field on both sides of the road, a few walkers could be seen in the distance walking in the same direction they were heading. "Where are we going?" Robert asks. "My parent's farm, we have peaches, cattle and chickens and a shit load of vegetables." As they continue down the dirt road a large pale blue farmhouse came into view with a large peach tree in the front yard. They had driven through a white picket fence and pulled into the large barn style garage. As they pile out they grab their gear and Venus takes off running and disappears. The group then follows Mad Dog to the front of the house where an older couple is waiting on the white wrap around porch. He goes up the stairs and is given a kiss on the cheek by his mother in which he reacts by pulling away wiping his cheek saying "ma! Don't embarrass me in front of my friends! This is my mom and dad Madeline and Tony, ma and dad this is Rob and his group, they are going to have lunch with us." "Oh, welcome," his parents said. "Come in, relax lunch will be ready shortly."

Robert goes to Mad Dog and gets in his ear "we need to get to Spearpoint now. We don't have time to waste." Mad Dog tells him that they needed a decent meal and that he was going to take them to his cabin in a couple of hours and there is an extra vehicle there that they could use. Robert agrees and enters the house. Mad Dogs mother offered them their bathroom to shower which the group gladly does.

After freshening up the call for lunch was given and everyone gathered around the table that was dressed with glasses of lemonade, plates, a bowl of fresh salad, mashed potatoes and homemade biscuits. A minute later Madeline came to the table with a platter of hot sizzling steaks straight off the grill and placed it in the center of the table. Everyone dug into the feast and was able to forget the world was going to hell. The laughs and the general conversation went on for most of the meal when everyone was brought back to reality as they jumped from the sound of a gunshot. Everyone ran to the front porch as a second shot cracked the silent afternoon. "Who is that?!" Robert asked. Mad Dog tells him that it was some of his Army buddies that came to stay and help on the farm when the shit hit the fan. Five of them are here with their wives or girlfriends and we take turns standing watch. They must have seen a few puss bags that got through the fence and are taking them out". A voice from the roof shouted down to Mad Dog "we're all clear! A couple got through the fence but we sent them back to hell by the 5.56 express!" The group came off the porch to see who was on the roof and two men stood up waiving. Mad Dog waives back and they go back inside to continue eating their meal. Madeline asks the group where they were going and that they were more than welcome to stay if they wanted, but Robert explains that they were on a schedule and needed to make it to another destination within the next few days. She still offered an open door invitation to the farm if needed as they all ate their fill of the rich country cooking. Afterward, the group took their supplies, thanked the hostess for her hospitality and went to the garage where Mad Dog was wiping off the stock of the shotgun and began jamming rounds into the magazine.

"You guys ready?" Mad Dog asked rhetorically. Robert, RJ, Jaylen, and Evangeline all nodded in accord and began placing their equipment into the red blazer and everyone jumped in. Mad Dog takes a portable radio from the floor console and radios that he was going on the mission to the cabin and would be back the next day. The voice on the other end of the radio was the voice of the man on the roof who replied that if they didn't see him by tomorrow afternoon they would come looking for him. With that, the vehicle was started and they began their trek to the cabin in the Hydracon Hills of South Carolina. As they headed down the dirt road they saw the couple walkers now prone with large head wounds caused from full metal jacketed NATO rounds. They take a left back out on the main road they had met just hours before and continue the hour drive into the hills.

Deep in the Hydracon Hills MRSV-32 made its way there too. The Providence family has been infected and all are in the final stages of the virus ravaging their bodies. Mr. Providence had instructed his family which included his wife Lisa, two daughters Christine and Amanda, his stepfather Harry that they would commit suicide rather than walk around after they died and they agreed. They all took their place under their individual noose stepped up into them tightening the rope around their necks. Mr. Providence sobbing as blood filled tears streamed down his pale sunk in the face as he went to each family member kissing them one last time. He then walks behind them as they step off the chairs causing the ropes to go taught as they began kicking their feet and grabbing at the crushing rope around their throats as their survival instinct kicks in. Within a minute they had stopped struggling and the only sound was the rope rubbing against the wooden crossbeam as their limp bodies slowly swung in the room. Mr. Providence tried to hold back his grief and cried aloud to himself in the living room. He can feel death beginning to cloak itself around him as he began to lose feeling in his extremities. The fever had become unbearable as he took his vintage Colt 1911 pistol from the table and struggles to load it. From the table, he could see his neighbors familiar red SUV making its way up the trail. Becoming dizzy Mr. Providence tries to put the pistol to his head but blacks out falling to the floor.

The old SUV made its way up the rolling hills from Hydracon valley when Mad Dog pointed out another log cabin that was coming up on the right. "That place is my neighbor up here on the right, good man. Mr. Providence is a Vietnam Vet wounded in the head, he got a Purple Heart and shit. I haven't seen him in a couple of weeks, I just want to check in on him real quick." The group pulls into the driveway next to a white sedan and Mad Dog exit's the truck and Venus follows. Robert gets out and tells the others to stay put as he stood near the front of the vehicle as he keeps a keen eye on Mad Dog knocking on the front door several times and waits with no response. He looks into the window and what he sees sends him into a panic. "God no!" he exclaims as he kicks in the front door and goes inside with Venus hot on his heels. Robert startled at the sudden outburst grabs the Glock 9mm and enters the house with the gun ready to shoot.

He peers into the living room and sees Mad Dog trying to hold up two of the lifeless hanging family members. "Help me!" he exclaimed. Robert hurries over to Mad Dog pulling him away from the corpses as they began to swing again. "Don't touch them, they're infected." Robert tells him, "Look at them". Venus begins barking wildly again gaining the attention of both Robert and Mad Dog who look to the far left of the room where Mr. Providence had reanimated and gotten back to his feet still holding the vintage 1911 in his right hand. His milky white eyes had the same saddened look like the rest of the dead as he began to sniff the air moving slowly in the direction of the two men. Robert takes aim and is pushed by Mad Dog as a shot strikes Mr. Providence in the right arm causing him to stumble back a bit. "The fuck is your problem!" Robert yells, "He's fuckin dead!" Mad Dog takes a second and then turns his back as Robert takes aim putting the front sight on Mr. Providence's snarling face as things seemed to slow down as he squeezed the trigger. The bang deafened the two inside the room and a spark was seen as a large chunk of flesh was ripped from the left side of the forehead sending blood splattering against the wall. Mr. Providence stumbled backward onto the ground from the impact. Mad Dog comes over and places a folded American flag over his body and salutes him. Venus begins growling again heightening Rob and Mad Dog's awareness but the house was clear, this time it was his family that had begun flailing their arms in an attempt to reach the men as they twisted freely in circles swinging from their twisted necks. "Jesus" Robert mumbles and sends a jacketed hollow point into each of their heads causing the backside of their heads to splatter blood, bone and brain matter on the floor and walls behind them. Mad Dog now stood with his back Mr. Providence as he looked at the remaining family. Little did he know Mr. Providence slowly sat back up as the red white and blue slid from face revealing a large gouge of flesh on his forehead revealing a shiny dented metal plate, he bore his overexposed teeth and before he could take a chuck out of Mad Dog Venus leaped by her owner pouncing on the zombie knocking it back to the floor. Mad Dog jumped out of the way as Robert quickly comes over pointing the pistol at the head area and began squeezing off rounds. After a couple of hollow points that sent sparks into the air the next four sealed the deal putting the walker down for good. Mad Dog takes a swift kick to what was left of the walker's skull "cock sucker!" he yells. "Let's get out of here," Robert tells him and both head outside, climb in the truck and take off up the rest of the hill to his cabin that was just another mile up ahead. "Are you guys ok?" Jaylen asked. "Fine" Mad Dog answered Robert, adds "a poor family opted out." The rest of the short ride was is silence when the road had straightened out and a large dark brown log cabin came into view with a beautiful lake.

"Whoa," Evangeline says under her breath. In the dirt driveway were two other sport utility vehicles that were parked in the gravel driveway and they pulled up blocking one in. They get out of the truck and follow Mad Dog through the front door into the cabin. The interior was like a typical cabin with all polished interior woodwork throughout the open lower level. There was a large wooden dining table with a half dozen high back chairs and stainless steel kitchen appliances with a marble island. The living room was also open and spacious with a couple of load-bearing wooden tree trunks with a high stone fireplace with two large ten-point bucks on either side of the mantle. The fireplace was surrounded with a plush large sofa and matching lazy boys and a large flat screen was over the mantle. The cabin was filled with various photos of Mad Dog and his family over the years and the stairway that lead to the bedrooms upstairs was filled with photos of the same. "Make yourself at home," he says to the group. "It's getting dark soon, we should stay the night and you can head out any time in the morning you want." He goes to the refrigerator and grabs a cold domestic beer cracking the can and swigging just about all of it. With a deep belch he licks the foam from his neatly curled mustache he tosses a set of keys "here" he gets out between belches. Robert grabs the keys midair and puts them in his pocket.

They settle down in the living room and turn on the television to find that emergency broadcast was on what seemed like every channel. The same news stories and the same repeated footage of civil unrest and violence. They cut the television off and decided to unwind as they lounge at the cabin and use the shower. By the time everyone was refreshed the sun had set and the night air was surprisingly cool which meant fall was around the corner. Robert makes the final security check of the doors and windows to ensure the cabin was locked up nice and tight. Everyone takes a spot on the living room couch or large recliner chairs and all drift off to sleep in the living room.

Early the next morning just as the birds began to sing everyone was woken up by the continuous ringing of the doorbell and pounding on the front door. "Help please! Open the door, they're coming! Open pleeease!"

Evangeline hurries to the door with her pistol ready and Mad Dog covers the door with the shotgun shouldered and gives the nod to open the door. She unlocks the deadbolt and turns the doorknob pulling the door inward as a female covered in dirt and blood falls into the cabin. She quickly scurried away from the door with a look of pure horror as Evangeline slams the door shut relocking it. The frightened woman looks up at everyone surrounding her and the five weapons pointed at her. She lies there is silence with wide eyes with her lower lip quivering. "Who's coming, the walkers?!" RJ asks. The woman shakes her head yes as she stares back at the door. Stammering her words

"Those…. things" the woman muttered. "There were so many of them, hundreds I think." "What happened!?" Mad Dog asked. The tattered woman goes into her story as she stares off into space.

"We were trying to get away like everyone else. Steven, that's my husband decided we should take the back roads to avoid traffic, looters and if there were fewer people that meant fewer zombies. We were doing alright until about an hour ago where we turned onto route 41 thinking the countryside would be our best bet. Back on a road about a mile from here our car

overheated as we came to a stop under a street light. We hadn't seen anybody the entire day so we figured it was safe to stop for the night and rest. About an hour ago Steven went to go to the bathroom and woke me up when he closed the door. I watch him as he walks toward the trees and I get out of the car too and stretch my legs. The cool air felt good when I heard a breaking twig in the bushes. I look around back into the darkness behind the car and just out of the umbrella of light the dragging of feet could be heard. The cool air was suddenly filled with the odor of death, like rotting meat. As I squint thorough the light out of the shadows staggered one of those dead people. His face and throat were ripped apart and he was wearing farmer's overalls. I was in shock and couldn't move when I heard Steven yell and come running out of the tree line. I looked back at the dead farmer and he was suddenly accompanied by more and more zombies that kept coming into the light exposing their mangled bodies. It was like an ocean of them. They began gnashing their teeth as they got closer and before I knew it Steven grabs and shoves me into the car. He jumps in and tries to start the car but all it does is skip as he turns the key. Start you piece of shit! He said but it didn't work. The dead were now at the back of the car and the farmer was biting at the window when the car magically started as we sped away. The problem was we only made it twenty feet or so when the car stalled again this time we hit a telephone pole head-on. I blacked out for a few minutes and when I came to, I hear Steven screaming as a warm squirt of his blood hit my face and neck immediately clearing the cobwebs. I see the farmer biting and tearing his Adam's apple out as another rips a large chunk of hair from his head from the broken back window. He looks at me telling me to run, run! So I did, I ran and ran, they were all around us grabbing at me but I pulled away and ran through the woods. They were behind me but I was able to pull away. I came to the cabin down the road but they were all dead too. I continued a little farther and saw this place."

The woman seemed to come out of the trance and looked at everyone. My name is Cindy by the way. With a look that she had processed what she just went through she covers her mouth saying "Jesus Christ, I left my husband to die!" and she began to cry again. RJ and Mad Dog go check the front of the cabin for walkers and Evangeline gets Cindy a glass of water and Jaylen gets her a warm rag to clean up. The men come back in and tell everyone that the coast is clear and Mad Dog offers Cindy the use of the shower. Jaylen shows her the way to the bathroom and makes sure she is ok. Cindy says that she wasn't bitten and just shaken up. As Jaylen was leaving the bathroom Cindy says to her removing her shirt "those things sure grab hard" as she gets into the shower. Jaylen notices that Cindy had deep scratches down her back that were caked with blood.

While she was in the shower Jaylen went downstairs and informed the group that was now having breakfast the fact Cindy was scratched and infected. "Bitch gotta go!" Mad Dog says without looking up from his breakfast. Robert tells him he can deal with her any way he saw fit and that the group was about to leave. He turns to the group telling them that they are less than ten miles from Spearpoint, and that is where they will wait for the Tribe's Emergency Response Team to take them back to the reservation on Hilton Head Island.

While finishing his coffee Robert's eyes grew to the size of saucers as he sees the legion of the dead making their way stiffly up the driveway of the cabin. "Shit!" he yells, "she led them right to us! Everybody down!" Everyone grabbed their weapons waiting to see what was going to happen next. They could see the dark shadows of the dead in the windows as they began to bump into the wall and door of the cabin. "They're all over the cars," Evangeline says gripping her pistol tightly as RJ nervously looks at his dad. Robert looks at Mad Dog saying "this truck is good right?!" and he responds "hells yes, check it once a week" and he gives Robert a confident thumbs up. Robert tells Jaylen to cover the front door as she trains the automatic twelve gauge in that direction. "We need a distraction, junior grabs the black bag" as he points to the gym bag in the kitchen. "Go up to the master bedroom onto the balcony and toss a flashbang as far as you can. Then wait until I tell you to throw the second one." RJ nods grab the bag and heads upstairs. At this time everyone was ready to make a run for it. Robert gets on the radio giving RJ the green light to throw the first grenade. Ten seconds later BOOM! The explosion rattled the windows at the back of the house and the dead moaned and hissed and seemed to move toward the sides of the cabin away from the front door. Cindy came running down from the bathroom and was met by Mad Dog who snatched her by her wet stringy hair putting her on her knees. "You fuckin led them right to us! Are you one of them? Are you infected?" He yells in her face. He forces her head down revealing her deep severely infected scratches. "Let's go!" he says as he picks her up and she follows, one hand on her head and the other holding up her towel. Mad Dog escorts her to the back door and tosses her out where she fell into the back yard. Crying she stumbles to her feet and sees dozens of walkers flow from both sides of the large cabin and begins gingerly making her way over the loose gravel. He takes aim with his shotgun and squeezes the trigger BOOM! He had peppered her upper right thigh and ass with the shot knocking her to the ground as she screamed in agony and all he did was close and lock the door. Back in the house, Robert asked, "what the hell was that?" Mad Dog simply stated, "we need a distraction, she was infected and had to go." The dead were now drawn to the commotion in the back of the cabin and only a third were now in the front but were following the crowd. "Toss the second one" he ordered RJ and three seconds later another explosion rocked the rear window.

Outside in the yard, an ear-splitting explosion had rattled Cindy's cage and all she could hear was a high pitch ringing in her ears. As she came to she turned over on her back and the burning from the hot lead in her subsided as she saw the hoard of zombies were closing in on her. One among the hoard was her beloved Steven missing his throat and a flap of skin peeled back on the right side of his head. He was wearing his favorite Dallas Cowboys shirt that was now covered in blood. The last thing she saw was his dark-colored teeth as he knelt down to take a bite. She let out a blood-curdling scream as he sunk his teeth across her forehead, left eye and cheek.

Back in the cabin the survivors anxiously wait for the herd of the dead to thin out. When there were less than a dozen they decided to make a break for it. "Alright, get ready to move!" Robert anxiously tells the group. He counts down from three and at one they all burst out the door making a straight line for the vehicles. The few zombies that were close enough began to turn their attention toward the survivors and began staggering back toward the vehicles. The group opened up on the walkers as they approached then got into the vehicles locking the doors. Robert turned the key and the blue trailblazer started without a hitch, and as the dead began to engulf the rear of the vehicles they took off down the road as Robert followed behind Mad Dog to the main road. RJ and Evangeline look back and could see the cabin and hoard of the dead backlit by the orange sunrise.

SPEAR POINT

Back on the reservation of Hilton Head Island Chief High Eagle was at the police complex where he was being briefed on the mission that was going to bring the survivors safely back. High Eagle sits in the conference room with Commander Eagle Tail and his top Lieutenant Eric Tall Tree who would lead the rescue mission.

The police complex is a modern building of stone and shatterproof glass. The conference room was located on the fourth floor just down the hall from Eagle Tails office and had a large heavy glass conference table surrounded with two dozen black high back chairs, gray walls with matching low carpeted floors. There were two large monitors on the walls and a refrigerator full of water and soft drinks. There was a small counter and sink with a coffee pot and mugs. On the walls hung pictures of the tribal chiefs and the highest-ranking members of the police department. Taking a swig from his bottled water Chief High Eagle looking at the two says "how are we going to get our people home."

Eagle Tail is a large stature and barrel chest man who is built like an NFL lineman. He wears his uniform of black combat boots, green standard BDU pants and a navy blue t-shirt with Tribal Police printed in gold lettering as he sips on a large mug of coffee. He answers by saying that he would lead the team from the control center vehicle and take two of the five Special Operations Teams led by SOT commander Tall Tree. The other Armored Personnel Vehicles will transport the teams to the meeting place where Robert, his son RJ, Vange and other survivors will be awaiting our arrival. Chief High Eagle then asks "where is the meeting place?" Tall Tree wore the same uniform as Eagle Tail except his t-shirt has SOT embroidered on it. He towers well over six feet tall and sits high in his chair as he interjects "we don't know yet and is awaiting contact from Robert. We have an active tracker signaling his current location and he is currently on the move north. Our latest Intel and if I know my brother he will go to Spearpoint and fortify a location and wait for us. Before this meeting, I checked and the last location he was just a few miles from Spearpoint and the beacon was getting closer. It's only twenty minutes from here that would make the most sense. I have my teams gearing up as we speak and we will be ready to go in a couple of hours."

Chief High Eagle nods at the two men and says "bring our people home, we need them. Our tribe and this nation need them. "The three men stand up and High Eagle wishes them luck and says he will be there before they go on their mission and shakes their hands. Eagle Tail and Tall Tree head out of the conference room and Tall Tree tells his uncle Eagle Tail that he would be in the SOT's trailer briefing the men and getting supplies ready for the mission. They agree they would meet in an hour as both men go their separate ways in the hallway.

Back on the road, the group comes to the end of the dirt road that leads to the cabin and pulls up alongside Mad Dog. Robert rolls down the window, "thank you, do you want to come with us?"

He answers "I need to get back home and defend the farm. Good luck my friend!"

Robert asks "what is your real name?"

"Tony" was the response out of the side of his mouth as he lit a cigarette. "My friends call me Mad Dog, see you again" as he peels off to the right heading down the road and out of sight. Robert takes the left heading toward the main roadway that ran parallel to Interstate 95 towards Spearpoint. Within a half-hour, a green traffic sign with white reflective lettering which read "Spearpoint 2 Miles" appeared on the right side of the vehicle and Robert tells the group that this is where they would make a stand and wait for the rescue team to arrive. "I was in contact with my brother and they are leaving the reservation in the next few hours to come to get us. We need to find a place we can fortify and wait for their arrival." As they approached the small city it was like rereading the same line in a book that told the same grim story. Thick black smoke bellowed from various spots throughout the city and some buildings had flames still burning in the windows. The group stared in amazement at the skyscraper which looks like it was shelled by the military with large holes in its side. They take the off-ramp to the city and are able to get a close look of the gruesome story that never seemed to end. The streets of the outskirts of the city had a few half-ass barricades by the Spearpoint Sheriff's Department with a few cruisers or saw horses here and there some of which were pushed aside or set on fire. The group made their way through the abandoned streets that were littered with papers and trash blowing in the wind and dead corpses splattered everywhere. The smell of death was strong in the streets from the dried blood and rotten meat that was festering in the sun. They weave around trashcans, walkers that were put back down and remains of bodies that were eaten by the dead. The closer in to the city they got the dead began to appear as they staggered after the passing vehicle. Robert stays clear of the downtown section certain that it would be congested with the dead and other headaches they didn't need. The group turns west and heads to the city's west end and the low-income housing area came into view. The first high rise building the group saw was the place they decided to barricade and wait for the rescue.

The vehicle makes a turn onto Hartford Avenue making its way into the heart of the housing projects littered with graffiti marking the city of Spearpoint with Hartford gang territory signs in black and white spray paint. The only high rise was getting taller the closer they got. The hulk of a building was fifteen stories high and shaped like a cross constructed of concrete, brick and steel doors. "This is it" Jaylen says to the group and Robert nods and says "my thoughts exactly." They were now in the shadow of the building and looked for the entrance to the parking lot. They make a right onto Whelan Road and pull into the lot and park right in front of the main entrance which was barricaded. Robert gets out of the vehicle checking the surroundings and approaches the door with his carbine ready and tugs on the door. Just as he figured, it was locked so he tries the other door and it was locked too. He looked around and could see a few scattered walkers across the street that were still wandering aimlessly about the other steel and mortar buildings so he signals for Jaylen, RJ, and Evangeline to join him on the building's walkway. They fall in single file behind Robert and come to a brown steel door with white lettering that read "maintenance." A check of the loose handle indicated that the door was locked but loose and with enough force could be pulled open. Robert has Evangeline go to the corner of the building and check for walkers to ensure it was safe which she does. As she peered around the corner she saw a little person who had turned and was standing over the cracked open skull of a male. The walker was no more than two and a half feet tall, he scooped a chubby handful of brains stuffing it into his mouth savoring the bloody brains as he reinserted his hand scooping another handful. The slopping sound of its chewing had caused Vange to splatter vomit loud enough to get the walkers attention as it hissed bearing its teeth, brains falling from his mouth. "Shit!" She exclaimed, as the zombie hopped over the head and began waddling as fast as his little chubby bowed legs would carry him.

Vange had run toward the group by the maintenance door with a horrid look on her face. "Go, go, and go!" she told them. RJ gets in front of the door and with a swift powerful kick, the steel door goes crashing inward. They look behind Vange and see a midget zombie hurrying behind her and as Robert and Jaylen head into the building, RJ takes aim at the midget with the Mossberg and with a loud BOOM he peppers the walker with shot sending it flying into the door of a parked car denting it and smashing out the window. The massive echo of the shotgun drew the attention the walkers that were across the street and they began to stagger toward their location. Vange and RJ make their way into the building behind Jaylen and Robert slamming the door behind them. Inside they make their way through the corridors that were still lit with fluorescent lights. The walls were painted light tan with gray cement flooring and brown stained drop ceiling. There were various tools in a small workroom on the wall above a steel workbench with a radio that was still on the as the radio host still broadcasting in Spanish. Robert enters the work office and grabs the keys off the desk. He tosses them to Jaylen and they head to the main lobby of the high rise and listen intently for what is on the other side of the door. Jaylen fumbling finds the right key and slowly unlocks the door allowing it to swing open. They enter the main lobby which was full of trash and the common sitting area furniture chairs and a few sofas were propped against the windows and doors along with a couple of well-worn stained mattresses. The lobby was clear and they could see the dead had now made their way to the main doors where they parked the truck. The midget that RJ blasted was front and center minus his right arm biting and clawing at the glass. "Let's get out of here," Robert says as he cautiously backs the group into the hallway leading to the elevators and stairwells. "Take the stairs," RJ says as he covers the hallway and he follows them after the last person and they make their way to up the stairs. "How high do you want to go, dad?" RJ asks as they cautiously climb the concrete steps. "Just a few flights buddy, we will need to get out of here in a hurry when the transport arrives." They settle on the fifth floor where the four stand on the landing again listening for anything on the other side of the door. To their surprise, they could hear the voice of a woman talking so they carefully open the steel door and peek into the outdoor hallway. They could see an older grey-haired woman talking to her neighbor from the threshold of her apartment. The elderly woman and Robert's eyes met and she slammed her door shut along with her neighbors. Robert and the group head down the walkway and knock on the woman's door. Seconds later she opens the door and the muzzle of a double-barred shotgun emerges causing Robert to shout, "Shit!" He stumbled backward just as a blast was fired from the shotgun. RJ pumps two rounds from his shotgun into the doorway as the group retreated to the stairwell unharmed. "Shit that was close!" Robert said nervously to the group. Vange adds "let's go up a few more flights."

The group agrees and heads to the sixth floor which was clear of any shotgun-wielding grandmas. They make their way to the end of the hallway toward the end apartment where they noticed a few of the doors to the apartments were open. Once they reach the end door they again stop and listen for anybody inside. They knock and wait for a response which there was none. Robert then has Jaylen use the large ring of keys to open the door. The door was eased open and the smell of must hit the group in their faces. They take their time entering and clear the small apartment and open every window to air it out. Robert immediately calls the tribal police and his brother Eric Tall Tree answers from the Special Operations Team's building. "Hey Bob, is everything ok? We're about to head out to get you in ten minutes." Robert tells Eric that they would be in the project high rise off of Hartford Avenue on the sixth floor and would signal their location when they arrived. Eric tells his brother that he was coming and to hang in there before he hung up.

Eric Tall Tree finished uploading his magazines to his Glock .40 and holstered his pistol. He takes an M4 from the weapons rack and heads to the waiting convoy outside. At the convoy, he is met by Chief Eagle Tail with the eighteen specially trained warriors who were in formation behind him. They are awaiting the medicine man to provide the smudge ceremony where they would be anointed by the burning of sage for protection. Each warrior was then marked with three stripes of black paint down their cheek which is the tribe's tradition for warriors going into battle. After the ceremony, he jogs to the lead vehicle and jumps into the front passenger's seat. There he gets on the communications band and tells Eagle Tail that they were clear to go as the lead vehicle lurched forward as the diesel engine roared and the five-vehicle convoy headed to Route 1 that led from Hilton Head Island to the barge that leads to the mainland of South Carolina. On the two-mile bridge of route 1 Eric radios ahead to the barge stand by and that the transport would be there in a couple of minutes. After the short ferry trip, they dock on land and the transport continues to the checkpoint. As the roadblock comes into sight Eric lock and loads his M4 and turns on the red dot optic. The convoy drives over the drawbridge and the tribe's warriors acknowledge each other as they pass and they head out into the land of the dead.

Back at the project high rise on Hartford Avenue Robert is at the threshold to the apartment keeping watch. RJ and Vange are working on setting up the GPS on the cellphone for Eric to track to their exact location. Jaylen was taking inventory of the remaining supplies the group had. She jumped at the sound of a gunshot. She ran to the front door of the apartment when she heard a second ear-splitting crack that rang in everyone's ears causing them to come running to the front door. CRACK! A third shot was fired as they came to the front door as Robert's Colt smoothly ejected a smoking brass casing onto the tan tile flooring. They come to the outside hallway and discover two walkers laying on their backs with a canoe-shaped wound in the top of their heads and their brains were splattered on the concrete floor behind them. "We have to clear the floor," Robert tells them. They fall in line behind Robert as they make their way to the next apartment which the dead stumbled out of and enter slowly. The apartment was filled with dried blackened blood that was smeared all over the floor with the slim remains of a female corpse. The remains were mostly a blood-soaked skeleton with minimal muscle tissue left and the body was devoured from the abdomen down and the poor woman's mouth was open as if she was screaming. It must have been painful they thought as she seemed to be staring sleepily at the group. The apartment was clear and they left closing the door on a gruesome scene moving on to check the next apartment.

One by one Robert, RJ, Vange and Jaylen checked each of the open rooms on their floor without incident. The others that were locked they decided to leave them alone, they figured that the zombies couldn't get out through the steel doors. If anybody was in the apartments they would have come out at the sound of gunfire. "We can use the furniture in the open rooms to barricade the hallway until uncle E gets here," RJ tells his dad. Without a word, all four began to remove furniture from the abandoned apartments and began piling it into the hallway creating a waist-high wall that should help slow any dead that might come their way. Once completed Vange and RJ began to cook food and Jaylen took watch as Robert took a nap while all was quiet.

Robert wakes up to the smell of soup in the air which reminded him of how hungry he was as his stomach growled. He gets up off the couch and goes to the kitchen area and sees nobody but the hot pan of soup so he turns the burner off and looking around says "hello? Where are you guys?" There was no answer. He looks in the bedrooms and nobody was there either.

Dumbfounded he goes into the bathroom and washes his face and hands before he eats. Robert then goes outside but there is still no sign of RJ, Vange or Jaylen. From inside the apartment, he could hear them laughing in the living room area where a table was set up where they all sat carrying on a conversation like they were there the entire time. "Where were you," he asked the group. They all look at him funny "we've been right here silly" Jaylen tells him. Robert shrugs it off and sits at the table taking a piece of bread from the plate on the table as Vange serves him his portion of the soup and he digs right in. After a minute or so Robert notices that nobody else was eating and just watching him. He stops mid spoonful, looks around and then stops eating altogether. "What?" Robert asks. "We're having a special guest for dinner tonight," RJ says. Immediately Robert could feel a presence in the room behind him as the sound of high heeled shoes echoed as they clicked against the floor. For whatever reason he could not bring himself to turn around to see who was behind him, in fact, he now realized that he was stuck almost frozen to his seat. "How's the food?" Vange asked. Robert looks down at the bowl and it was no longer a bowl of ramen noodles it now was a bowl of blood with eyeballs, brains, fingers, and chunks of human flesh. The smell of rotten flesh fills the room as the person now makes their way opposite of Robert and sits down. It was Leese! She sat there with her drawn in skin which was now decaying and flesh was now visible under the tears in her skin, her eyes were cataract and bloodshot. Her hair was oily, stringy and patched. Her lips were nonexistent exposing her large gums and teeth as she slowly puts her head down scooping the bloody flesh with her hands taking a mouthful of brains. Robert looks in horror around the table and RJ, Vange and Jaylen were now zombies and eating the flesh in their bowls as blood squirt all over the table as Robert struggles to get up. His struggling seemed to get the attention of the dead eating at the table and simultaneously slowly turn their attention to him and began closing in on him reaching out with their bloody hands. Frantically struggling to get up he tries to scream but nothing comes out as the four sets of bloody meat-filled teeth are opened wide just about to bite him he shuts his eyes as everything goes black.

Robert jumps up and falls off the couch getting a belly laugh from the group. Breathing heavily he looks around wide-eyed as he gets to his feet and wipes the sweat from his brow. "Bad fuckin dream," he says between pants. "It was just a dream," Jaylen tells him as she gives him a hug assuring him everything is ok. They each take a bowl of soup and sit in the living room for dinner.

The convoy was now about three hours from the group's location as Eric calls the mobile phone they were tracking to check in with them. RJ answers and informs his uncle that they were alright and holding on the sixth floor of the high rise.

The ride to get the group held up in Spearpoint was for most of the members of the special operations their first time they had gotten a real taste of how bad everything had gotten. Most of them had spent most of the apocalypse defending the reservation from swarms of the dead alongside the U.S. Military but haven't ventured much past Hilton Head Island. The convoy had passed several buildings and homes with either white towels or sheets hanging from the windows indicating that people were alive inside and in serious need of help. Some even saw people hanging out of the windows waving frantically screaming for help when they heard the roar and felt trembling of the armored vehicles as they passed by. These screams had gotten the attention of the dead causing them to gather under the windows reaching up clawing in hopes of a treat to fall from above. The dead that were in the roads were easily crushed beneath the heavy steel bodies and large tires of the convoy that kept rolling as countless dead were flattened like empty beer cans. Eric kept a look at his watch eager to reach his family that is waiting for his rescue in hopes that he wasn't too late. He yells to the driver "can't this go any fuckin faster!" All of a sudden the convoy came to a halt as the brakes squeaked and the trucks hissed jolting everyone inside. The voice of Eagle Tail comes over Tall Tree's communications set "Why the hell are we stopping?" Eric gets on the radio "stand by sir, I'm on it."

Eric quickly checks the immediate area then orders an officer to man the turrets machine gun and cover him. He opens the door and steps onto the platform of the truck and asks what the problem was to the lead truck over the radio. "Sir, come take a look at this shit!" Came over the radio in an unsure tone and Eric's eyes opened to the size of saucers. The two-mile main artery of Broad Street that ran through town the convoy needed to traverse was clogged with abandoned cars that were pulled to the sides of the street and several hundred dead that were slowly shambling directly at the convoy. Chief Eagle Tail met Tall tree at the front of the convoy and had the same reaction. "Holy Shit," they said.

"We gotta go through," Eric says.

"Do what you have to do, just get us to the pick- up location."

Eagle Tail shoulders his assault rifle and walks back to the APC and climbs in. Eric orders the fourth vehicle to pull up adjacent to the first vehicle and to use the miniguns that were mounted on the top of the vehicles. Eric hops back into his vehicle climbing onto the roof and orders the gunners to open fire on the dead that was still about fifty yards away and to aim high. The electronic six barreled guns began to spin and a second later each spit a three-foot flame with a deafening roar as they dropped hot brass down the side of the vehicles. From his vantage point, Eric could see the bodies of the corpses burst into large chunks of hamburger and heads popped like balloons as the hoard seemed to part like the Red Sea did for Moses in the Old Testament. Eric began taking shots with his carbine scoring headshots more often than not. The hoard oozed back into the path made by the guns and continued moving forward. A second-order was given to open fire and the electric guns began turning again a second before the giant flames and roar cut the dead apart again this time creating two smaller paths this time with the same results. This time when the hoard filled in again it was significantly smaller and Eric gave the command to move forward knowing well they could drive-through and crush the rest. He climbs back in through the turret and the convoy once again lurches forward and reaches high gear as exploding walking corpses popped as they are plowed over by the vehicles.

Before they knew it the convoy had made it through the sea of zombies with each vehicle lower half completely covered in splattered blood and meat as if they had run through a large red puddle. The convoy was now making their way toward the end of Broad Street which was now mostly walker free. They finally came to the onramp of I95 South and proceeded to the next city of Spearpoint that was an hour away according to the green and white sign they passed on their right. Eric anxiously checks the monitor and the red beacon they used to track his family's location and it was slowly getting closer on the monitor. He looks out the window at the passing trees in anticipation and hopes they reach them in time.

Back at the high rise the group had finished their meal when the cell phone rang and Vange answers. It was Eric on the line who was checking in and to let them know that they were almost at their location and he could see the high rise off in the distance. Robert takes the phone from Vange and confirms the information that was relayed to him and his brother confirmed that they were now about fifteen to twenty minutes away barring any incidents. Just as he was about to hang up the buildings security alarm had sounded which sounded like an old school bell. "Shit!" Robert says on the phone, "I gotta check this out" he says as he hands the phone back to Vange leaving Eric hanging in suspense. Robert takes his M4 and makes his way through the barricade and to the stairwell on the left. He pushes open the door and trots down a few stairs looking over the edge and stops. Three floors below he sees the dead had broken into the building and have now flooded the stairwell that was slowly making their way up. Robert trying to control his rapidly growing panic as he quietly made his way back up the steps then to the room.

RJ, Jaylen, and Vange see the sick looking expression on Robert's face and all ask rhetorically "what is it." Robert takes the phone and tells his brother to pick it up and get here. He gives Eric the frequency to turn to when he gets closer to communicate via the military radio and that he would signal their exact location when they had gotten close enough.

"See you soon," Rob says before hanging up. Robert tells RJ to grab two grenades from the bag and tells the group that the walkers made it inside and were coming. Hearing this caused fear to rise in everyone face but was met with resolve as Robert looked all of them in the face telling them that the convoy was close. "Look, guys, we have enough ammo and the will to survive, if not we wouldn't have made it this far! This is a small hallway and they will have to bottleneck down to a few at a time and we can handle them, only shoot at what you can hit. Cover each other and we will get through this. RJ, you take a smoke grenade and pop it when you hear the convoy on the radio. Vange and Jaylen, you guys will help me cover the hallway and if need be we can fall back into the apartment." Everyone knows their assignment and gets down to business. Robert takes the fragmentation grenades and goes back to the stairs. The dead had made it up another half flight where he had pulled the pin on a grenade dropping it into the crowd of zombies then ducks out behind the door. A couple of seconds pass then a large concussion rips through the stairwell that shakes the building as smoke pours from under the door of the stairwell. Robert opens the door inspecting the damage. Dozens of the dead were torn to hamburger and limbs that were strewn about painted the stairwell red and pink. He goes down a flight and rigs the other grenade to a string rigging the booby trap to detonate when the string was tripped. He checks the stairwell and sees walkers that weren't hit by the blast began to make their way up the stairs slowly so he begins to make his way up the stairs. The smell of burnt rotten human flesh fills his nostrils and he loses his lunch all over the stairs. He closes the door behind him and he makes his way through the furniture barricade and joins the group. "This is it, after the explosion, we'll have two to three minutes before they reach our floor. They may go right past our floor, just be ready."

The group sits in silence behind the furniture in the hallway when the booby trap went off again rocking the floor under their feet causing them to jump as their hearts seemed to beat through their chests. The focus seemed to sharpen as tunnel vision began to affect everyone who was the intent of the steel door leading to the stairs. Everyone kept their weapons trained on the door for what seemed like an eternity before the moans of the dead could be heard in the stairwell. In the distance, the roar of diesel engines could be heard and RJ goes to the end of the hallway pointing down Hartford Avenue "I see them!" He exclaimed. Eric's voice came over the radio "Be ready guys, just down the street." RJ responds "I see you! Hurry we are surrounded! Sixth floor!" RJ hears "Pop smoke!" Yelled by his dad so he wedges the smoke canister in the opening of the gate pulling the pin. The spoon clicks off the canister and a second later a large orange plume of smoke begins to bellow from the sixth-floor hallway marking their location. The unmistakable, deafening, high pitched crack of the 5.56 Nato round caused RJ to jump and turn abruptly as he saw walkers head to explode from the high-velocity rounds from the M4. The dead had pushed the door inward and spilled into the breezeway. Gunfire erupted as the group opened up dropping the dead.

On Hartford Avenue from inside the lead vehicle, Eric excitedly points to the orange smoke "There they are!" He yells as he tries to contain his emotions of joy. "Hurry up for fuck's sake!" He orders his driver who immediately floors it revving the engine. Eric orders the gunners to ready the miniguns as they could now see that the dead were clogging the entrance. Quickly accessing the situation Eric tells three of the vehicles to stay on the street and keep the engines running and that two would go into the parking lot shutting down the engines. He hoped that would draw some of the walkers away from the building. The first two vehicles burst through the gate of the high rise coming to a screeching halt and turn off their engines. The other three pull alongside the parking lot and several SOT officers climb onto the tops of the vehicles and take up shooting positions facing in a 360-degree circle. The rumbling of the engines in the street began to gather the attention of the dead who began to turn around and shamble toward the noise. Eric gets on the radio telling the group they are in the lot and if he could to make his way down. "Negative!" Robert answers, "get your ass up here bro!" The sound of gunfire could be heard in the background of the transmission causing a sinking feeling in Eric's stomach knowing his family needs him. "The first stairwell is clogged with walkers! What about the second one?" Robert asked Eric over the radio.

By now half of the dead had passed the two vehicles in the lot and began to surround the ones in the street as the officers began firing in the sea of the dead. Eric orders the gunner of his vehicle to open up into the remaining dead in the front of the building which was cut down in short order. He gives the command to move and six men including Chief Eagle Tail dismounted from the vehicles tactically making their way into the building dropping the dead with precise headshots. They make their way through the lobby and down the long hallway to the secondary stairwell and open the door. To their surprise, it was clear and began making their way up to the sixth floor. Eric gets onto the radio "Bob the far stairwell is clear, get there! I'm on my way up!" Robert tells the group as he slams another magazine into the breach. Run for the far door, I'll cover you, GO!" He yells at the group as he continues firing from his smoking carbine. Vange and Jaylen take the bags with the remaining supplies and made a run for it as they high step over the corpses and brain matter then sprint to the end of the breezeway.

He realized RJ was still there running the Mossberg with carefully aimed shots. Robert yells at RJ to go but he yells "no, I'm not leaving you!" Robert grabs the last bag slinging it over his shoulder. He takes RJ and pushes him in front of as they both take off running. Robert raises the M4 firing a steady stream of lead at the doorway scoring three more headshots as they both sprint pass the door and join Jaylen and Vange at the far end door then they all head down the stairs.

"Bob!" Eric yells as his deep voice echoes in the stairwell. "Uncle E!" RJ exclaims. They all meet up on the landing between the 2nd and 3rd floors. After a brief hug, Eric tells them to follow him and they began their trek back to the ground floor in a single file. They get to the bottom of the stairs where Eric radios to the men "jackpot, I repeat jackpot. Everyone accounted for, we're coming out." "10-4" was the response. They head out into the main lobby area where dozens of corpses littered the floor where every step the group took was on the body of a zombie. Gunsmoke still hung heavily in the air and the metallic stench of stale blood made their mouths water.

The two vehicles in the driveway were now running and waiting by the front door with the heavy steel door open where Eagle Tail was waiting with a smile. The group exhaustedly climbs into the belly of the heavily armed beast and the door is closed shut and locked. The dead slowly began to close in on the transport as the convoy slowly takes off and picks up speed as they make their way back up Hartford Avenue and back to Hilton Head Island.

THE RESERVATION

Inside the vehicle, the group was given rags to clean up with and cold bottles of water. "Are you guys ok?" Eagle Tail asks as he looks back from the front passenger's seat. Everyone responded by either shaking their head yes or giving a thumbs-up as they were examined by the corpsman. Another officer came behind the corpsman with some meals ready to eat handing each survivor two advising them to eat. Robert taking a long swig of water he notices that Eric is just looking at them holding back tears. "We're ok, bro. Thanks to you guys" he tells him patting him on the shoulder. "You remember" he continues before being cut off by Eric "yeah, you guys were" then paused as he noticed RJ intently listening as he ate the candy in his MRE. "You guys are old friends. Any word from Leese?" With tears welling in his eyes RJ answers "she didn't make it. We tried to save her but we couldn't. We took care of that asshole though, huh dad." Shaking his head yes with a saddened look on his face said it all without saying a word.

From the front Charles, Eagle Tail shouts over the diesel engine "We have your laboratory ready and all the assistants you will need to continue your work. Lead medicine man Twin Oaks made progress and believes that the citrus flower that grows in the mountains of the reservation has the key characteristics that he believes can help with your work. He thinks that is why our people have not contracted the virus since we use the citrus flower in our daily diet of teas, soups etcetera." He pauses as if listening to a broadcast on his earpiece nodding his head up and down then responds "that's affirmative sir, we have Mr. Babcock, his son, assistant, and one survivor. We are en route to Hilton Head now. 10-4." He turns back continuing "D.C. has been in contact with us inquiring if you were alive and if you had made it back safely." "I bet they are! Assholes need me to save their ass" Robert replies shaking his head. "Only by the grace of God we made it to my office at the CDC but it was overrun by the dead. My other department heads Miller and Stanfield had trashed my lab and destroyed all my lab work. Luckily I saved all the hard data on a couple of flash drives, here." as he hands his hard drive to his uncle Charlie who takes it placing it in his left front breast pocket.

With the adrenalin dump, the survivors begin to feel drained and begin to settle in for the ride back. Sleep closed in on them heavily as they shut their eyes which unexplainably immediately felt they weighed ten pounds and fell into a deep sleep.

Robert was awakened as the vehicle skidded to a stop. "What the fuck is this" Eagle Tail says as everyone gets up to get a look. From the front window, they see a military roadblock with hummers and men dressed in fatigues with M16 rifles ordering the convoy to stop. The leader raised his hand palm out and the other half dozen men with their weapons at the ready.

Eagle Tail orders the second transport vehicle to slowly approach and make contact with the men. The second to last vehicle in the convoy breaks formation and pulls within thirty feet of the roadblock and comes to a stop. "Stay sharp" Eagle Tail orders over the radio. The vehicle in front of the command vehicle that contained the group had pulled forward a bit and angled to the right as to protect the command vehicle. By now the officers in the lead vehicle had exited and approached the men cautiously. "What are they saying?" Evangeline asks as everyone intently looks out the front window. Peering over the hummer blocking the command vehicle from the roadblock only the upper half of the men could be seen as a discussion was taking place. The leader of the roadblock could be seen pointing at the convoy and the officer could be seen motioning with his hands for them to move their vehicles apart. The contact officer turned to look back at the convoy keying his mike as he began to transmit the issue. "Sir, they" he was cut off as the leader drew a pistol shooting him in the head. Everyone witnessed this in slow motion as his face had exploded into a red meaty cavity as his lifeless body fell to the concrete. "Oh shit! What the fuck! Came from everyone inside the vehicle as muffled gunfire could be heard from the front. PING! PING! THUD! Could be heard as the bullets bounced off the armor of the command vehicle. The officers returned fire and scrambled to cover behind the hummer as immediate calls for help began pouring over the radio "SHOTS FIRED! SHOTS FIRED!" Another voice cut the first guys off "Steve and Tahj are down, Christ they're fucked up!" The lead hummer was taking the brunt of the gunfire as white sparks could be seen as the bullets pinged off its side. The officers returned fire from behind the vehicle as another vehicle from behind the command vehicle pulled forward opening up with the large belt-fed minigun. After a short burst, everything was eerily quiet as gun smoke hung heavily in the late afternoon air. The officers in the security vehicle had exited and cautiously approached the roadblock. "Clear" could be heard over the radio in the command vehicle as everyone piled out and went to check on the wounded officers. Six total of the tribal police were killed in the ambush and another clung to life as Eric began chest compressions. The group looked in disbelief at the carnage that they had witnessed and the realization that the dead were not the only threat out there. A minute later Eric had given up as the fallen officer was not responding to the aid. The lead vehicle was completely destroyed riddled with bullets as the engine was leaking every kind of fluid imaginable, the engine smoked and tires were flat. "Now what?" an officer asked of Eagle Tail. Looking around he orders " place our guy's bodies in the back of the second vehicle so we don't ring the dinner bell for the zombies and pull it off the side of the road. We need to keep moving, but we'll send out another recovery team and give them a proper ceremony and burial on the Rez".

"Sir!" could be heard from the other side of the roadblock as Eric and Charlie hurry to the other side of the destroyed blockade. There sat slouched against a hummer bleeding profusely from his stomach was the leader. "Why did you do this?!" Eric asked and the man looking up at them tears streaming from his eyes, he began coughing up blood and refused to talk. He just gave them the middle finger mouthed the words fuck you and turned his head away. Eric takes a shotgun from the officer who found the leader pressing it against the man head yelling "why the fuck did you do it!" Charlie pulls Eric away from the man "no, he's not worth it man, let him bleed out." Tears welling in his eyes Eric looks at him shaking his head in understanding giving the shotgun back. Looking down the road about a half dozen walkers could be seen staggering in their direction as the burnt orange sun began to set behind them. Eric kneels down spitting on the ground and whispers "you're going to have some friends over for dinner" as he yanks the man's head forcing him to look at the walkers approaching. "Let's get outta here" orders Eagle Tail and everyone makes their way back to the remaining operational vehicles and begin their way down the road speeding past the dead continuing on to the reservation. Eagle Tail gets on the radio "Eagle Tail to base" a female voice answers "Base here Chief, go ahead." Taking a second he continues "we need a recovery team sent to route 37 at about mile marker 4. We lost team four and their vehicle to an ambush. The package is safe and we are on the way home." The dispatcher replies "10-4 chief, recovery team to mile marker 4 on route 37."

Back at the roadblock the leader was now leaning to his left head almost touching the ground. Wincing in pain as blood flows from his stomach and mouth he struggles to open his eyes as he heard the moans of the dead approaching. Through squinting eyes, he sees the dead staggering in his direction as their foul stench fills his nostrils then everything goes black. Seconds later he reopens his eyes the best he could and all he could see now was the zombies within arm's reach crouching and reaching for him as the last thing he saw was a rotting set of teeth bearing down on him. He closed his eyes tight as a child would hide under their blanket hiding from the boogeyman hoping whatever it was would just go away. He then felt several hands-on him followed by intense pain on his chest, arms, and legs. He gave a scream of agony as the walkers took large mouthfuls of flesh and ripped his apart with their bare hands.

Back in the transport vehicle, Charlie Eagle Tail is listening intently shaking his head in acknowledgment before answering "copy" ending the conversation. He turns back to the group and informs them that the medicine man has created dozens of samples of the citrus flower serum and prepared the laboratory for your arrival." Robert shakes his head in acknowledgment as they continue their ride. The next couple of hours had passed without incident as RJ and Evangeline were now fast asleep and Jaylen was on her way out too. Eric and Robert were reloading the magazines for their carbines and placing them back in the carriers. "Less than an hour to Hilton Head Island. We're coming up on the town of Manville now" the driver of the transport vehicle yells to the group. Eric begins to tell Robert that he was glad that they were alright and he was able to reach them in time. Robert begins to answer but is startled as the vehicle comes to a sudden stop. A voice came over the radio "truck two is overheating and the engine is seized." Smoke could be seen flowing from the engine of the lead vehicle as well as the dead that were closing in on the stranded vehicle. "Get em outta there!" RJ yelled. Eagle Tail gets on the radio "vehicle three, pull alongside two and open the hatch. Take as many as you can and we'll grab the rest."

Without hesitation, the vehicle pulls alongside the damaged vehicle as the dead had swarmed both vehicles and were clawing at the sides. Eric, Evangeline, and Jaylen had crawled on the top of the transport vehicle and began taking carefully aimed shots into the crowd of walkers striking the occasional headshot. The sound of the gunfire had gotten the attention of the hoard as several began to slowly shamble towards them. They redirect their fire on the approaching infected dropping them as their heads burst apart like water balloons. Over the radio in the vehicle "we're full, come get the rest of the guys!" was broadcast as the lead vehicle had pulled off making room for the next vehicle to make the pick- up. The rain was still coming down hard and was no relief from the thick humidity and the road was now covered in bright orange mud. The second vehicle had moved into position stopping with the front pointing toward the front of the vehicle forming a wedge as it slid just colliding with the parked vehicle due to the muddy road. The collision had pinned three walkers between them causing their eyes to pop out of their heads. The dead continued to moan and blindly claw at the vehicle as the smell of fresh meat filled the air and the survivors climbed back into the vehicle in anticipation of the convoy moving again. "We have to help them," Evangeline said. Eagle Tail steps in "no, everyone stay put. You guys are too important and I will not risk your safety for anyone."

The remaining Special Operations Team members had carefully made their way from one vehicle to another transferring bags of equipment that they couldn't leave behind all while the dead were surrounding reaching up at them. Two of the officers had taken their assault rifles and opened fire into the crowd of the dead dropping the ones in the tiny wedge between the vehicles. Two had jumped back across and climbed back into the vehicle to retrieve the last of the gear. "Let's go, guys, enough fuckin around!" Tall Tree orders over the radio. "Just grabbing the last of the gear sir! Coming out now." Gunfire continued from the third officer who had taken out all the walkers between the vehicles. As the men climb out of the vehicle they toss a bag to the waiting officer who catches it and drops it through the hatch of the vehicle and climbs in following it. The second officer jumps across slipping onto his back grabbing onto the railing as he started to slide across the top of the vehicle. The dead were now frantically grabbing at the officers' boots snarling and chomping in attempts to get a bite. The closest zombie had finally gotten a decent grip on the officer's boot and chomped down. The officer screams as he frantically shakes his foot loose from the walker's mouth then gives a sharp kick snapping off its lower jaw. He scrambles to his feet checking his foot which was fine. Some of the dead were making their way between the vehicles again and he opened up with his Glock pistol scoring headshots dropping the dead one by one.

He gathers the bag and tosses it into the vehicle and yells for his friend Jim to jump across "C' mon Jimmy!" motioning with his pistol in hand. Jim looking nervously at the distance and takes the leap. He lands on the edge of the vehicle falling to his knees dropping his bag to the ground. His partner helps him to his feet and begins to climb into the vehicle when he notices Jim jumping off the side of the vehicle to retrieve his bag and not following him. "Jim!" he yells and begins to climb out of the vehicle again to help his partner.

On the ground, Jim is gathering the supplies that fell out of the bag when he does a double-take as he notices the walkers began making their way between the vehicles again. He struggles to take out his pistol as the dead approach. He finally gets it clear of the holster as the closest walkers head spurts blood from a bullet from his partner's pistol. Another shot drops the next and another then another. Jim gets to his feet and begins shooting as well before his weapon is emptied at which point the tosses the bag to his partner. He grabs onto the support bar to climb up the ladder when he hears "Jimmy!" as walker grabs him taking a mouthful of meat from his forearm. "AAAAH!" Jim screams punching the walker as blood flows from the gaping wound. He climbs the latter missing the last step causing his legs to scrape against the slippery metal edge and hang over the side. Jim lets out a second scream as another walker takes a chunk from his right shin exposing the tibia. His partner pulls him up shooting into the crowd of walkers. From the command vehicle, Eagle Tail orders the over the radio to move out and the convoy pulls off and the three remaining vehicles continue their way to Hilton Head Island.

The convoy gets a few miles down the road and Chief Eagle Tail asks for an update on the injured officer. The driver of the vehicle came over the radio "Jim's been bitten twice, sir. He's in a lot of pain but we applied tourniquets to minimize the bleeding." Hearing the news Eagle Tail turns to ask Robert and Evangeline if he will make it. Evangeline shakes her head no as Robert explains that without the viable antidote he was as good as dead and making a serum could take from weeks to months if at all. Jaylen interjects "he's a threat to the group, we can't allow him on the reservation. Tell your men they have to leave him behind." Eagle Tail looks at her considering her argument then gets back on the radio addressing the commanding officer "Jim is infected and is a danger to us all. Pullover, we need to deal with him." There was a moment of silence on the other end as Eagle Tail hastily added: "do you copy!" The driver finally came over the air "we can't leave him, sir! No more discussion, he stays. That's final" and the communications were turned off in the vehicle. Eric tries his portable radio to contact the driver but there was no answer. "Now what?" RJ asks. "The road is too narrow for us to get around him." Eric tells the driver "wait for the road to open then take him then." The driver acknowledges nodding his head.

About a half-hour passed and the middle vehicle begins to swerve sharply to the right the hard left running headfirst into a large tree. "Oh shit!" Eric exclaims looking wide-eyed at the crash that happened right in front of his eyes. Both vehicles came to an abrupt stop and every officer from both vehicles exited and approached with caution weapons raised. As they got within reach of the vehicle Jim had suddenly smashed his face against the blood-splattered window causing everyone to jump. He had turned and attacked everyone in the vehicle killing them. Lowering his head in disgust Eric tells everyone to mount up and prepare to move out. He takes a thermite grenade from his vest and climbs up the ladder pulling the pin tossing it into the belly of the vehicle.

He jumps off and trots back to the command vehicle. BOOM! The vehicle is engulfed in a silver ball flame as it began to burn white-hot from the inside out. The convoy once again began its final leg to Hilton Head Island.

Outskirts of Hilton Head Island Reservation

South Carolina- 90 minutes later; after the incident of the breakdown the convoy was able to get within a mile of the reservation where the barricade protecting the entrance of the reservation was coming into view. The command vehicle could see from a distance that the police were holding off a good-sized hoard of walkers as muffled gunshots could be heard in the distance. As they get closer radio chatter could be heard from Sergeant Dave Hamlin who was giving orders to his men to hold the line. Chief Eagle Tail comes over the radio "Sgt.

Hamlin, get your men down. We are coming up on you and will clear most of the dead." From the vehicles, the men on the wall could be seen ducking behind cover. "All clear chief" came over the radio and the order was given for the miniguns to open fire on the hoard that was clawing at the gate. The convoy pulled into a line formation and the electric machine guns were manned as the six barrels begin to spin as the three-foot flame spit from the barrels. They roared spitting a heavy wall of lead into the thick wall of walkers causing their bodies and heads to explode into chunks of meat mowing them down with a long burst. The bright orange tracers marked the path of the bullets as they flowed back and forth a second time into the wall of the dead as more fell as their heads exploded into pink mist.

At this point, most of the dead were cleared from the entrance. The convoy made their way towards the entrance where they could see the officers back on their feet opening fire on the remaining dead. The zombies fell lifelessly to the ground with each headshot blowing the brains out of the back of their heads.

The gate was slowly swung open allowing the vehicles to pull in as gunfire continued by the other officers to keep the remaining walkers at bay. The vehicles come to a screeching halt as their heavy doors swung open as the group and the remaining officer's bailout to help hold the line and secure the gate. Now with the gate secured everyone takes a breath and gathers around the vehicles where they welcomed the group back. Dave had asked his cousin "can you really fix this cluster fuck we're in? The head medicine man is all set up and thinks you guys have a good chance." Everyone in the circle looked at Robert awaiting an answer. "Well my job at the CDC was to maintain viral control via antidotes to the viral weapons created. I was on the right track to completing the anti-virus when the MRSV-32 got out. With the proper conditions and equipment I know I can get this turned around." "Where is everyone else, the other trucks?" another officer asked. Eric answers "we lost them, the men and the vehicles," he looks somber "it's getting bad out there." The officers at the gate all had looks of disbelief and desperation when Sergeant Dave ordered them back to their posts. "Good to see you guys safe and sound, we'll catch up later," he says to the survivors. As the group begins to enter the vehicles Sergeant Dave approaches Chief Eagle Tail and the rest of the group telling them "we lit the lamentation fires for the men we lost and will keep them burning for the next three days and we are preparing to have a pop-wow in celebration of your return."

"Alright" Eagle Tail announces. "Let's get to the station." The group shakes hands with the officers at the gate and mount up as the vehicles pull off headed to Hilton Head Island that was now in sight. The vehicles came to a stop at the ferry port and the command vehicle pulled onto the ferry. The other two vehicles parked and the officers loaded into a zodiac and followed the ferry as it made its way the third of a mile to the dock of the island.

Back at the main administration building Sachem High Eagle welcomes the tribes' elders as he holds the door to the cafeteria open for them. The crowd made of forty or so men and women slowly made their way to their seats after making their cups of coffee and taking their share of fry bread. Taking a sip of water Sachem High Eagle clears his throat and addresses the elders "Our people are back safe and sound. We can get to work on healing the population and making it safe again." One elder male voicing his opinion "Why should we help the white man! This is The Creator's way of giving us back our land." Everyone began talking amongst themselves nodding in agreement. "Listen, everyone, listen. Please!" High Eagle firmly tells the elders. "It is our way to protect Mother Earth and all who live here. That is the way The Creator would want us to act." Again the people began talking among themselves. An elderly woman interjected as she raised her hand as if in elementary school "I heard that we lost several of our warriors on the recovery mission, are we going to burn the lamentation fire for the departed? And one more thing, we hear the medicine man figured out the citrus flower in the Hilton Head Mountains may help Mr. Babcock find the antidote for the sickness that is plaguing the Earth. Shouldn't we be gathering the citrus flower to help with their work?" Nodding in agreement Chent Sachem listens intently to their concerns and answers "yes the fire is lit and will burn throughout the weekend in their honor and sacrifice, the citrus flower is being harvested as we speak and being taken to the medical center." What can we do?" another elder asks. "The tribal council has decided to have a pow-wow to celebrate the return of our people which we preparing for now and we need you to prepare the feast and sweat lodge for cleansing of their souls so they could get to work as soon as possible on the cure. Let's get to the church grounds and gather to welcome back our people with the rest of the tribe." With that everyone slowly got up from their chairs and began to shuffle out of the cafeteria and down the hallway.

After docking from the short ferry ride the command vehicle makes its way up the road of Hilton Head Island and heads to the Tribal Police Station. It pulls in front of the sally port where it comes to a jolting halt and waits for the steel door to raise to let them in. It enters the building hissing to a stop and shutters as the diesel engine is cut off. The heavy doors of the rear of the beast slowly swing open and everyone climbs out. Everyone takes a deep breath and sighs in relief as the cool air conditioning hit their skin and they are met with cold bottled water. Some of the officers cry in mourning and some in thanks they made it back alive, and Robert, RJ, Jaylen, and Evangeline hug each other as well as Tall Tree and Eagle Tail. While they all took a moment to gather themselves, stretch and hydrate they gathered their bags and headed to the elevator that would take them to top floor offices where they would be met my Sachem High Eagle. As the elevator door opens there were a couple of police officers that greeted the group as they exited and escorted everyone to the restrooms where they could take a warm shower followed by a hot meal in the cafeteria where Sachem High Eagle and the medicine man would welcome the group and begin talks of combating the virus. The restrooms were large with rows of blue lockers wooden benches and matching blue carpeting with white walls. The shower area resembled that of your local Y and had the same bleach and chlorine smell. Each thoroughly enjoyed the hot shower and took their time coming out. When they came to the changing room changes of fresh clothing was neatly folded and waiting. While getting dressed Eagle Tail turns to his nephew "Rob, can you really turn this thing around? I mean is the answer on this little disk?" as he holds the microdisk up. Looking at his uncle in his eyes "I hope so. We were on the right track before all this went down, and hope Mack has the answer with the citrus flower."

As the group finished getting dressed they leave the dressing rooms and head down to the main floor where another officer was waiting by the front door in the lobby who opens the door to an awaiting suburban where everyone piled in. "Indian Church Grounds," Eagle Tail tells the driver. They begin the two-mile drive through the reservations residential area, the center of town and then to the outskirts into the wilderness where the church grounds were. You could tell you were close because the paved road ended as you turned off onto a rocky dirt road that jolted everyone about. Soon they came to a clearing and the evergreens parted as the sound of drums beat loudly seemingly in rhythm with your heartbeat. Smoke could be seen billowing from the fires that burnt in the center circle and the lamentation fire in the corner near the burial ground. The native yells and war cries could be heard as thousands gathered they came from their teepees and tents to see the arrival of the survivors. The truck stopped short of the sacred circle and everyone piled out of the vehicle. The crowd parted making a path that leads to the center of the circle where Sachem High Eagle stood. Sachem was a short rugged man with bronze skin who motioned for the group to enter the circle and stand before the fire. Everyone watched with anticipation as Mack handed a bundle of sage to Sachem as he lit it in the fire. From there he conducted the smudge ritual and prayer over the weary survivors as he anointed each one going down the line from Robert to RJ, Jaylen, Tall Tree, Evangeline, and Eagle Tail.

Once the ceremony has completed a roar came from the crowd as men and women gave their individual war cry as they raised their assorted weapons of assault rifles, bows, knives, shotguns, and hatchets. The drums began beating in unison again as everyone began to crowd the survivors shaking their hands and embracing them. The elders led the group to the sweat lodge for prayer and fasting before the pow-wow and feast begin. The tribal members went on about their business enjoying themselves with family at the pow-wow as they danced in the center circle and made traditional native foods in preparation of the feast. As the group was led to the sweat lodge they had noticed that the entire reservation was unchanged thus far by the zombie apocalypse as the group almost seemed to forget that Hell must be full as the dead walk the Earth.

Inside the sweat lodge, the temperature had risen to at least 115 degrees inside where everyone sat around the fire as Mack began the prayer once the drums began to beat the Praise song four times. There he added hot rocks to the circle in the lodge and pour water from the brook that caused a sauna-like atmosphere. They prayed and worshiped God through the playing of the four songs and once the ceremony was completed Mack had given the group the final blessing before leaving the lodge. Once outside, the humid afternoon air seemed like a cool blanket that wrapped around them. The sun was setting as the sky faded from pale blue to light violet and the fire burned bright orange casting a warm glow in the early evening. The drums beat steadily into the night and everyone enjoyed the bountiful feast and each other's company until the food and firewater were gone. Sometime in the middle of the night, the last person went home leaving only the family members of the departed to keep the lamentation fire going through the weekend.

The next morning Robert wakes up and checks in on RJ who wasn't in his bed. Robert smells the familiar scent of coffee filling the air as he makes his way down the brightly lit hallway to the cafeteria. There RJ was dressed and bringing his dad a cup of coffee. "You're going to need this to help you work, it's going to be a long day," he says as he hands the cup of steaming java. "Thanks, buddy," Robert says smiling at his son. Jaylen comes staggering into the cafeteria definitely in the need for caffeine and waives silently to the two as she pours a cup of coffee. "I gotta get to work at the medical center with my cousin Mack. I'm going to head over soon and see how we're going to kick MRSV-32's ass. RJ, I want you to stay close to the medical and police buildings." Rolling his eyes "Alright dad." he says sarcastically. "I'll keep an eye on him," Jaylen says sending a wink to RJ. "Maybe we can check out the shopping mall in town, lots of girls there." Smiling, "just be careful" Robert reminds them as he walks out of the cafeteria to get Evangeline to head off to work.

Meanwhile at the Tribal Medical Center Mack is fast at work in the laboratory pulling up Robert's work from the flash drive and downloads the information. He takes the citrus flower serum from the freezer as well as specimens of infected blood from walkers taken for research. Robert and Vange knock on the shatter-resistant glass and Mack smiles waiving in acknowledgment. The lab is eerily similar to his back in Atlanta, and Robert shakes the image of the destroyed lab and heads to the cleanroom. There they decontaminate before donning the level five hazardous material suit and pertinent precautionary equipment. They meet at the door and ensure each other's suit is properly sealed before entering the lab where they join Mack and begin their work to kill the Mutated Rabies Strain Virus.